IN THE COUNTRY OF THE MIND

Bayley opened his eyes and found himself on flat white concrete under a pure blue sky. He squinted in the glare. He seemed to be in the center of some kind of gigantic circular plaza, a high wall marking its perimeter. Suddenly, he remembered.

His last moments of consciousness on the operating table were vivid in his mind, and he could almost hear the echoes of his final shout for help. Where the hell was he? Had the experiment failed? Had he been revived somehow, somewhere?

There was a loud noise behind him. He turned quickly, staring across the plaza, searching for the source of the sound. There was a faint black speck in the distance, growing closer. Some sort of animal—a dog? Instinctively, he ran.

The straps of his sandals cut into his skin as he pounded across the hard concrete. His lungs ached. His vision wavered. He glanced behind him and saw the creature gaining on him, a big black shape, its mouth hanging open. It howled again, and the noise echoed all around him.

"A GREAT READ. . . . Will we ever make a machine that is a person? Lots of smart people argue it can never happen. Yet with sufficiently powerful hardware, there is a direct approach to the question that is very hard to deny. The Silicon Man explores that approach."
—*Vernor Vinge, author of* True Names

BANTAM SPECTRA SPECIAL EDITIONS

FULL SPECTRUM 2 edited by Lou Aronica, Shawna
McCarthy, Amy Stout, and Patrick LoBrutto
NO ENEMY BUT TIME by Michael Bishop
SYNNERS by Pat Cadigan
VIEWS FROM THE OLDEST HOUSE by Richard Grant
WINTERLONG by Elizabeth Hand
POINTS OF DEPARTURE by Pat Murphy
THE SILICON MAN by Charles Platt
UNIVERSE 1 edited by Robert Silverberg and Karen Haber
A HIDDEN PLACE and MEMORY WIRE
by Robert Charles Wilson

SIGNATURE SPECIAL EDITIONS

MINDPLAYERS by Pat Cadigan
LITTLE, BIG by John Crowley
STARS IN MY POCKET LIKE GRAINS OF SAND
by Samuel R. Delany
EMERGENCE by David R. Palmer
PHASES OF GRAVITY by Dan Simmons

The Silicon Man

CHARLES PLATT

BANTAM BOOKS

NEW YORK • TORONTO • LONDON • SYDNEY • AUCKLAND

THE SILICON MAN
A Bantam Spectra Book / March 1991

SPECTRA and the portrayal of a boxed "s" are trademarks of Bantam Books,
a division of Bantam Doubleday Dell Publishing Group, Inc.

ISBN 0-553-28950-0

Published simultaneously in the United States and Canada

Bantam Books are published by Bantam Books, a division of Bantam Doubleday
Dell Publishing Group, Inc. Its trademark, consisting of the words "Bantam
Books" and the portrayal of a rooster, is Registered in U.S. Patent and Trade-
mark Office and in other countries. Marca Registrada. Bantam Books, 666 Fifth
Avenue, New York, New York 10103

PRINTED IN THE UNITED STATES OF AMERICA

RAD   0 9 8 7 6 5 4 3 2 1

*In memory of Fred Beyer,
friend, computer programmer, and mentor,
who died too soon.*

Acknowledgments

I am indebted to Vernor Vinge, a mathematician and important science-fiction writer in his own right, for helping me with some of the details and implications of the central idea in this novel. I hope he doesn't feel I played too fast and loose with the science.

Roberta Lannes read the early drafts and played an indispensable role encouraging me to develop the human qualities of the narrative. John Douglas gave valuable advice after reading an initial outline of the novel. Jonathan Post advised me on the policies and procedures of aerospace contractors. Robert Frenay, Richard Kadrey, and Bruce Sterling read the manuscript and were good enough to take the time to offer valuable suggestions for improvements. My editor, Betsy Mitchell, offered helpful advice. Nancy Weiner provided medical information. Many others have assisted me by discussing and/or disputing the ideas in the book.

Although electronic immortality is pure fiction at this time, there are real possibilities for achieving longevity by being frozen after death in the hope of subsequent resuscitation. For details contact the Alcor Life Extension Foundation, 12327 Doherty Street, Riverside, California 92503, telephone (800) 367-2228.

I must emphasize that I have extremely high regard for the ethical codes followed by Alcor, and the cryonics organization that plays a minor part in the plot of my novel is not in any way intended to resemble Alcor or any other organization in the real world.

Author's Note

The equipment and procedures that I have described in this novel do not yet exist. In fifty to one hundred years, however, such techniques may be possible, and at that point they will enable us to achieve a form of immortality.

I believe that not everyone will welcome this. Indeed, pioneers in the field may be forced to conduct their research under clandestine conditions in order to escape restrictive regulations or conservative backlash.

One way or another, though, there surely will come a time when the mind may outlive the body; and I myself look forward to this as a form of liberation—for future generations, if not for my own.

PART ONE

Obsession

At first LifeScan had been a challenge, luring her with the promise of freedom and power. Ten years later it had become an obsession, ruling her days, haunting her nights. When she lay in bed alone, restlessly seeking sleep, her mind still fretted at unsolved problems: how to obtain materials for the next phase of development, how to hide purchase orders, how to lay false trails and store fake data. The project had long since violated ethical guidelines and federal law; if they were found out now, it would ruin their careers. But even the prospect of prison sentences seemed trivial compared with their biggest fear—that LifeScan would be dismantled and their work would be lost.

Each morning, muzzy from too little sleep and too many pills, she ate a breakfast of instant eggs and soy toast, thinking about it still: how to filter out noise that was corrupting the data, how to suppress vibration from the refrigeration unit, how to refine the scanning resolution of the probes. The project was like a metronome setting the rhythm of her life.

Her name was Rosalind French and she worked at North Industries, a defense contractor just off the Long Beach freeway. Her laboratory was a big, bare, high-ceilinged room with beige walls and a black plastic floor, barred windows looking onto a courtyard of eucalyptus trees. It was cluttered with monitoring and diagnostic gear in gray aluminum cabinets, metal-working tools, a scanning-tunneling electron microscope, tissue samples in a large freezer, sheets of steel and bar stock, keyboards and flat-panel data displays. At the center of the space, ringed by the other equipment, a Cray-12 computer stood like a small black tombstone beside a cylindrical stainless-steel tank the size of a baby's crib.

Tonight, like most nights, two other scientists shared the lab with her: Michael Butterworth, a tall, skinny neurophysiologist who looked down on the world around him with an enigmatic air of detachment, and Hans Voss, a Polish-born engineer and craftsman of the old school. Butterworth was something of a mystic, a dreamer who once told her he'd chosen his vocation after a two-hour stint of meditation followed by a session with the *I Ching*. By contrast, Voss was a little old man with a pink bald head rimmed by wisps of white hair. He was shy and unimposing, yet he had a special rapport with machinery. To Rosalind it almost seemed as if systems sensed his authority and surrendered to his special, gentle touch.

This, of course, was irrational nonsense. But the more time she spent in the lab, the more each piece of equipment seemed to acquire a personality filling the void that friends had once occupied in her life. Sometimes she even found herself talking to the hardware—praising it for performing correctly, scolding it for defying her.

Strange behavior for someone who believed in the scientific method, and yet as the months passed she was growing more and more superstitious. If she sensed there were bad omens—if the mix of people and equipment wasn't *propitious* in some mystical way she couldn't even explain—she'd cancel a test run without hesitation. Her burden of responsibility had grown so heavy, the only way she could deal with it was by going with her gut feelings.

Tonight—a warm spring California night—the setup did feel propitious. She waited beside the stainless-steel tank, a tall woman in her early thirties with alert gray eyes, black hair pulled severely back. Her self-control and her formal posture—the product of a venerable East Coast finishing school—allowed no clue to her inner anxieties.

She waited, and Hans Voss waited with her. Butterworth got ready for the run, settling into his seat at the control desk, his head hidden beneath the black hemisphere of the viewing hood, his hands groping inside waldoes—metal gauntlets lined with pressure and motion sensors.

"Ready," he said finally.

Rosalind pressed the on-button of her log unit. It functioned like an airplane's flight recorder, tracking the real-time status of more than two hundred key components. Company policy specified that archival facilities in the basement were the correct place to store this kind of data, but LifeScan's experimental results had long since been taken off the official record.

"Looks okay," said Butterworth. "I'm starting the peel."

Rosalind stared through the observation panel in the side of the tank. It was cold in there—minus 170 degrees Celsius—and there were tiny ice crystals on the inside of the glass. Metal clamps were holding a gray lump of tissue the size of a child's fist, glistening in the light from two halogen lamps. The razor-thin red beam of a laser scalpel flicked into life. Hundreds of gossamer-thin, gleaming probes swung down, moving so slowly they seemed to be drifting through oil. Delicately, they touched the slick gray surface of the tissue sample, conforming to it, preparing to tease secrets from its cells.

The laser edged forward, mimicking Butterworth's hand movements on a microscopic scale. Carefully, it began peeling a layer of cells like skin from a plum—skin so thin, it was transparent. Metal clips like tiny clothespins lifted the peel, and a second set of probes started exploring its underside, digitizing the information and transmitting it from the tank along a wrist-thick cable to the Cray alongside.

Rosalind had long ago learned to suppress her expectations. This was just another test run, and it could founder like those before it. But tonight—tonight it really did feel propitious. She stood peering intently into the tank like a stern mother observing her child's attempts to walk.

The laser completed its pass. Voss, beside her, gave a little grunt of satisfaction. "Good," he said. But she hardly heard him; she was aware of nothing but the gleaming red line of the laser and the clusters of whiskery probes performing arabesques around it. The muscles in her neck and back were rigid with tension.

"There's some mistracking." Butterworth's voice was muffled by the viewing hood, but the words were clear enough. Rosalind glanced quickly at a display depicting the operation in false colors at high magnification. It showed the surface of the tissue as a landscape of lumpy, rolling hills, probes dancing over the terrain in a complex ballet. But one of them had fallen behind, out of step with its neighbors. It was searching dumbly from side to side like a blind man's cane.

She let out her pent-up breath in a groan of frustration. She hit the off-button of her log unit. "Damn it, Mike!"

The laser winked out and the probes slowly retracted. Butterworth pulled back from the hood and withdrew his wrists from the gauntlets. He sat there for a moment, restlessly flexing his fingers like a synth musician whose solo performance had been aborted by a loose connector. He gave Rosalind a faint, ironic smile. "Too bad," he said.

"There has to be some dumb little thing that we missed." The night wasn't propitious anymore; that had been an illusion, a deception, and she felt betrayed, determined to find out how or why the hardware had conspired against her. She turned to Voss. "Hans—"

"Is not the stepping motors." He hunched his shoulders as if bracing himself for bad weather. "Please, we don't strip them again, okay?" Even though he was twice her age, he looked like a kid facing a school principal.

She studied him with her steady gray eyes. "You're really certain?"

"I think Hans has it right," said Butterworth, pushing back from the control desk and getting calmly to his feet, seemingly unaffected by the tension between Rosalind and Voss. He was a Zen Buddhist, and he preached fatalism, yet in his own quiet way, Rosalind sensed he was as tenacious and ambitious as she was herself. She wished he kept less hidden; it meant he was that much outside her control.

"So what's the problem?" she said. "We've wasted three weeks trying to find the source of this malfunction. I want to know what's wrong."

He shrugged, turning away from her. "You want to strip it down again, go right ahead."

It was that time of night, Rosalind realized, when it was easier to snap at each other than cooperate. She tried to control her irritation. "Am I right in thinking that both of you still believe there's a bug in the terrain-tracking software?"

Butterworth nodded. "Yep."

"Jeremy has checked that software, line by line. He's done

simulations, he's run it under—" She paused, sensing his adamancy. "All right. Maybe you should go upstairs and tell Jeremy to check it again."

Butterworth shook his head. "It's getting kind of late."

Rosalind knew from experience that he tended to dig in his heels if she was too aggressive. "Michael." She switched to her softer, be-reasonable voice. "With all that we have at stake here . . ."

Butterworth wandered over to the Cray. He methodically erased the persistent RAM, then started powering the system down.

"He's tired," said Voss. "It is a strain, you know, working the waldoes. We all need some rest. Even you, perhaps."

His tact was almost more irritating than Butterworth's detachment. Nothing could really please her, right now, short of the equipment magically fixing itself. She felt like screaming, *Why doesn't it work?*

Butterworth finished with the Cray, picked his way across the tangle of power cables, and started shutting off servo systems under the tank. The faint whine of motors gradually died away. A vacuum pump chugged briefly, then fell silent. "You know, it's just a matter of days," he said laconically. "We've done some excellent animal scans, we've verified our model, we know it works. All we have to do is shake out the last couple of bugs, and then—" His eyes had a distant look, as if he could already see the world that LifeScan promised to open up.

Rosalind succeeded in repressing her anger. "All right, I'll go upstairs and tell Jeremy you think it's the software." She unplugged her log unit and slid it into the pocket of her lab coat. "I'll see you both tomorrow." She flashed them a brief, stiff smile. "Good night."

Codeworld

The building was silent, this late. Sometimes she would encounter a security guard checking each office and laboratory through the wire-glass windows in the gray steel doors, but tonight she had the hallways to herself. The quick tap-tap of her footsteps sounded loud in the stillness.

She started up a flight of stairs to the second floor—and stopped, gripping the handrail, gasping involuntarily as pain gripped her legs and radiated from her hips up her back. She propped herself against the wall and closed her eyes. The pain was so intense, it made thought almost impossible.

The condition had a name—systemic lupus erythematosus—but its origins were still not understood. It was an autoimmune disorder, usually ending in renal failure. Along the way, it could cause severe arthritis. It had been diagnosed in her just over ten years ago, which was when they had told her that ten years was the median life expectancy after diagnosis. She tried as much as she could to forget that fact; but the bouts of crippling pain were getting more frequent and more severe, and sometimes, when she was tired, she feared that her muzzy-headedness might be the first sign of kidney dysfunction.

Just a few more weeks, she thought to herself, as if begging one last favor from her body. After that, it won't matter. After that, do anything you want.

She stood waiting for the stabbing sensations to diminish. She imagined how it would be to live without pain, in a future where all physical ailments were eliminated and the spirit was free. The fantasy frightened her. She wanted it too much.

When she was able to, she went on up the stairs moving slowly, tentatively, afraid of doing anything that would trigger another attack.

Finally she reached the next floor and made her way to Jeremy Porter's office.

It was a little windowless cubicle, and since Porter had removed the fluorescent tubes from the ceiling panel, the only light came from a low-wattage bulb in a battered metal desk lamp that he'd scrounged from a thrift shop. Beyond its dim circle of radiance the room was lost in shadows.

Cardboard boxes of hardcopy and stacks of technical magazines were scattered across the floor like a minefield to trip intruders. The plain beige walls had been papered with a mosaic of charts listing specifications of computer components. Company-issue bookshelves had been engulfed with heaps of loose-leaf reference manuals. Once the cubicle had been no different from all the others on this floor; but now it was Porterized.

He was a fat man with unkempt frizzy hair and a black, bushy beard. He wore white shirts that were rumpled and stained with coffee, corduroy pants that were baggy at the seat, and he peered out at the world through antique wire-framed glasses whose lenses were never clean. When Rosalind had first started working with him she'd been exasperated to see him squinting at his computer screen through a patina of grease, and she'd gotten into the habit of wiping his glasses for him. Bit by bit, she'd found herself taking on other chores he never seemed to notice were necessary: cooking him real meals once in a while, buying him a new pair of socks, even trimming his beard. He'd received her favors with shy, confused gratitude. Though the two of them had absolutely nothing in common beyond their dedication to LifeScan, a bond had been created. When Porter's landlady filed plans to turn his building into condos, Rosalind offered to let him stay temporarily in the spare room at her home. Her husband had left her the year before, and she felt she needed some company. Of course, Porter was no company at all; he seemed to have trouble remembering that she existed. Yet she liked having him there, and he'd stayed ever since.

She waited in the doorway of his cubicle. He was slouched in his chair staring at a screen full of program code. His fingers rattled briefly on the keyboard, and he addressed a couple of muttered commands to the system. Finally he squirmed around in his chair, blinking in the light from the hallway. "Uh, Rosalind." He slid his fingers under his glasses and rubbed his eyes. "You were going to do another run, is that right? How'd it turn out?"

She walked in, pushed a couple of dirty coffee cups out of the way, and perched on the corner of his desk. It was heaped with scribbled notes, crumpled sheets, documentation, RAMcards, and unanswered memos.

"One of the probes lost acquisition again. Mike and Hans are more convinced than ever that it has to be a software problem. They swear they've eliminated everything else."

Porter didn't say anything. He continued staring up at her. He spent most of his life living inside the programs he wrote.

Codeworld, she called it. Once, with an embarrassed smile, he'd told her he even had dreams in program language. The real world was of secondary importance; he put it on hold, in some sort of mental input buffer, till his brain found time to process the interruptions.

Porter blinked, which was generally a sign he was coming back online. "So what exactly—"

"Maybe you should review the event sequence." Distantly, she was aware of sounding severe and impatient. The pain that she often felt made it hard to project human warmth. But she assumed Jeremy knew her well enough to ignore her manner.

She handed him her log unit, and he took it from her with obvious reluctance. The last thing he wanted was to go back to a problem that he had solved, so far as he knew, six months ago. He rummaged in the papers on his desk, found the wire he was looking for, and attached it to the unit. He turned toward his console. "System, external device, port five, upload data, encrypt, store in RAMcard, alpha-test folder, filename May 12, 2030." He waited a few seconds for the acknowledgment, then returned the log unit to her.

"Thanks," she said. She cleared its memory and put it back in her coat. "You know, apart from that one probe mistracking, it was . . . really a promising run."

Porter rooted around some more, pulled out a single white sheet, and handed it to her. "This isn't so promising."

She saw that it was a memo from the State of California, Office of Science and Technology, Military Research Division, Department of Finance, Board of Audit and Review—part of the bureaucratic infrastructure that had been imposed on North Industries since it had been taken over by the government in 2019. Shorn of the bureaucratic vocabulary the memo's message was simple: management wanted to know what, if anything, the LifeScan program was good for. Porter had been concocting false test data for years—results that always looked vaguely promising but never amounted to anything definite. In the past, this had been enough. But now, someone in government was getting impatient.

She stared at the paper, not really seeing it. "When did you get this?"

"Um, this morning. Horton brought it in. He said he doesn't

think there's much he can do this time. It's gone too high up. There's no way to avoid the funding review." Porter paused as if replaying the meeting in his head, making sure he hadn't lost any of the data. "He was also pretty pissed about the memory modules. You know, the ones that, ah, disappeared."

She closed her eyes for a moment. Just a few more weeks, she thought to herself.

Porter fidgeted. He pushed his glasses up his nose. "What do you think?"

"I'm too tired to think." She dropped the paper back on his desk. "Let's go home. We can talk more conveniently on the way." She meant, more safely. They swept his office regularly for bugs, but surveillance was always a possibility. North Industries felt no great need to spy on personnel, but the state bureaucracy was notoriously suspicious of scientists involved in classified research.

"Can you work on the software at home?" Rosalind asked.

Porter looked disoriented. "Software?"

"The terrain-tracking software that controls the tissue probes. Don't you want to compare it with the event sequence you uploaded from my log unit?"

"Oh. Yes. I can do that." He was back in Codeworld, she realized. His eyes had strayed toward the monitor screen as it called to him in a language that only he could understand.

"Time to power down, Jeremy." She said it with a smile.

He grunted. Finally, he forced a smile in return. He issued a shut-down command, took the RAMcard out of its slot, and flipped the switch. She noticed that there was a slight tremor in his fingers. It wasn't just her, she realized; the tension was getting to all of them.

Human Error

She drove along back streets, following one of several zigzag routes that they'd established years ago. Freeways were out of the question; the traffic density made her too nervous. Another vehicle could be following behind, or even alongside, without her realizing it. From nearby it would be easy to detect their conversation; a laser scan of the vibrations of the car windows would be sufficient. She was, of course, paranoid to think that anyone would take so much trouble, but it was better to be paranoid than risk getting caught.

"You know, maybe we should show them some of our real data," Porter said as the little car moved along a residential back street. "If we told them even a little bit of what we can really do, they'd give us all the money we want."

Sometimes, he could be touchingly naive. "No, Jeremy," she said.

The car's motor whined, and the tires thumped over potholes in the highway. The gutters were littered with garbage and old leaves, and half the streetlights were dead. It was a run-down low-rent neighborhood, but it was close to the lab and the rent was cheap. The less they had to pay in everyday expenses, the more they could spend on equipment for their after-hours activities.

"We could show them some stuff from a year ago," Jeremy persisted. "I can fake a fault to explain why they never saw it originally."

"No," she said again. "That might fool Horton, but not the board inspectors. And besides, if we let out even a hint of what LifeScan can really do, we'd have management breathing down our necks, and we'd have extra personnel assigned to the project. We'd never have a chance to—to do what we want to do."

She turned onto the street where they lived. Behind security fences, the barred windows of small suburban homes glowed yellow in the darkness. "You know," she went on, "maybe Horton was trying to tell us something by passing the memo to you at the same time he complained about the missing memory modules. We've stolen so much equipment, the disappearances must make him look bad. If we could 'find' those modules for him, he might try a little harder on our behalf."

Porter moved uncomfortably in his seat. He looked unhappy. "We can't give them back. They're essential."

Rosalind parked beside her house and pulled her key card out of the ignition. "I can go to Little Asia and trade for some new modules. Kai could get them for us."

He looked at her doubtfully. "I don't like the risk that entails."

She shrugged. "Neither do I." She paused, brooding. "So let's leave it for now. Hold it in reserve as an option."

Later, they ate microwaved soy steaks while Rosalind took the mail out of the fax and Jeremy scanned program code on a portable editor. They barely noticed their surroundings, spartanly furnished with thrift-shop chairs and drapes, as neutral and characterless as a motel room. In the kitchen, the stainless-steel sink was dry and dusty, and there were bags of TV-dinner dishes waiting to be taken to the recycling center.

Rosalind came here only to eat and sleep, and Porter used the place even less than she did. Often he spent the night in a private lab that they maintained in a safe house in San Pedro, working through till dawn, napping intermittently on an air mattress in the glow from his computer screen.

"I see a possible error," he said, after a while. "I did a patch, then a second patch when we enhanced the equipment after the last animal scan. There's a shared variable—"

Rosalind looked up from the text in front of her. Slowly, she put the page down. "But Jeremy, you absolutely swore to me—"

"Well, I'm still not entirely sure. The code is extremely complex. But an error does seem possible." He fidgeted, looking embarrassed, avoiding her eyes.

"So we wasted three weeks stripping and rebuilding the hardware." She sounded more weary than angry. It was hard to get mad at him, perhaps because he seemed so vulnerable. In any case, scolding him was pointless. It would be more likely to paralyze him than galvanize him.

"Sorry," he said. His expression was hidden behind his beard.

She walked over and put her arm around his shoulders. "All that matters is finding what's wrong and fixing it," she said quietly.

"Right." He nodded to himself. "I'd better get over to San Pedro and do a full simulation. Is the other car recharged?"

"I think so." She handed him the key. Their second vehicle was reserved for special trips only. It was protected with the best antisurveillance equipment they knew how to devise. "Be careful, Jeremy. We can wait an extra eight hours, if you need the sleep."

"No, I'm fine." He paused as if doing a quick self-test. He smiled. "Fine," he confirmed.

Human Needs

Alone in her bedroom, she lay listening to intermittent traffic humming past along the street. A warm wind bent the branches of the tree outside her window, and leaves rustled against the glass. The trees should have been cut back, she realized. Another entire year had gone by—a year under the flat glare of the fluorescents at the lab, working against time. On rare occasions when she stepped back and looked at her life it seemed empty and joyless, an endless series of self-imposed deadlines and obligations.

Yet that was just an emotional response. Other people's lives were far emptier. In fact, to her, most humans seemed little better than cells under a microscope, jostling one another in random motion, pairing, procreating, because that was what their DNA told them to do.

Procreation, to Rosalind, was merely a function of biology, a distraction from priorities that were infinitely more important. Sex, likewise, seemed an animal ritual. And yet, trapped in her flesh, there was no way she could completely suppress her needs.

She ran her hands over her body, feeling its contours. She touched herself, masturbating gently at first, imagining a baroque palace—maybe a Greek temple—in a land where the air was clean and the water was clear and platters were piled with fresh meats and fruits, and there were dozens—hundreds?—of servants, all men, half-naked, clustered around her where she sat in her chair. Or was it a throne? Yes, she was their monarch; they worshipped her. Her life was pure sensual indulgence and it would last forever.

She came, then lay there in the darkness feeling embarrassed by her own fantasy. How would it feel if there were no mental privacy and other people could monitor her thoughts as readily as computer data? This was a concept that made her extremely uneasy. Better not to think about it; and so, in the afterglow of her orgasm, she drifted into sleep.

Weapons

The sky was the washed-out color of a concrete highway, brown around the edges. The sun was near the zenith, pale and hazy, glaring down, making James Bayley sweat under his headware and body armor. He glanced at the time displayed in sharp green numerals beside one of the microscreens inside his mask. Not yet noon; still a couple of hours for the heat to grow more intense, reverberating between the old brick buildings. Here in Little Asia, just a few blocks from downtown, the air always seemed heavy and rank, pollution overlaid with odors of greasy food and disinfectant. The tiny streets were packed with people: illegal immigrants, beggars, hookers, traders, tourists, hustlers, and businessmen clad in robes and privacy masks like his own. Not that Bayley himself was a businessman; he worked for the government, and his mask was merely a means to an end.

He paced the stained sidewalk, monitoring the view on his fore and aft microscreens: the shifting crowds of people, three-story buildings hidden behind a mosaic of posters and neon, wallscreens blaring sales messages in Japanese, English, Korean, and Chinese. In the street itself teenagers were hawking tech toys, imaging systems, sense-players, and microcomponents off market stalls improvised from planks laid across oil drums. Loud music from cheap radios in bars and tea houses mingled with the shouts of the traders.

Bayley paused and checked his reflection in the aluminized armor-glass windows of the Chinju Merchant Bank. In his headware and flowing black robe he looked like Doctor Death.

He flexed the muscles of his face. Gray plastic grinned back at him.

The bank's greeter, a doll-faced Korean, clasped her hands and bowed. "Good morning, sir. Nice day! Open new account, sir? Safe-deposit box? No name, no ID number, sir, very private."

And probably a violation of federal law, Bayley thought to himself. But here in Little Asia a lot of laws were tacitly ignored. Gray-legal import-export companies did business side-by-side with pachinko parlors, tattoo emporiums, drug houses, and psychic healers. The Los Angeles Federal Center was less than half a mile away, just the other side of the freeway, and Bayley's own office was in one of those tall glass towers. Yet Little Asia was permitted to survive in all its quasi-legal squalor for the same reason that Hong Kong had once been tolerated by communist China: It helped to vitalize the nation's centralized, planned economy.

A fat woman tried to sell Bayley barbecued soy steak off an aluminum handcart. A teenage mulatto girl started tugging at his arm, offering sex disks. He studied her face for a moment, wondering about her life—where she'd been born, who she worked for, how she would survive as she aged.

But the address he was looking for lay just ahead, a tenement whose windows were covered with steel shutters, themselves obscured under layers of spray-paint graffiti. Green neon displayed a business name in Kanji script, an English translation below: Kai's Personal Defense Mart.

Bayley checked his aft video. So far as he could tell, he wasn't being followed. He slid his hand around under his robe and loosened the 9mm automatic that he carried in a shoulder holster. Against the inside of his left leg, just above his ankle, was a second weapon: a miniature pistol less than a centimeter thick, containing just a single round of plastic ammunition. It was fabricated from carbon fiber to be as difficult as possible to detect, and was intended strictly for emergencies. Bayley carried it not because he expected to use it, but merely because it felt good, like a rabbit's foot or a lucky penny.

He went over to the tenement's door. The wooden panels, long ago painted red, had been reinforced with steel rods embedded in transparent resin. He thumbed an old-fashioned plastic bell push and waited.

A steel disc slid aside, a lens looked down at him, and a synth voice told him to state his business.

"I'm here to see Mr. Kai. I'm Frank Morello. I'm a friend of Terumi Kobayashi."

Bolts shunted aside and the red door swung inward, powered by a motor that made a low growling noise. Bayley stepped in feeling a little surge of adrenaline, not so much from nervousness as from anticipation. He upped the sensitivity of his mask's optic amplifiers to compensate for the gloom and saw a narrow hallway, dusty gray floorboards, wallpaper mottled with mold. Immediately to his right was a door faced with riveted steel plate, a reinforced window in the center revealing a room beyond, yellow paint lit by naked fluorescent tubes.

The street door shut itself behind him and he waited passively, his arms by his sides, his pulse and his breathing sounding loud inside his headware. Finally, the second door opened, and he moved forward across the threshold.

His microscreens showed glass-fronted display cases stacked to the ceiling, crammed with weapons. The opposite end of the room was blocked off by a massive wooden counter and a wall-to-wall slab of milky Lucite layered with wire mesh. A wrinkled, silver-haired Japanese man was sitting on a stool behind the barrier, peering at Bayley. He gave a perfunctory little bow. "Good morning, sir." His voice was amplified through a cheap loudspeaker.

"You're Mr. Kai," said Bayley.

"I am Mr. Kai, yes." He grinned, showing nicotine-stained teeth. "And you are Mr. Morello. You are referred by Miss Kobayashi."

Bayley glanced again at the cases full of equipment. Handguns, rifles, and grenade launchers; billy clubs, nunchucks, and samurai swords; gas guns, bolos, time bombs, and ceremonial daggers—the place was a weapon freak's wet dream. "That's right, I'm Morello," he said, pacing himself, deliberately taking his time. "Terumi said you could help me out." His voice sounded alien, modified by his mask's scrambler.

"Ah." The Japanese paused. His smile became stiff, as if the subject embarrassed him. "You are aware, of course, of her untimely death."

Bayley blinked. For a moment time seemed to gel around him. "She's dead?"

"You are not aware?"

"No." He tried to keep his voice level. "Ah, how long ago did it happen?"

"Six months." The little man removed his glasses and polished them on his tie. "Two reports appear in the newsfax. And her family notify all close friends. How strange, you do not know."

Bayley decided to take the risk. He forced a laugh. "Come on, Kai. I saw Terumi just last week."

The Japanese put his glasses back on and clasped his hands. Suddenly he laughed and inclined his head as if conceding the loss of a couple of stones in a game of Go. "Please excuse, Mr. Morello. My, little story. I must make sure my clients are . . . sincere. So, you a genuine friend of Miss Kobayashi. What can I do for you?"

Bayley realized he'd been holding his breath. He let it out, angry at Kai for inflicting the little initiation but pleased with himself for not having fallen for it. "I hear you've got something new," he said. "Some kind of electronic handgun—"

"Stunner in display case, there? Very popular item."

Bayley turned and inspected it, then shook his head. "The thing I'm talking about is a lethal weapon. I understand it matches phase somehow with brain activity, and blanks it."

"Ah." Mr. Kai paused carefully. "Of course, if such device exists, it is illegal. Not for sale even in Little Asia."

"Of course." Bayley reached under his robe and pulled out a stack of metal disks rolled in oiled brown paper. He held them up so that Kai could see them through the Lucite barrier. "I do have hard currency."

Mr. Kai eyed the disks. "One kilo platinum?"

"Right."

Kai seemed to reach a decision. "Please put there." He pointed to a little turntable set in the surface of the counter, subdivided so that the inside half was accessible to him, the outside to his customers.

Bayley set down the coins and waited.

Kai reached under the counter, took out a small pistol, and placed it on the inner half of the turntable. He spun it, and the weapon and the coins switched places.

Bayley picked up the gun. It was fashioned from stainless-steel plate bent into a box shape, a length of tube serving as a hand grip. The design was crude but the workmanship was good—surprisingly good. "What's the range?"

"Five, six meters. Please observe, grounded metal-mesh screen is complete protection to your target."

"Is it directional?"

"Highly directional." Kai had placed one of the coins in a small weighing-analysis unit and was speaking abstractedly, watching the readout. The unit made a soft musical chime, and he nodded to himself, satisfied.

Bayley slid the gun under his robe. "How many hits is it good for?"

"Only one, Mr. Morello, and not rechargable."

"But if I want more of these, I can come back to you?"

Kai smiled happily. "I am sole source of supply."

"You got any more right now?"

The smile reversed itself. "Very sorry, Mr. Morello. As it happens, is last one. But it is fortunate, today I expect new shipment quite imminently."

Which meant . . . what? "I could come back this afternoon and buy another?"

"It is possible, I think."

Bayley considered his options. He could complete his assignment right now—identify himself as an FBI agent working in the Department of Technology-Related Crime, notify Kai of his rights, and take him in. The entire transaction had been monitored on the systems in Bayley's headware, and the recordings would be admissible as evidence.

But something about the gun was—wrong. It wasn't a street item. The technology was too slick. It had a pedigree. He sensed a mystery behind it, and that alone was enough to sway his judgment.

"Maybe I'll come back later," he said. "Thank you, Mr. Kai." He turned toward the steel exit door.

"Thank *you*, Mr. Morello."

Modules

Bayley walked back into the noise, the color, the smells of the street. He pushed through a group of tourists, ducked into a tea house directly opposite, and climbed creaking wooden stairs to the upper floor. A red code started blinking in his mask's data display as sensors detected narcotics nearby—opium smoke, probably, from private rooms on the top floor. He killed the telltale; in this part of town, the bureau had no interest in casual drug use.

He sat at a small table by the window, ordered a pot of peppermint tea, and looked through grimy glass at the street below. The permissive atmosphere in Little Asia was deceptive; there were limits that all the traders understood. Recombinant DNA or radioactive isotopes were forbidden. So were lethal weapons such as the one he'd just purchased.

He upped the magnification of his headware so that the entrance to Kai's Mart filled one of the microscreens, then sat quietly, sipping his tea through a straw that fit the mouth slot in his mask. The room was quiet, almost empty. Two preteens in motorcycle jackets were drinking beer laced with vodka at a table by the door, and a geisha sat watching a vidbook, glancing up occasionally, maybe waiting for her pimp. In Little Asia early afternoon was always a slow time.

Bayley told his headware to connect him with his home. The system at his apartment recognized the origination code and picked up. "One message for you, Jim," it said, "from Sharon."

His wife's face appeared in one of the microscreens. "Hi, honey." She smiled, making dimples. She wasn't conventionally beautiful—her face was a little too round, her features not quite symmetrical—but there was an alive, enticing quality about her. She had bright eyes, a wide, expressive mouth, black hair in a pageboy haircut. "I'm at work. I just had my meeting. Looks like there's some good news. I'll tell you when you get home. Don't be late! I love you!" And the screen blanked.

Bayley replayed the message, then erased it. She worked in the news department at KUSA, the government-owned channel, and she'd been hoping for a promotion for months now. He wondered if she'd finally got it. It was like her to tease him a little, make him wait for the facts till he got home.

He thought of their apartment building in Granada Hills, beige stucco walls shaded by elms and jacaranda trees, flowering cactus in the courtyard, new cars in the basement garage. Compared with the grime and sleaze of Little Asia it seemed impossibly remote, a middle-class fantasy.

A kid in gangland colors paused in the street, looked each way, then pressed Kai's bell and disappeared inside. Bayley decided that the kid was of no interest to him. He took another sip of his tea, and he waited.

An hour passed. More customers arrived in the tea room. He ordered sushi sandwiches: thin-sliced tuna substitute on nutty brown bread. He widened the mouth slot to feed himself and waited some more.

Finally he spotted a prospect, a slim figure striding through the crowds, moving purposefully, lugging a black Fiberglas suitcase with dented corners and scuff marks down the sides. The man was wearing a blue robe, his face concealed by a mask like the one that Bayley wore.

Bayley jumped up, hurried down the stairs to the street, then paused by a market stall as his suspect was admitted through Kai's grimy red door. Time passed: one minute, two.

The caped figure finally reemerged, still toting the suitcase. But he walked with a straighter posture, as if the case was no longer so heavy. Bayley started walking quickly, threading his way through the crowds till he was a couple of paces ahead of his target.

He watched the aft screen to judge the moment precisely, then turned without warning. His shoulder caught the man high in the chest, just under his jaw. He made a muffled sound of surprise, staggering backward, tripping over Bayley's foot. He fell heavily onto the sidewalk and his suitcase tumbled free, bursting open as it hit the ground.

Bayley bent down, quickly maneuvering his mask to face his adversary. "Sorry. My fault. You okay?" As he spoke, he activated camera systems built into the headware. "Here, let me get your case."

"No." The man scrambled up.

But Bayley was already bending over the suitcase. He'd expected it to be empty or maybe to contain some cash; but instead he found ten little electronic modules packed in antistatic blisters. He glanced at them long enough to vid their serial numbers. "Hope I didn't break anything," he said.

The other man seized the suitcase and snapped it shut. For a moment he confronted Bayley, mask-to-mask in the crowded alley under the fierce sun. Then he strode away down the sidewalk without looking back.

Bayley followed at a slower pace. He saw the blue cape turn the next corner, onto a main street. By the time he caught up the man was getting into a car parked in a loading zone. Bayley zoomed in on the license plate, and then the vehicle was gone, receding into the mass of traffic.

Mysteries

Much later, when the day had spent itself and the land was softened with long purple shadows, Bayley drove north on the San Diego freeway, a straggler in the great commuter convoy heading home.

For eight years now, ever since he'd finished college, he'd maintained a basically nine-to-five routine. But it still felt just a little strange. No matter how he tried to adapt himself to it, it never quite fit him.

As far back as he could remember, he'd had trouble blending in. Growing up in a small town in northern California he'd been a shy, quiet kid who was always slow to understand the social rituals that everyone else seemed to understand instinctively. He didn't date many girls, and he never made it onto the football team. He didn't even do well academically; he was too much of a dreamer, staring out of the window, wondering how insects communicated with each other, or what made the sky blue, or how much you'd weigh if you were in the center of the earth, when he should have been learning the names of U.S. presidents or how to say "Good morning" in Japanese. His teachers complained he had a short attention span, but what they meant was that he kept asking strange, difficult questions instead of sitting quietly and viewing his lesson programs.

At the age of eight he'd found an antique alarm clock in a neighbor's trash. He'd cleaned it and taken it apart, just for the pleasure of discovering what was inside. He had no interest in putting it back together; instead, without really knowing why, he sorted the gearwheels, the levers, and the tiny machine screws, bagged them, and then labeled each bag.

Almost twenty-five years later he was still asking questions and taking things apart. The difference was that now he was getting paid for it. Unraveling mysteries, learning how the world worked, that was his motivation, his greatest pleasure. Catching felons and putting them in jail was a secondary priority as far as he was concerned.

He took the Granada Hills exit and drove past neat little houses nestled amid lush vegetation. He could have lived closer to downtown, but government aid had enabled this suburb to survive better than most, and he liked the comfortable rituals: evenings spent reading or talking or watching interactive video, Saturdays at the supermarket or the shopping mall, Sundays lying in bed with the fax-*Times*. It almost made him feel, sometimes, that he had found a place where he truly belonged.

His apartment building came into view, and he pressed a button on the dashboard to gain access to the basement garage. The gate slid aside, rusty wheels squealing, and he reminded himself to do some maintenance on it. It wasn't his responsibility, but he was the kind of man who generally believed the job would be done better if he did it himself.

He parked his car and climbed the two flights of stairs to his apartment, feeling pleasantly unfettered without the burden of the headware and body armor he wore during field work. The security system recognized him, the door opened, and he heard loud music—some sort of nursery rhyme played on a synth—blaring out of the new DVI system he'd bought a couple of weeks ago.

"Daddee!" Damon, his four-year-old, came running across the carpet. Bayley lifted him up and hugged him. "All Macdonald," Damon said, wriggling in Bayley's arms. "Mommy bought me All Macdonald. Look!"

Now Bayley recognized the music. "You mean *Old* Macdonald." He set Damon down, stepped in front of the wallscreen, and found himself surrounded by cows and chickens, a bright red barn in the background, puffy white clouds parading across an impossibly blue sky.

Damon picked up the remote. "That's what I said: All Macdonald. Let's go see the pigs!" He pressed buttons, the viewpoint tracked forward, the music recycled, and the animals started grunting and mooing on cue, taking turns to sing along.

Bayley winced. He retreated into the kitchen and found Sharon standing at the sink, chopping vegetables. She lifted one wet hand, wiped her bangs away from her forehead with the back of her wrist, and gave him a guilty grin. "He really wanted it, and I didn't have the heart to say no. Can you stand the noise?"

"Barely." He hugged and kissed her. Little Asia was still haunting him somewhere in the back of his mind, but less, now, as he keyed into the familiarity of home.

"I got off early," she explained. "So I let Mrs. Lopez go home, and I took Damon shopping."

He nodded, saying nothing. It was part of their game that if she was keeping a secret, he wouldn't come right out and ask what it was.

She bit her lip. Her cheeks were a little flushed; she was excited. "I got the promotion," she said, finally. "They liked my test video. I won't be editing wire copy anymore. I'm going to be covering city hall."

He raised his eyebrows. "For real?"

She nodded. Her smile widened. "Your wife's going to be a TV personality."

He laughed and hugged her again. He looked at the apartment, the life they'd been gradually establishing. Sometimes it all seemed too good to be true—like a trick, or a trap, as if he was being set up. Holding Sharon, he felt himself holding onto all his good fortune, so tightly that it could never be taken away.

Identification

Later, while Sharon was putting Damon to bed, he sat on the couch with his briefcase on his knees and took out the weapon that he'd bought at Kai's Mart. He turned it, studying it, taking care not to touch the power switch. The stainless steel was neatly welded. There was no way to open the piece, short of cutting it apart, which he guessed might initiate some internal destruct mechanism.

Gingerly, he placed the gun on the coffee table. Even though he was no stranger to firearms, something about it made him uneasy.

Sharon came in, sat down beside him, and saw what he'd brought home. "I guess this means you found the source. Was it in Little Asia? The way you figured?"

He nodded. "The tip turned out to be good."

She peered at the gun but didn't touch it. "It looks like a toy."

"It kills people. Instant loss of brain function. No noise, no evidence, no apparent cause of death."

She pulled back and gave him a doubting look. "Were you authorized to bring it home?"

He shrugged. "No. But I didn't want to log it. Not yet. I'm . . . still following my own track."

She leaned against the cushions at the end of the couch, kicked her shoes off, drew her knees up, and slid her feet under the side of his leg. She watched him earnestly, her eyes alert. "Going to tell me about it?"

"Of course."

Most agents at the bureau didn't take their work home with them or discuss it with their wives. But Bayley wasn't like most agents, and Sharon wasn't like most wives. Her journalistic perspective, her ability to analyze and criticize, were valuable to him.

She listened while he described the alley in Little Asia, the interior of the Personal Defense Mart, his decision to conduct surveillance from across the street.

"Wouldn't it have been easier to plant a bug?" she interrupted.

"Yes, but Kai could have had detection gear, and I didn't want to risk my cover."

"But you didn't know he was telling the truth when he said he was expecting a new shipment. You could have sat there all day, watching and waiting for something to happen."

He shifted uneasily. "I know." It bothered him when he didn't have a logical explanation. "I just had a feeling that it was the right thing to do."

She laughed softly. "Male intuition?" She slumped down in the deep cushions, making herself more comfortable. "So, you watched and waited. Then what?"

He told her about his encounter with the masked, robed figure.

Sharon shook her head in mock disapproval. "Are you telling me that your suspect voluntarily waived his constitutional rights against unreasonable search and seizure?"

"I didn't search him. We just happened to bump into each other," Bayley said, straight-faced.

"Sure, Sherlock. So, you managed to sneak a peek into the case. What did you find?"

"Electronic components. Computer memory modules of a type I've never seen before. Looked to me as if he'd delivered the guns to Kai and picked up the modules as payment."

"That's a big supposition, isn't it?" She fixed him with her sharp, bright eyes. "He could have been trying to *sell* the memory modules. Or he could have left something else with Kai. Some other kind of gun. Maybe even something legal."

"It's a possibility. Want to bet on it?"

She wrinkled her nose. "Hell, no. You're probably right. As usual." She paused, verifying everything they'd discussed so far. It was a ritual that they both enjoyed. "Okay, what happened then?"

"I followed the suspect to his car and got a picture of the license plate as he drove away. I didn't have a chance to plant a trace on the vehicle, and when I went back to the office I found that the plate wasn't listed."

"So that's a dead end. What about the modules in the suitcase?"

"From their serial numbers I traced them to a shipment that went missing a couple weeks ago. State-of-the-art, very exotic, very expensive. You'd have to be doing classified research to have any use for them."

"Really." She paused, thinking. "It's strange, isn't it? I mean, this doesn't seem like some kid selling homemade guns to support a drug habit."

"Exactly. And that's what interests me about it."

She thought some more. "But it seems to me you've reached a block. Kai probably doesn't know who his supplier really is, and even if he did, he wouldn't tell you."

Bayley shook his head. This was the part he enjoyed most. It was his turn, now, to have a secret. "I've already identified the supplier."

She looked puzzled. "How? You said he was masked."

"I shot a couple of pictures, one infrared, one scan-focused ultrasonic. It's a new technique. We put the two together, with image enhancement, and reconstruct the primary facial features under the mask. When I did that, the first thing I found was that the guy wasn't a guy at all; he was a woman. I uploaded her picture to the Department of Motor Vehicles, they pattern-matched it with driving license photographs on file, and I got back three possible hits. Two of them I could rule out right away because the other physical stats didn't fit. The third was the right height and weight. Her name's Rosalind French, she's a biochemist, and she works for North Industries, which is an aerospace lab in Long Beach. She's doing some kind of military research."

"My god." Sharon looked shocked. "She's a scientist with a security clearance, and she's dealing homemade handguns?"

"It doesn't make sense, does it?" Bayley stared across the room, considering the deeper mystery that he'd stumbled upon. "It makes you wonder why a person with so much to lose would get involved in street crime."

"But you plan to find out?"

"Oh, yes." His eyes narrowed as he contemplated the path ahead. "I'll find out."

Homecoming

She felt a sense of dread as she entered the Federal Airlines Building. So many bad memories here amid the rows of chairs, the gift shops, the flight announcements, and the Muzak. As a teenager she'd shuttled back and forth between one parent and the other, one house and the other, neither of them a home. She couldn't count how many times her father had met her here in Los Angeles, aloof, preoccupied, hugging her but never kissing her, avoiding her eyes.

Yumi saw him as soon as she was through the arrival gate. There at the back of the crowd, the eminent man of science, tall and thin, with a deeply lined face and long, thick, bushy white hair. He looked just as she remembered him, despite the passage of time—six years? seven?

He hadn't yet noticed her, and she hesitated, clutching her flight bag and wondering if there was still time to change her mind. Maybe there was a seat on the next flight back to Hawaii. Suddenly she knew she should never have come here. There would be nothing for her but pain.

But then he saw her and waved. It was a stiff, awkward gesture; he wasn't a graceful man. Once a computer nerd, always a computer nerd, she thought. They never change. They never learn how to be human.

She walked over to him, weary and fatalistic now, ashamed of herself for not having the nerve to turn and leave. He put his arm around her shoulders and gave her a clumsy squeeze. "Yumi. Thanks so much for coming."

"How are you?" she asked in a small voice.

"Fine. And you?"

"Okay."

He started walking, taking long strides that meant she had to hurry to keep up. All around them friends and relatives were meeting and being met, laughing, embracing each other. She looked straight ahead, demure and composed, her face showing nothing.

"This terminal certainly hasn't improved over the years." He was frowning at the decor: grimy carpet, stained ceiling tiles, palm trees dying in their tubs. "You know, I can remember when it was still Pan Am—no, TWA. The government never had a clue about how to run the airline industry." He stopped and turned to her, noticing that she was lagging behind. "Shall I carry that?" He gestured at her canvas bag.

"No thanks." She tightened her grip as if she half expected him to take it away from her. "It's not heavy. And I don't think chivalry makes much sense at this point, do you?"

He looked disconcerted. "What do you mean?"

"You are fifty years older than I am."

He drew back a fraction, and she realized she had probably hurt his feelings. That gave her a little twist of malicious satisfaction, and yet surely there ought to be a better way to cope with him than this, rejecting him because he made her feel rejected.

"Do you have any checked baggage?" he asked stiffly when they were almost at the exit.

"No. I always travel light, remember?"

"Yes, of course I remember." He sounded testy, now. "I just thought it was conceivable, Yumi, as you enter your—middle years?—you might have become a little less bohemian."

They were back in their old roles, as if they'd never been apart. But he was always better at it than she was. He hit harder, because he cared less.

"I'm sorry to be a disappointment," she said, "but I'm just as bohemian as before. How about you? Have you changed at all, Father?"

He was silent for a moment. "Yes," he said finally. "There have been some significant changes. That's why I needed to see you."

Outside in the parking lot she waited while he unplugged his car from the charging outlet and put her bag in the trunk. His movements were a little slower and stiffer than she remembered, but he still seemed in remarkably good shape for a man of eighty-one. Of course, he'd had access to the best possible medical care, and he'd always exercised even though he didn't enjoy it. He treated his body like a piece of machinery that he was obliged to maintain so that his mind could survive.

Neither of them spoke as he drove out of the lot, displayed his credit disk to the reader at the exit, and joined the traffic heading toward the freeway. Soon they were traveling north on the upper level, his little car among all the other little cars, a river of steel flowing over a bed of patched concrete. To the left, as the highway climbed, she could see as far as the ocean, or at least to the Santa Monica sea wall. New construction seemed to be in progress on the barrier, keeping pace with the steadily rising water level.

She turned her attention back to the highway. He was an impatient driver, always switching lanes, and it made her nervous. "You were so mysterious when you called and asked me to come here," she said, talking to distract herself. "You made it sound as if something serious had happened."

He didn't answer right away. The silence lasted so long, she started wondering if he'd heard her. "You know, you and I have never been very close," he said finally. "I've had a lot of time to think about it, and I've come to the conclusion that it's largely my fault."

She opened her mouth to answer, then realized she didn't know what to say. He had always avoided discussing their differences directly. It was more his style to circle around the gap between them, sparring with her.

"Your mother wanted children," he went on. He was speaking rapidly, now, as if he wanted to get the words out and over with. "Kazuko was always a very determined woman. It was difficult to deny her anything, and I believed I could be competent as a father, so I agreed to her demands." He shook his head, pressing his thin lips tightly together. "I should have had this talk with you long ago, Yumi, and I regret that I didn't."

She felt confused. Without her permission, without any preliminaries, he was changing the most fundamental rules that they had always played by.

"I realized, recently, that I wanted to reach some kind of

understanding with you," he went on. "And if I kept putting it off, it might be . . . too late."

"I see," she said, not sure whether to trust what he was saying. "But you make it sound as if—I mean, are you okay?"

Another long silence. "No, I'm not. They've diagnosed a cerebral tumor. Even now, with all the techniques available, it's inoperable." He held up his hand. "Please, we will not discuss possible modes of treatment and therapy. And in particular, don't lecture me about alternative medicine. I've reconciled myself, Yumi, and all I want now is to put things in some kind of order before I die. Can you help me to do that?"

"Of course." The words came out automatically. She didn't know what to think, so how could she know what to say? "I'm sorry," she said. "I know that that doesn't sound like much. But I really am."

He glanced at her for a moment, and she looked up into his face. Even now he was an enigma. He had described his impending death in a matter-of-fact way, as if he was talking about an annoying mechanical malfunction. He was exposing himself to her as he never had before; yet still she saw the distance in his eyes.

Idyll

Several hours later he turned off the coast road and took a deeply rutted dirt track up a forested hillside. She heard birdsong and smelled wood smoke. As they gained altitude the track divided and small homemade cabins came into view, scattered among the trees. Most of the people here were descended from back-to-the-roots hippies who'd settled the land almost seventy years ago, back in the 1960s.

The little car rounded a series of tight bends. Stones and dirt scraped under the floor. A line of mailboxes came into view, and she saw her father's name on the last one in small, neat black lettering: Leo Gottbaum, private and unobtrusive, showing no awareness of style, no interest in presenting an image to the outside world.

The car's power cell was almost completely discharged, and it climbed the last, steep section of the track slowly. Finally they emerged from among the trees and passed between two concrete posts, entering a deforested area of tall grass. A steel-framed geodesic dome lay directly ahead like a blister on the rounded summit of the hill, glass facets glowing red and orange in the light of the setting sun. Two steel towers stood nearby, one of them festooned with satellite and microwave dishes, the other supporting a huge three-bladed windmill, its blades slowly scything the air.

He stopped the car beside a couple other electric vehicles and an old gasoline-burning Jeep. Yumi got out, grateful for the freedom to move. Rolling, tree-covered hills stretched away below and either side, and in the far distance, beneath gilt-edged clouds, the ocean was the color of copper. It was idyllic, and yet she could never forgive the blemishes. The blades of the windmill made an insistent *whush, whush* sound. There was a faint buzzing from the power lines that led to the dome. No matter which way she looked, technology intruded.

"Coming in?" he asked her.

She hesitated. "Is my garden—"

"It's probably still there."

"I'll just take a look." She walked away down the south side of the hillside, past a concreted area where a field of black solar panels tracked the sun. Long ago, at the edge of her father's land, she had established a little plot of her own—an organic vegetable garden—its edges marked with round white stones.

It was almost lost, now, under tall grass and brambles. She squatted down, staring at it, imagining herself as a shy little ten-year-old trying to find some sense of identity, digging with her hands in the powdery soil. She sighed. Even now, in her thirty-first year, her father still made her feel like a child.

A faint mechanical click intruded on her thoughts. The sound seemed to come from the edge of the forest just ten feet away. She stood up and peered into the shadows. She heard it again, and this time she located its source. A fat concrete pillar five feet high had been erected among the trees, painted olive-drab to blend with its surroundings. Recessed in a slot she could see something round and black, like the muzzle of a gun.

And mounted on top of the pillar was a camera in a heavy steel housing, its lens gleaming as it panned slowly from side to side.

Darkness

The living area occupied half the dome. It was a huge space littered with computer hardware, spare keyboards, printers, monitors, RAMcards, old-fashioned CD-ROMs, a huge flat-panel TV, virtual-reality rigs, a surround-sound stereo, stacks of magazines and technical papers, scribbled notes, unopened correspondence. She stood in the doorway surveying the space and saw that nothing much had changed. There was some new equipment, more gadgets than she remembered. That was the only difference.

Her father was sitting in front of one of the computer systems, talking on the phone. "Excellent, Jeremy," he was saying. "No loss of function at all? That's actually better than I'd hoped. Yes. Yes, of course. I just wish you could all receive the credit you deserve."

There was warmth in his voice—admiration, even—which struck her as unusual.

"Definitely, Email me the transcripts," he went on. "But let's use the revised encryption protocol, yes? Don't want to slip up at this stage in the game."

Leo Gottbaum had stopped doing research ten years ago when they'd made him retire from the lab at Long Beach. But inevitably he'd gone on working at the dome, playing with his toys, his hardware and his hardcopy. Even now, he was so engrossed in his tech-talk that he hadn't noticed her standing there.

"So you're all set. Yes, yes. Me too. And thanks again for your efforts." He hung up the phone, turned, and saw her watching him. "Yumi." There was a momentary hesitation before he spoke. "That was Jeremy Porter. Perhaps you remember him."

"The fat one with the frizzy black beard," she said.

"You could characterize him that way, I suppose. Or you

could refer to him as one of the most gifted computer scientists alive, depending on your system of priorities."

She told herself not to be baited, not to start arguing with him. "I was down by the forest," she said, changing the subject. "I saw your—your new defense system, if that's what it is."

Again, a slight hesitation. "Yes. I suppose I should have warned you about it."

She looked at him in bafflement. "Are you afraid that someone's going to come all the way up here and steal your computers, or what?"

"Well, you know, the fact is, I suppose I don't really need a defense system after all, the way things have turned out." He gave her an ironic smile.

She realized he was referring to his illness. His impending death. How long did he have, anyway? And would it be very painful? She wanted to ask, but at the same time, she was afraid to talk about it. "Maybe I should cook dinner," she said, averting her eyes.

"That would be nice." He made it sound as if the idea of someone cooking something was an unexpected novelty. "You're still a vegetarian, I suppose? We have some soy patties, I think, and there are some vegetables, though they're probably irradiated and I doubt they're organically grown."

She sensed he was mocking her, but she couldn't be sure and it was easier not to think about it. "Fine," she said, retreating to the kitchen.

A little later she set out paper plates on the table by the window. The pottery that she'd made, long ago, wasn't where she'd left it. Maybe it had been broken, or maybe he'd thrown it away. He had no interest in domesticity.

Gottbaum rummaged in a cupboard and found a dusty bottle of red wine. "Perhaps we should celebrate," he said. He applied an old-fashioned corkscrew with methodical precision as if he were still in a laboratory, calibrating a piece of equipment.

"What are we celebrating?"

"Your being here." He poured the wine into a couple of disposable acrylic glasses. "And, to be honest, I'm happy about Jeremy's news. All this time, he's been working on my old LifeScan project. He's finally validated some ideas that I put forward thirty years ago."

"That must make you happy," she said, although she couldn't understand why he should care anymore. She watched him take a big swallow of wine, then dig into his food. She didn't like the way he ate. He shoveled the food in quick mechanical movements, efficient, insensitive.

She glanced up as the lights switched themselves on, responding to the onset of darkness outside. The dome seemed unusually quiet, and suddenly she realized why. "Where's Sam?" she asked.

"Ah, Sam." He chewed and swallowed, then set down his fork, avoiding her eyes. "Sam died, I'm sorry to say, a while ago."

"Oh." She felt a wave of sadness. "That's a shame. He was a nice dog. I always liked him."

"Well, you know, he was getting very old." Gottbaum gestured vaguely. "His teeth were going, he had kidney trouble."

Her eyes narrowed. "You mean you had him put to sleep?"

"Well, it was for the best. He was incontinent. It really wasn't very practical."

There was something in his voice that made her skin prickle: callousness; contempt, even. She'd always suspected he hadn't kept the dog as a pet in the usual sense—more as a specimen, a semi-intelligent organism whose behavior was of interest to him.

"There really isn't anything to get upset about, Yumi," he went on. "It was a painless death, and he'll be a lot happier up there in doggie heaven."

"You think so, Father?" She felt her anger rise up too quickly for her to control it. "Well, before too long, you'll have a chance to—to verify that hypothesis for yourself."

There was a moment's silence. She seldom spoke out against him, and he looked mildly surprised. "You mean—I'll be up there with him?" Unexpectedly, he laughed. It was a loud, fractured sound.

Her anger died, and she felt ashamed. "I shouldn't have said that. I'm sorry."

"No, no, don't apologize. You're absolutely right." He was watching her shrewdly. "Sam has died, I will die, and for that matter, one day, so will you. That's a fact, plain and simple. Should we really allow ourselves to get upset over facts?"

Field Trip

Moments like this, Bayley thought to himself, were so ordinary yet so special. He lay in bed, his eyes half-closed, watching his wife in dim morning light filtering through the red drapes. She buttoned her blouse, peered at her reflection in the mirror, brushed her hair with the palm of her hand, then stepped into her pants and her shoes. He loved the way she moved, quick and precise. He loved the curve of her jaw, her mouth, her breasts.

She walked across to the bed and kissed him on the forehead. Her hair brushed his face and he smelled her perfume.

He lifted his arms and pulled her close. "Good morning," he said.

She drew back so that she could focus on him and narrowed her eyes, mock-serious. "Hey, were you already awake?"

"I can't deny it."

"Were you watching me?" She tilted her head to one side, a dimple forming at the corner of her mouth. "Keeping me under surveillance, Agent Bayley?"

"Observing your movements." He kissed her again.

She laughed and stroked his stubbly cheek. "Well, Sherlock, it's past eight, and I have to interview a councilman at city hall. How about you?"

"I figure on making another field trip today," he said.

"To check up on your scientist-suspect? What was her name, Rosemary somebody?"

"Rosalind French." He swung his legs out of bed.

"I thought you once told me that aerospace companies have their own law-enforcement agency."

"The Defense Investigative Service. Yes, we could see a turf battle with them over this one. I already had to get rid of the Bureau of Alcohol, Tobacco, and Firearms, because there are guns involved. That's why it's really a whole lot easier if I just keep a low profile, and—"

"Follow your own track?"

"Yes, follow my own track. How'd you know I was going to say that?" He walked into the adjoining bathroom and turned on the shower.

"Mom?" A small voice called from the living room. "Mom, Mrs. Lopez is here."

Sharon sighed. "Damn, I still haven't paid her for baby-sitting last week."

"I'll deal with it," he called above the sound of running water.

"Thanks. Listen, Jim? Can you hear me?"

"I can't hear you. The shower's running."

"Be careful!" she shouted.

A half hour later, after Sharon had left, he was holding a glass of instant breakfast in one hand, typing on his home terminal with the other, while the DVI system in the living room played Old Macdonald again, and again, and again, and Damon shouted above the noise, telling Mrs. Lopez the names of *all* the animals. Another typical working day, Bayley thought to himself as he downloaded names and numbers of personnel at North Industries from the terminal to his compad, then slipped it into his briefcase.

Ideally he should call ahead to set up his visit right now. But life was less than ideal. The screams of protest he would cause by switching off *Old Macdonald* would be even louder than the video itself. So, he'd have to make the calls while he was on the road. His car was one place—maybe the only place—where he could be sure of getting some peace and quiet.

He left a "love you" memo for Sharon on the message base and went into the living room.

"Daddee!" Damon turned away from the DVI and came thumping across the rug, clutching a teddy bear. "Fix it, Daddee! Fix it!"

Bayley swallowed the last of his instant breakfast, set the

glass on the dining table, and kneeled beside his son. "What's the problem?"

"Talking Teddy won't talk anymore." Damon dumped the bear on the floor.

Bayley picked it up and squeezed it. It made a scratchy, grumbling noise. "Maybe he just needs a recharge." He thought, It shouldn't need to be charged so often. And it's supposed to say "Plug me in, please!" when its power pack ran low.

"Can you fix it?" Damon looked up at him.

Bayley nodded. "Later."

"Tonight?"

"That's right, tonight. Look, I have to go. Give me a hug."

Obligingly, Damon wrapped his arms around his father's neck. Bayley disentangled himself after a moment and headed for the door. "Good-bye, Mrs. Lopez. I won't be at my office number this morning, but you can get me on my pocket phone if there's any problem."

She nodded and smiled, a plainly dressed lady in her fifties with a dignified, honest face. "Good-bye, Mr. Bayley."

"Bye, Daddee!"

As the apartment door closed behind him and Bayley ran down to the basement garage, the sounds of Old Macdonald finally receded into the distance.

Setting up his visit to North Industries occupied most of his ninety-minute drive to the installation. He hated the ritual of verifying his identity, asking for someone in authority, and persuading them to deal with him. There were too many echoes of his childhood, when he'd felt excluded from all the cliques and clubs that the other kids set up. As a loner, he had ultimately learned that the only comfortable way he could deal with institutions was from a position of power.

He finally got through to the assistant manager of investigations at the plant, only to be told that for such an impromptu visit, higher authorization was necessary. Colonel Ellis Horton, chief scientist, was the man to ask.

Fortunately, Horton started work at eight and was already at his desk. Unfortunately, he was an old-fashioned bureaucrat who distrusted fax—even encoded fax—and wanted signed documents delivered by bonded courier. In exasperation, Bayley persuaded Horton's secretary to call the Los Angeles FBI office, who verified his identity by transmitting his employment history to her terminal. At which point the chief scientist agreed to donate a half hour of his time.

Irregularities

The research facility was a sprawl of boxy brown two-story buildings surrounded by grassy knolls and clusters of trees that looked spare and undernourished. The perimeter was marked by a ten-foot chain-link fence topped with razor wire, with observation towers and large red signs warning intruders to beware of security robots. Overall, it reminded Bayley of a prison camp that had been face-lifted by a landscape architect.

He had to show his FBI shield at the main gate, and he had to give his fingerprints and have his photograph taken before they would grant him a visitor's badge. Only then was he allowed inside.

An armed guard led him along austere beige corridors to a bare little waiting area where a male receptionist was working a text scanner. After checking via an intercom, the receptionist ushered Bayley into Ellis Horton's office.

Austerity ended here. The room was paneled in dark oak, and there was an oriental rug on the floor. Two leather armchairs faced a massive mahogany desk. An American flag stood in one corner, a rubber plant in another. On the walls were framed pictures: Horton shaking hands with generals and senators, Horton cutting a ribbon on a remotely piloted-vehicle assembly line, Horton with his hand resting on one wing of a cruise missile. The decor was Aerospace Traditional, Bayley thought to himself. So traditional, it looked like a museum.

Horton was in his sixties, a big man, tall and slightly stooped, with a jowly face and a large head that was totally bald. He had a powerful presence, standing with his feet placed well apart, as if the office was a square of territory that he had personally commandeered. He clamped Bayley's hand in his and gave him a penetrating look. "Good morning," he said, in a tone that suggested he was quite prepared to *make* it a good morning, if necessary. "Take a seat."

He walked back behind his desk, lowered his pin-striped suit into an antique leather-upholstered swivel chair, and selected a briar pipe from a rack beside an antique blotter. "Don't mind telling you, we normally appreciate some advance warning for this kind of thing," he said, filling the pipe methodically.

"That would have been my choice, too, Colonel," Bayley said, trying to sound polite because he knew an old Air Force man like Horton would expect some courtesy. At the same time, he didn't want to sound apologetic in case that was interpreted as a sign of weakness. He hated dealing with military people; there was too much jockeying for position, too many unwritten codes of conduct. He told himself to feel his way carefully, neither hurrying nor allowing himself to be hurried.

Horton set about lighting his pipe. It was a lengthy operation using a series of wooden matches. "So what's this all about?" he asked.

Bayley leaned forward, maintaining eye contact. "Briefly, Colonel, my department has obtained circumstantial evidence suggesting that one of your employees, Rosalind French, may be involved in something that would jeopardize her security clearance."

"French?" Horton looked as if the accusation offended him. "I've always considered her a woman of extremely high integrity."

The pompous tone, the affectations of dignity, irritated Bayley. Chief scientist was a misleading title; the man probably knew next to nothing about science and spent most of his time negotiating appropriations from the Pentagon. That was his real function: begging favors, winning contracts.

"This is only a preliminary inquiry, Colonel," he said, relaxed but deliberate. "No formal charges are being made. At this point, I wouldn't want it to impact on Dr. French in any way." He paused. "I certainly wouldn't want her to know anything about it."

Horton nodded. "Understood."

"We do have to pursue it, though."

Horton puffed on his pipe, then set it aside. He leaned forward and clasped his hands on the blotter. "Well, we're always willing to cooperate with you people. Goes without saying, our concern for security is just as great as yours." He sounded genuinely, tiresomely sincere. "But what exactly do you want?"

That sounded a little more promising. Bayley decided to spell it out. "To begin with, I'd like to know if Dr. French was here at her job yesterday between noon and two P.M. I'd also like to know if she or her team have been involved in any significant irregularities. Anything at all."

Horton's eyes narrowed as if he was trying to decide how much to say. "She wasn't here yesterday," he said grudgingly, obviously wondering what, if anything, he was giving away. "When I tried to reach her, they said she was out sick." He paused and rubbed his jaw. "As for irregularities, I suppose there's one thing has to be mentioned." He didn't look very happy about mentioning it. "There've been some equipment losses in her lab during the past year. In fact our security people wanted to run a facilities audit. You know, numbered tags on the equipment, requisitions double-checked, the usual thing. I told 'em we didn't have time for that nonsense." He moved one fat hand as if waving away a fly.

Bayley nodded as if he sympathized. He said nothing. Best to let the man run on, now that he had started to open up.

"As far as I'm concerned, the losses are trivial. They may not even *be* losses. Scientists get involved with a project, they get a little sloppy sometimes, the stuff gets misplaced. A few months later, they find it again." He leaned back in his chair. "But you asked, so I've told you."

Bayley thought to himself that a facilities audit obviously should have been done. Horton was wrong; this wasn't just a case of an absent-minded professor forgetting where she'd put a handful of components. "I'd like a chance to meet Dr. French, and her team, just to get some personal impressions. But you do understand, it mustn't look as if there's an investigation in progress."

Horton grimaced. "Yes, you've made that clear. But . . . what are you really after?"

Bayley didn't much enjoy the man's steady stare, but he forced himself to return it. "Dr. French was observed in a— possibly illegal act. That's about all I can say right now."

Horton drummed his fingers on the desk. "Well, I suppose

. . . how about if we tell her you're here from our head office in San Diego. Say you're an auditor, verifying compliance with company regulations. Time cards, sales order numbers, that kind of thing. Good enough?"

Bayley nodded. It was more helpful, in fact, than he'd expected. "I assume you've had to deal with situations like this before."

"Once in a while. Not with French," he added sharply.

"Do you have a name that you'd like me to use?"

"Let's see, Richard Wilson. He's on the company payroll in San Diego, in their security department. Never been here in Long Beach that I know of."

"Fine." He was a little surprised that Horton had capitulated so easily. He guessed the man must be worried enough about the losses—whatever they were—to want to cover his ass, but confident enough of his staff to be willing to have the FBI check them out. "One other thing, Colonel. Can I have some background on the research that French is doing for you?"

Horton gave a short bark of a laugh. "I thought you people were supposed to know everything about everything."

Bayley looked dutifully chagrined. "In this case," he said, "I'm afraid there wasn't time for me to receive a comprehensive briefing from my squad supervisor."

"Well, you have SCI clearance, don't you? Yes, it was on your profile. All right, I suppose I can fill you in. And I'll have my assistant transmit a summary of the project to your office this afternoon, is that satisfactory? Good. Come with me."

Deceptions

He led the way out of his office, across a glass-walled bridge, into a neighboring building. "All the research is done in this section," he said, over his shoulder. He took Bayley down a flight of stairs, along another corridor to a metal door identified solely by a number. He punched a code on a combination lock, pushed the door open, and switched on the light.

Bayley found himself in a windowless space about twenty

feet square, with a floor of bare gray concrete and cinderblock walls painted white. Crates and cartons were stacked on metal shelves up to the ceiling. The center of the room was cluttered with heavy equipment wrapped in plastic. The place had a dry, dusty smell; it was like a high-tech mausoleum.

Horton carefully closed the door behind them, then walked over and started pulling the wraps off an object the size of a refrigerator. Its body was of black anodized aluminum, tapering from four feet wide at the base to two feet at the top, where video and audio scanners sprouted from a plastic dome. Articulated arms were mounted on opposite sides, and the unit rested on four fat rubber tires. There was a homemade look about it, obviously a prototype assembled in a hurry.

"The LifeScan program," Horton began, "was initiated by Dr. Leo Gottbaum in 1999." He raised an eyebrow. "Ever heard of him?"

Bayley hated it when people assumed he was technologically illiterate. "Gottbaum won a Nobel Prize in the late 1990s," he said, "for research into artificial intelligence."

"Quite correct." Horton looked irritated, as if Bayley had somehow trespassed on his turf. He cleared his throat and raised his voice slightly. "Gottbaum did some work for us on imaging systems—target acquisition, terrain scanning, that kind of thing. But what he really wanted to tackle was a general-purpose AI that could display initiative and judgment."

Bayley told himself to be patient. "Go on," he said.

"A lot of people were working on that problem. Still are, for that matter. But Gottbaum figured he'd take a short cut. Instead of designing a system from scratch, he'd steal the answer from Mother Nature herself. The goal of LifeScan was to copy an entire animal brain, neuron by neuron. Not a new idea, of course; but he was the only one at that time with enough clout to persuade D.o.D. to fund it properly."

Bayley frowned. "He really thought he could model an entire brain? All the neurons, the ganglia, and all the electrochemical states?"

Horton allowed himself a smug little smile as if the ambitiousness of the program appealed to his can-do philosophy. "They began by using chicken brains, although, of course, even a chicken has several million neurons. Take you the rest of your life just to draw a map of 'em."

"But this wheeled vehicle, here, was that supposed to—"

"Ah, yes. ADVENT." Horton paused, taking pleasure in making Bayley wait for an explanation of the acronym. "Autonomous Demonstration Vehicle with Experimental Neural Topology. This was the vehicle their synthetic brain was supposed to control. They built it back in '05, to show the top brass, make it look as if the project was getting somewhere."

"But it wasn't?"

Horton turned back to the vehicle and started carefully rewrapping it in its plastic shroud. "Gottbaum's approach was fundamentally sound. I've always said so, and I stand by that." He sounded defensive, as if he'd staked his reputation on this research a long time ago and couldn't afford the loss of face if it ever turned out to be a dead end. "The trouble was, people expected too much too soon. By the time Gottbaum retired and Rosalind French took over from him, Congress was fed up with it. They cut the budget just when it was beginning to show some results. Right now, there are only four full-time staff. They're making good progress, though. Brilliant people—although I must warn you, they might seem a little nonconformist. Come next door, I'll introduce you."

Bayley followed Horton out and waited while the chief scientist made a show of verifying that the storeroom was securely locked. Then they went a little farther down the hall, to another door. Bayley experienced a good, tense feeling of anticipation, the way he always did when he was progressing to the next step in a case. Here, in this lab, was the woman he'd seen leaving Kai's: the woman who'd taken it into her head to risk her work and her reputation—for what?

Horton opened the door into a high-ceilinged room cluttered with equipment, metal cabinets gleaming dully in gray light filtering through tall windows. Four people were working in the lab, and as they heard the door open they all stopped talking and looked up, sharp-eyed, like forest animals scenting an intruder. No one said anything. No one needed to.

Horton showed no sign that he'd noticed the charged atmosphere. "Dr. French," he called to a tall woman standing beside a cylindrical tank in the center of the lab. "Just a moment, if you please."

She put aside a pocket computer and walked toward him. "Yes, Colonel?"

Bayley watched her. Five feet ten, maybe 140 pounds. Without a doubt, the same build as the robed figure in the street. And her features matched the photocomposite. So here they were, face-to-face again. He felt oddly vulnerable without his privacy mask, even though she could have no possible idea of his identity. She gave him a careful, evaluating look; he kept his expression neutral.

It was hard for him to believe she was really the one. Her posture, her poise, gave her an air of dignity and breeding, even while she was wearing a white lab coat. She seemed very self-possessed, but he noted a couple of rapid eye movements, some tension in the little muscles around her mouth. Something was making her nervous.

Horton gestured toward Bayley. "This is, ah, Mr. Richard Wilson, an auditor from head office. He's visiting several of the labs, just doing a floor check, making sure we're following regulations. Dr. French, here, is in charge of our LifeScan program."

Bayley saw her shoulders move almost imperceptibly, relaxing a fraction now that the intruder had been identified. "Pleased to meet you, Mr. Wilson," she said. Her voice was elegantly modulated, as if she'd had speech training at some time in her life. She shook his hand, brusque and businesslike. She turned to Horton. "Does this have anything to do with those memory modules?"

Horton looked disconcerted. He seemed cautious of her, maybe because she was tough, direct, and female, violating his archaic ideas about chivalry. "Why, no," he said. "In fact, I hadn't specifically mentioned to Mr. Wilson—"

"You see, I just sent a memo up to you," she interrupted. "We found the modules this morning. They're over there." She gestured to a workbench.

"Oh. Really." Horton walked over to the bench, and Bayley followed him. Ten blister packs were lying on the white Formica. Bayley noted the serial numbers. They were identical to the ones he'd seen in the street. So there was no possible doubt: she'd traded for them yesterday, she'd brought them back here, and she was lying.

"They'd slipped down behind the racks in the corner," she went on, watching Horton steadily. "It turns out there's a half-inch gap between the racks and the wall."

"Is that so?" Horton nodded to himself. "Well, I'm glad you found them. Very glad." He turned to Bayley. "You see, as I was saying earlier, there's no real problem here. Maybe a bit of carelessness about cataloging the inventory, that's all."

"It's really not a matter of carelessness," she said, calmly contradicting him. She didn't like the man, Bayley realized. In fact, she didn't like anyone who had the power to come in here and check up on her. Her tone of voice and her body language suggested that she felt she should be exempt from this kind of petty annoyance. "We've simply been very busy," she went on, "which leaves little time to take care of minor details." She gave the barest hint of a shrug.

Bayley was trying to place her accent. Boston, he decided. California had softened it, but she had that old-world, old-money twang, and she expected people to defer to her.

"If you don't mind," he said, polite but firm, "I'd still like to have a look around."

She waited to see if Horton would object. When he didn't, she turned away. "Help yourself. We are, of course, quite busy."

Bayley admired her act, for it was, indeed, an act. He wondered what would happen if he pushed a little harder. "Perhaps you'd like to introduce me to your coworkers," he said.

Her face showed a faint flicker of irritation. She gestured. "Hans Voss, Michael Butterworth, Jeremy Porter."

"Pleased to meet you." Bayley walked over and shook their hands in turn. Voss said, "How do you do," but he didn't meet Bayley's eyes. Butterworth seemed remote, in some other space and time altogether. Porter hunched his shoulders as if he felt threatened, and he pulled his hand back as quickly as he could.

"I understand you've all been employed by the company for several years," Bayley said.

"All of us were hired about a decade ago," Rosalind French said from behind him. "I'm sure the personnel department has the details if you're really interested." She stepped past, taking care not to brush against him. "I hope you won't mind if we continue calibrating this equipment. We're a little behind schedule."

"What's in the tank?" said Bayley, amiable but persistent.

"A tissue sample." She spoke without looking up.

"Brain tissue? Colonel Horton told me—"

"It's a section of an animal brain, yes."

"So you're scanning it into the Cray, there?" He nodded toward the black slab standing nearby.

She gave him a sudden, sharp look. Her eyes moved quickly, as they had when she had first been introduced, and he realized she was reevaluating him.

Bayley realized his slip. "I've worked with computers," he explained, "back before I went into the security division." She was very alert; it would be a mistake to underestimate her. He turned to Voss, then Butterworth, looking for an easier adversary. "One of you writes software?"

"Um, I do," said Porter.

Bayley seized the opening. "So with your program inside that computer, you can actually model the animal brain?"

Porter coughed nervously. "It's not nearly so simple, I'm afraid. Even for a cubic millimeter of the cortex, the Cray isn't adequate. We just use it as a holding area during the scan. It's fast, but it doesn't have the right architecture—"

"I doubt that Mr. Bayley is really interested in the technical details," Rosalind cut in.

Porter stopped talking. There was an uncomfortable silence.

She really seemed quite dangerous, like a mother lion defending her cubs. "You're right," he said, deciding to back down gracefully. "I should be taking care of business. May I look at your time cards?"

She inclined her head as if accepting his apology. "They're over there."

He took the long way around, skirting a tank of liquid nitrogen and squeezing past a bench covered in offcuts of aluminum and metal filings. He glanced at neat racks of tools and a miniature welding torch lying beside a set of C-clamps. "You make your own equipment, here? Isn't it rather unusual not to use the company's machine shop?"

"We require special instruments of great precision," said

Hans Voss. He moved closer. This was Voss's turf, evidently. To test the man's reactions, Bayley picked up a delicate ribbon file, like something a dentist or a surgeon might use.

"Please." Voss stepped up and laid his hand on his arm. "I would prefer you not to touch my tools."

"Sorry." Bayley surrendered it to him. At the same time, taking advantage of the distraction, he dropped his other hand over a scrap of stainless steel lying on the bench. He palmed it and slid it discreetly into his pocket.

He continued around the lab till he came to the rack of time cards. He rifled through them, looking at the neat notations, and raised his eyebrows. "You're billing the company for all these hours?"

"By no means," said Colonel Horton. He was still standing by the door, looking ill at ease. "Dr. French and her team have an unusual arrangement whereby they work additional hours at their own discretion. They feel this project means enough, they're willing to donate some of their time."

"Really." Bayley nodded. "Well, the cards have certainly been completed conscientiously." He put them back in their rack, turned, and scanned the laboratory. "And I don't see any safety violations." He headed back toward the door. "I'm sorry to have disturbed you all," he said.

"Quite all right." Now that he was backing off, Rosalind French seemed to have less trouble being polite to him. Maybe if someone capitulated to her on a habitual basis, Bayley thought, she could be downright friendly.

He looked once more at the three men. Voss was still standing by his metal-working tools, guarding them. Butterworth was nearby, still looking distant, although that could be an act. Porter was peering suspiciously at Bayley from the dense cover of his hair and beard.

Horton opened the door and he and Bayley walked out.

"Satisfactory?" Horton asked, as they started back toward the stairs.

"Yes, thank you," said Bayley. He drew a slow, measured breath, methodically relaxing the tension that had gathered in him while he was in the lab. "Of course, as I said before, we're still in the preliminary stages."

"Yes. So is there anything else you want?"

Bayley paused. He shook his head. "No. Not at this time."

"Well, I'll wait for your report." Horton seemed impatient to get rid of his visitor now that the official business was over.

Bayley saw he could take advantage of the situation. "I can walk out directly to the parking lot from this building, can't I?"

"Yes. Yes, you can just go down this corridor to the exit sign. It's a shortcut, in fact."

"Well, thank you, Colonel, for your help." He submitted once again to the severe handclasp and the penetrating gaze. Then Horton nodded curtly and disappeared up the stairs.

Bayley waited till the footsteps were no longer audible, then turned and went back along the corridor. When he reached Rosalind French's laboratory he paused and glanced behind him. The corridor was empty and silent.

In his lapel was a microphone no larger than a pin head, linked with a tiny audio recorder in his pocket. He pulled the microphone up, trailing a gossamer wire, and quickly pressed it against the glass pane in the laboratory door.

Seconds ticked by. He stood there feeling unpleasantly vulnerable. It was one thing to demand information, backed by the authority of the bureau. It was something else to conduct unauthorized surveillance inside a defense contractor's research facility.

He heard someone coming and quickly moved away from the door, reeling in the microphone. As a figure appeared at the far end of the hallway, heading toward him, Bayley made for the exit.

He felt a sense of relief as he emerged into the sunlight. He paused for a moment, reorienting himself, then headed for his car.

He'd achieved most of his initial objectives: getting Horton to cooperate, meeting Rosalind French, checking out the laboratory. And yet, there was still a conspicuous lack of evidence. The most that Rosalind French could be charged with at this point was driving a car with unregistered plates and possession of stolen goods—the memory modules in the suitcase.

That alone would probably end her career at North Industries; but Bayley was beginning to suspect it was just the tip of the iceberg. The clannish, paranoid mood in the lab, the bizarre work schedule, and the history of missing inventory, all implied something much bigger than street crime; and whatever it was, Horton's bombastic incompetence would have enabled it to flourish unchecked.

Bayley's visit to the lab had actually created more mysteries than it had solved, and they tantalized him. What had happened to the modules that French claimed to have "lost" previously? Why had she gone to the trouble and taken the risk of manufacturing high-tech handguns in order to get black-market replacement modules from Little Asia? And what had happened to the other equipment that was missing?

Lastly, there was the matter of the research itself. Why were French and her team working so obsessively on a project that had begun thirty years ago and still hadn't fulfilled any of its initial objectives? And what, exactly, were they keeping inside that stainless-steel tank?

Trust

Long sunbeams slanted between the trees. The air smelled of wildflowers and sap and dry dead leaves, and the forest was alive with birdsong. Yumi walked slowly, pausing often, feeling at peace for the first time since her arrival the previous day.

She shifted the bag of groceries from one arm to the other. Only halfway up the hill, and already she was out of breath. When she'd been a kid she'd run most of the way; but now she was past thirty she didn't have that instantly available energy. Too many lazy days in Hawaii, sitting at the beach, or sitting watching TV, or sitting in her little workshop.

She heard an approaching vehicle. She stepped to one side of the track and waited till it came around the bend, bumping toward her, an ancient pickup streaked with rust, its fenders dented, its windshield spattered with dirt. She shaded her eyes, trying to see who was driving, and suddenly she smiled. "Jack!" she shouted, waving her arm. "Hey, Jack!"

The pickup stopped beside her and its bearded driver frowned at her from under a red gimme cap, one hand resting on the wheel, one elbow on the open window. "G'morning," he said, gruff and a little suspicious, sizing her up.

"You don't remember me, do you?" She laughed. "We were neighbors. I'm Yumi. Yumi Gottbaum."

"Well, shit." He trod on the emergency brake, threw open the door, and stepped down, a big man in a lumberjack shirt, Levis, and work boots crusted with mud. He grabbed her and hugged her, and she felt herself being lifted off her feet. "Hell, Yumi. Jesus Christ. What is it, five years?" He set her back down and put his hands on his hips. "What the hell happened

to yer hair? Used to be halfway down your back. Well, I'll be."
He laughed, took off his cap, slapped it against his thigh. "I'll
be damned!"

"I cut my hair when I relocated in Hawaii," she said. "To be
with my mother. It was seven years ago."

"Seven years. Goddam. Hey, have you had breakfast?"

"Not yet. I just went down to the store on the coast road to
buy groceries. You know my father, he never has anything except frozen string beans and TV dinners. I'm on my way back
up to the dome, now." She hesitated. "Can you give me a
ride?"

"Well, hell, yes. Step in, princess."

He drove slowly, taking his time, glancing at her once in a
while, grinning. She gave him the bare details of her life in
Waikiki, her small business making jewelry that she mostly sold
to tourists. She'd lived with her mother till her mother died of a
sudden heart attack; and then she'd sold the house and moved
to an apartment of her own.

"You got a boyfriend?" he asked.

"Not right now." She shrugged. "You know how it is with
me and men. The ones I can have, I don't want, and the ones I
want, I can't have. I'm just a hopeless case, Jack. But what
about you, are you still with Emily?"

"Oh, yeah. And three kids, now. Got a new one. Sally. She's
four already."

"What about the animals? You still have them, too?"

"Well, let's see." He scratched the side of his jaw. "We shot
the goat, fed him to the pigs. Then we ate the pigs. Hate to have
to tell you that, you being a vegetarian, but ever since they
legalized marijuana, it ain't the cash crop it used to be." He
grimaced and spat out the window. "But how come you're here
in California? Thought you said you wasn't never coming
back."

"My father. He's . . . got a brain tumor. He says he doesn't
have long to live, and he wanted to see me before he dies."

"Oh, jeez." Jack stopped the truck. He leaned on the wheel
and looked across at her. "That's real bad." He gave her shoulder a clumsy squeeze. "That's rough."

Yumi shrugged, hoping it might dislodge his heavy hand. She
knew he meant well, and he'd opened his home to her over the

years as if it were her own. But his awkward sympathy she could do without.

"I've been so cut off from him," she said, "it . . . doesn't really touch me very much."

"You know, I hate to hear you talk like that." He started the vehicle again and drove in silence for a while. As he rounded the final turn in the track and emerged onto the hilltop, he forced a laugh. "So here you are. Dome sweet dome." He paused. "Looks just the same, I guess, even after all the work."

"The work?" She gathered up her groceries.

"He had a whole lot of hard hats up here. Putting in his damnfool defense system, and some kind of a new power generator, so they said."

"Really? So now he can run his gadgets even when the municipal supply cuts out, the sun isn't shining, and the wind isn't blowing." Yumi smiled at Jack, then kissed him on one grimy cheek. "Thanks for the ride." She opened the door.

"Come visit," he called after her. "Six can eat as cheap as five, right?"

She waved. "Maybe tonight." She waited and watched while he turned his pickup and headed back down the trail.

Inside the dome, Leo was waiting for her. She saw his face and knew immediately that she'd done something wrong. The knowledge gave her a tense, grabbing sensation in her stomach. She ducked her head and walked quickly into the kitchen, but he came after her.

"Where have you been?" His voice sounded matter-of-fact, but she could hear the underlying irritation. She hadn't been where he expected her to be. For a couple of hours, she had been an element of his environment that had been out of his control.

"You seemed to be sleeping, and I didn't want to disturb you, and I went shopping," she said, unpacking the groceries and putting them away. "I thought you might like a proper breakfast."

"Breakfast." He waved his arm. "I already had breakfast. It's past ten o'clock, Yumi. If you had to go to the store, why didn't you take one of the cars?"

"I still don't drive," she said, in a small voice. "Cars make me nervous."

Gottbaum grunted in exasperation. "Come in the living room. I have a document to show you."

She started after him, then checked her automatic tendency to do whatever he wanted. "But *I* haven't had breakfast yet."

"This will only take a moment. Really. Think of it this way: in a few days' time, you'll be free to eat breakfast whenever you want."

Bastard, she thought to herself, following him.

"Sit down," he told her, gesturing toward the table. Obligingly, she took a seat. She looked out of the window, trying to calm herself, and saw that in the distance the sea was shrouded in mist. It looked like a soft, white meadow beneath the vivid blue sky.

Gottbaum picked up some papers from his desk, then walked back and stood looking down at her. "Enjoying the view?" He seemed slightly more cordial now that she was obeying him again.

"It's pretty."

"But I expect there are some bad associations here, aren't there?"

He was doing what he'd done yesterday, bringing up topics that they never normally talked about. Was it the prospect of his death that made him want to address the issues? "There are some unpleasant memories here," she said, treading cautiously, afraid of a trap. "Of you and Mom arguing all the time, and . . . there's a lot of stuff that I try not to think about."

He nodded. "So, I assume that even though you are my sole heir, you have no interest in inheriting this land and the structures on it."

Why couldn't he talk normally? Why did he have to say "structures" when anyone else would say "buildings"? And then she grasped the meaning of what he'd said. "You mean you're cutting me out of your will?" She almost laughed. Was *that* what he was worrying about?

"I want to establish this dome as an educational trust," he said, still very serious. "There'll be annual awards to enable students to come here and pursue their work. A retreat, for serious study. Call it an old man's vanity if you will, but I want to leave something that will be useful, with my name on it."

She nodded slowly. It made sense. "I can see you might like

that," she said. "Well, it's your dome. You should do whatever you want with it. Frankly, it never even occurred to me that I should inherit something from you."

"You will receive some cash," he said. "But anyway, from what you say, I gather you'll be willing to sign these." He placed the documents in front of her. "This is a waiver, stating that you understand my intentions, find them agreeable, have read my will, and won't contest it."

She looked at the printed pages. Then she looked up at him. The same impassive face as always, controlled and controlling. What was he thinking? What did his thoughts actually sound like? She imagined them clicking and beeping, like a computer in an old Hollywood movie. "I wouldn't have contested anything anyway," she said. "Why are you making such a fuss about this?"

He pulled out a chair and sat down opposite her. He leaned forward as if trying to be more intimate. "My dear, I don't have a lot of money anymore. I've spent most of my savings. If there was a battle over my estate it might cost so much in legal fees that the property would have to be sold to raise the extra cash to pay the lawyers. Do you see?"

Yes, she saw. Even after he died, everything still had to be the way he wanted it. Yumi clenched her fist. It would be some sort of justice, wouldn't it, if she defied his last dying wish—although just the thought of that gave her the tense, grabbing sensation again.

He reached out and turned the pages. "Here, you see—fifty thousand new dollars, your share of the cash and investments. I have provided for you, Yumi. All I ask is that you leave me my home to dispose of as I wish." He put a pen into her hand. "Sign at the bottom, there."

For a moment she did nothing. She imagined herself pushing her chair back and saying no. His face would go pale, the way she remembered it. Even though he was over eighty he could still fly into one of his rages, she had no doubt of that. She closed her eyes, trying to suppress the adrenaline that was surging through her. Would it really be worth it to refuse, just to get back at him? To endure the subsequent arguments, threats, recriminations? She had her own life, now. The battles of the past were over, and if she had any sense, she'd let them go.

She drew a deep breath, focused on the page in front of her, and signed.

"This copy, also," he said, giving her a duplicate.

She signed that, too.

He took back the documents, and his pen. "Mrs. Wright will be here sometime today to do the cleaning, and I'll have her witness these." He gave Yumi one of his rare smiles. "Thank you."

She'd pleased him, she realized. Was that the real reason she'd signed? No, that was too upsetting to think about. "Can I have breakfast now?" she asked, feeling somehow drained.

"Of course, of course." He was walking away; she could do whatever she wanted, it was no longer of any interest to him.

"Talking about your will, you . . . make it seem as if you're going to die tomorrow," she said.

He opened his fireproof safe in a concrete stanchion in the north wall, put the documents inside, and swung the door shut. "Not tomorrow." He spun the dial on the safe. "But very soon after that."

Suddenly she felt like crying. She ran into the kitchen, cursing the way her emotions eluded her control whenever she was around him. She took eggs from the refrigerator and broke two of them into a bowl, spilling some of the white onto the counter. "I just do not understand you," she said, seizing a fork and beating the eggs. "There could be some new cancer treatment you've never heard of. Why do you have to give up and assume it's all over?"

He came and stood in the doorway. "It seems to be upsetting you to talk about this."

"Of *course* it's upsetting me!" Yumi switched on the electric stove, found a frying pan, and poured the eggs into it. "You're planning your death as if—as if it's a new piece of research, or something. How can you talk about it like that?"

"Because," he smiled faintly, "I don't regard it as permanent. I still have my contract with Cryonic Life Systems. I'm in regular contact with my friends there. The techniques have advanced a lot in the last two decades, and I'm confident I can be frozen with minimal tissue damage. In another fifty years or so, with some further advances in nanotechnology, I believe it will be possible to cure my condition and revive me."

Was *that* the real reason he wanted to leave his dome to a trust? So he could repossess it when he "came back"? She shook the frying pan violently. "I remember you used to talk about stuff like this—being frozen, cheating death. I should have known you really believed in it."

"Yes," he said. "You should."

She told herself to be calm. She looked out of the window at the trees. But she couldn't focus on them. She turned and glared at him instead. "So what are you going to do, get your cryonics friends to dump you in one of their freezers while you're still alive?"

"Yumi, you know they can't do that." He paused. "The, ah, eggs are sticking to the pan."

"Thanks." She switched off the stove with an abrupt motion and pushed the pan aside.

"On Monday," he went on, "I will be admitted to a hospital. I will refuse all food and fluids. It will take about four days for me to die in this way, from dehydration; not a pleasant process, but I will be given morphine. As soon as there are no further vital signs, the cryonics people will take over."

"Monday? You mean, the day after tomorrow?" She stepped back, instinctively touching her fingers to her throat. "This is the most cold-blooded thing I have ever heard in my life."

He spread his hands. "Yumi, it's merely rational. There is very good reason to believe that I'll be able to return, in the future, if I arrange my death properly now. Why, in another fifty years, we should have immortality."

"But starving yourself—"

"If I do it any other way there will be an autopsy, which would damage my brain. The whole idea, Yumi, is to act swiftly and in such a way that no further brain damage occurs . . . from the tumor, or from anything—or anyone—else."

She stared at him. Slowly, she recovered herself. "You're right," she said. "Of course, as always, you're right. It's totally logical. You'll come back in fifty years and start all over again." She rolled her eyes. "Excuse me. I have to go outside."

He watched her as she pushed past him, threw open the door, and walked out into the sunlight. Her legs brushed through the tall grass. She breathed deeply and tasted the clean air.

After she'd gone a little way she sat down on the curve of the hill and stared into the distance.

From inside the dome, she heard a melodic tone. His phone was ringing. Not many people knew his number here; if anyone called, it was always something important. That meant he would answer it and leave her in peace.

She lay on her back in the grass, feeling the lumpy earth under her body, and looked up into the featureless bowl of blue sky.

Faintly, she heard his voice. "Could be just a coincidence, Jeremy," he was saying, "but I agree, you'd better cross-check his identity with the records at San Diego. We shouldn't take any chances."

Chance; that was what he abhorred most of all. Uncertainty. Random factors. Human error. People who acted without thinking. Emotional women. Aging pets. Young children.

She closed her eyes and rich red replaced deep blue. She crossed her arms over herself, feeling the sun press down on her. She realized, suddenly, that it was quite possible that she'd still be alive when her father was revived from his deep freeze. She didn't know which disturbed her more: the certainty of his imminent death, or the possibility that it might not be permanent.

Intruder

Rosalind drove into San Pedro past abandoned storefronts, derelict gas stations, apartment buildings that had been looted and burned many years ago. With Porter sitting beside her, Voss and Butterworth in the back, she made a right turn off Pacific Avenue and headed up into the hills overlooking the town.

A huge fence of rusty barbed wire came into view, twenty-foot concrete gate posts planted in the sidewalk. The gates themselves had long since been removed, and the only real barrier that remained was a tangled mass of vegetation that had engulfed the street.

Thirty years ago, when the AIDS retrovirus had mutated and mass hysteria had precipitated drastic measures, this whole area had been made into an internment camp. Those years were over and almost forgotten, but the neighborhood had never recovered from the stigma, and in an age when population growth had turned negative, no one felt any need to live in houses haunted by the specter of a bygone plague.

A handful of artists, writers, and social rejects had migrated to the fringes of this no-man's-land where homes were free for the taking and government interference was virtually nil. Deeper into it, though, thousands of houses still lay empty, fractured by earthquake damage, weakened by termites and rot, slowly collapsing in on themselves.

Rosalind drove the car slowly along the overgrown street, bumping across vines, scraping through tall grass and brambles, a cloud of insects rising up either side. After a couple of blocks she slowed and checked the rearview mirror. As always, the neighborhood seemed devoid of human life. She swung the car around, turned into the overgrown driveway of a house that looked as derelict as its neighbors, and parked out of sight under the drooping branches of a fig tree that had run wild. "You know," she said, "I can't remember the last time we arrived here in daylight."

Behind her, Voss chuckled. "You want that we should work some more. You think we are getting off too lightly, leaving the lab before midnight."

She smiled. "No, Hans, that is *not* what I think." She opened the car door. The air smelled of lush foliage and wild blossoms. Birds sang; a light breeze stirred the kudzu that had engulfed the front lawn. In the distance, Catalina Island was a hazy gray shape in the sweep of the ocean. "I think we all deserve some time off," she said. "My only trouble is that I seem to have forgotten how to take it. I mean, after ten years, it's like—like moving into a psychological vacuum. Not empty space, but empty time."

"In zen, there's a state of being called *dyana*," said Butterworth, unfolding his lanky frame from the rear of the car.

"Really?" She looked at him, deadpan. "Are you going to spell that for us, Michael?"

"Spell it?" He treated her to his faint, ironic smile. "I could tell you how to attain it. Although, you might not like it much. It'd make you kind of mellow."

Voss grinned. He looked from one of them to the other. "It is pleasing," he said, "to see you two pretending to be human again."

Rosalind laughed. It felt good, and she realized how long it had been since she'd been untroubled enough to let go and spend some time—even just a few minutes—trading jokes, releasing tension. "Hans, are you implying that I've been inhuman?"

He became mock-serious. "Rosalind, is not my place or my nature to imply."

She got out of the car and went over to Porter, who was opening the trunk. "Jeremy. Give us an objective assessment. Have I been an inhuman team leader?"

He heaved out an aluminum suitcase, set it down in the long grass, and paused, giving the question his usual thorough examination. "I would say you have been somewhat difficult," he said. "The only times you have been actually inhuman were when you had to deal with outsiders."

"Yeah, like with Horton," said Butterworth. "Or that guy he brought into the lab today. The auditor."

"You mean Richard Wilson?" Rosalind waded through the vines and grass to the front door of the house, unlocked it, and disabled the two alarm systems. Out of long habit she glanced quickly behind her before walking in. But the neighborhood was still silent: no traffic, no one on foot to notice or observe them. "I suppose I *was* a bit rude to him," she said as the others followed her into the ruined front hall, its carpet matted with dirt, its walls stained brown with water damage. "And he didn't really deserve it. I mean, he wasn't as bad as most auditors. I just didn't want him around, least of all today."

Voss was last into the house. He shut the front door and secured it. Rosalind unlocked a fireproof steel hatch, turned on the lights, and went down concrete steps to the basement. The original owner of the house had evidently had a security fetish: the basement was a bomb shelter with walls, floor, and ceiling of reinforced concrete, its own emergency generators, a filtered air supply, a freshwater well, and a recycling sanitation system.

Now it was filled with electronic hardware. This was where Porter came when he worked through the night. Voss and Butterworth had accumulated equipment here, also: a magnetic resonance neuroimaging system, an ultrasound scanner, customized focused-field sensors to monitor brain function, and an assortment of basic medical supplies. Some of the materials had been bought, some stolen, some homemade, some obtained through sources in Little Asia. All of it was pushing the limits of current technology.

Porter laid his aluminum case on a stool, opened it, donned antistatic gloves, and started carefully removing circuit boards. Butterworth went to the neurosensing gear and started switching it on. "You know, you're right," he said, picking up Rosalind's comment as if, in his head, no time had passed. "That guy, today, wasn't as bad as most auditors. In fact, when you think about it, he hardly acted like an auditor at all."

She nodded absently as she linked her log unit with Porter's database and started uploading the morning's figures. Then, as

she waited for the transfer to complete, she realized Butterworth's implication. "He *was* an auditor, though," she said.
"Jeremy checked him after he left. Didn't you, Jeremy?"

Porter nodded. "I called Leo, as you said. Leo told me we
shouldn't take any chances, and I should verify that there was a
Richard Wilson in the San Diego office. I accessed their personnel directory and he was listed, current." He paused as if mentally reviewing the sequence of events. "Yes," he said. "That's
what happened."

"I already know that," Butterworth said, still calmly going
about his business. "I don't question that there's someone
named Richard Wilson in San Diego, employed by North Industries, who has a position as an auditor. What I'm questioning is whether Richard Wilson was the guy who came and
visited us today."

There was silence in the basement broken only by the humming and clicking of equipment, the whisper of filtered air
through the vents. Finally, Rosalind laughed. It wasn't the
same laugh that she'd enjoyed outside in the front yard. It
sounded forced. "You're being very paranoid, Michael."

"But Michael is correct," said Voss. "We have been less thorough than usual with this visitor, this Richard Wilson, because
we are so happy to be nearing the end of our work. But this is
no time to be careless. We still cannot afford to take anything
for granted."

Rosalind walked over to Porter. "Jeremy, please get online
with the Long Beach facility right away. Check their visitor log
for this morning. That's the first thing we should have done. I
blame myself for not thinking of it." She glanced over her
shoulder. "Thank you, Michael, for reminding us of our re-
sponsibilities."

"Hey, look, it's probably nothing." Butterworth broke open
a pack of vapor syringes and started idly stowing them in a
drug cabinet. "It just seems to me we ought to make sure, you
know?"

Porter dialed through and started typing passwords and access codes, entering security records via a back door that he'd
long since installed in the computers maintained by the defense
contractor. Rosalind looked over his shoulder as the screen
filled with a list of names. "I don't see a Richard Wilson there,"

she said. There was tension growing in her voice. Get a grip, she told herself. Check it again.

"I'll sort the list," said Porter. He typed a code, and the names rearranged themselves alphabetically. "No. No, there's no Richard Wilson."

Rosalind made herself take a slow, deep breath. "Let me make sure there's no misunderstanding. You are certain that this is the complete list of all today's visitors to the plant. Including people who may be employed by North Industries at their other facilities."

"That's correct," said Porter. His fingers fidgeted on the keyboard. He blinked up at Rosalind through his thick-lensed glasses. "What do you want me to do?"

There was a moment of uneasy silence. "Access their affiliations," she said. "Find out who they represent or work for."

He thought for a moment. "All right, I can do that. They have to give that information at the front gate." He typed more commands. The screen cleared, then filled again.

"Hold it." Rosalind pointed. "Look there. Federal Bureau of Investigation, Department of Technology-Related Crime. Name: James Bayley."

Butterworth carefully set down the syringes he'd been holding. He turned toward Rosalind. "You're kidding."

"But it is maybe just a coincidence, nothing to do with us," said Voss.

"We'll find out." Rosalind turned back to Jeremy. "Is there some way to get a picture of this Bayley? Don't they vid them on the way in?"

"Yes, but they don't file that data centrally," said Porter. "There's no need to. They just put a RAMcard in a cabinet somewhere."

"All right. Let's see; would there be telephone records that would show if Bayley called the plant recently?"

Porter stared above the screen at the blank concrete wall. Rosalind knew he had heard her; it was just a matter of waiting for his response. Even so, as the seconds dragged by, it was hard to be patient.

"The only communications that would be stored accessibly to me would be those that were faxed, of a sensitive nature," Porter said finally. "Anything encrypted."

"If North Industries has been dealing with the FBI," said Rosalind, "that's probably the kind of communication we're after."

"I'll see what I can do." He sounded doubtful. "I did some snooping a few years ago in the general archives. I think I remember how to get in there from a remote terminal. But there are a lot of different fax encryption systems, and data in bulk storage isn't indexed. There's just this one big holding area, like a dumpster, where they put stuff that's not important enough to be cataloged."

"Well, give it a try," she said. She put her hands on his shoulders and gave a little squeeze. "Begin with this morning and work backward."

Porter didn't answer. He simply started typing. First he went through his own files retrieving code-breaking programs that he'd accumulated over the years. Then he downloaded a bunch of data from the North Industries archives and went to work cracking the codes. It was a time-consuming process; a half hour slowly passed while the other members of the team watched and waited.

"Here," he said, finally. "Bayley's office must have been asked to verify his identity this morning, before he arrived. It looks as if they transmitted his entire employment history."

Rosalind, Voss, and Butterworth clustered around him, peering at the screen. "My god," said Rosalind, "they sent just about everything, didn't they?" She scanned the text. "There. Look there. The physical description."

"Identical to the man who visited us," Voss said softly.

Rosalind nodded. "There's no possible doubt."

"Here's his most recent assignment," said Porter, screening the last page of data. "Investigate distribution and source of electronic handguns employed in homicides in Los Angeles, California, and Las Vegas, Nevada."

Voss swore softly.

"But there's no way they could have traced the weapons back to us," said Rosalind. "We were always so careful. Even Kai, in Little Asia, never knew my identity."

"Maybe Bayley saw you going into Kai's store yesterday," said Butterworth, "when you took him the new batch of guns to get the replacement memory modules, so Horton would stop hassling us."

"No." She shook her head. "He couldn't have identified me. I was masked. Completely concealed."

"Maybe they've developed a way to penetrate that."

Rosalind fell silent. She remembered bumping into the other masked figure, dropping her suitcase, seeing it fall open on the sidewalk.

"We should be thankful," said Voss, "this man is interested only in some illegal handguns. He knows nothing about our real purpose."

Rosalind stood up. She paced to the other end of the basement and back again. "But he was very inquisitive. He's not a pompous ass like Horton. The way he looked around, he may have guessed there was something bigger involved. Otherwise, why would people in our position take the risk of dealing in street weapons? But either way, if he starts an investigation, they'll revoke our passes. We'll be locked out of our own laboratory." She turned back to Porter. "We need to know how much Bayley has deduced. Is there a way to get into the FBI database and see if he's filed a report?"

Porter stared at her as if trying to understand what she had just said. "What?"

Her face was pale. Her thoughts seemed to be chattering uncontrollably in her head. It was almost impossible to keep her emotions under control; and yet she had to. She had always been the source of stability for the team. They oriented themselves around her, whether they realized it or not. "Jeremy, please pay attention, this is very important. We have to get into the FBI records."

He shook his head, looking at her blankly. "I have no idea how to do that."

She clenched her fist. "Then you must *find out* how."

"Rosalind." Voss laid his hand on her arm. "Calm, please. Jeremy is a computer programmer. He is not a magician or a criminal. Police files will be isolated, extremely difficult to access from outside, maybe impossible."

She stared at Voss. It took her a moment to grasp what he was saying. "Yes. Yes, I suppose you're right." She pressed the palms of her hands to the sides of her forehead. "So what are we going to do?"

"Better give Leo another call," said Butterworth. "Maybe he has some idea. You know, these old sixties guys, they grew up fighting the system. He probably cracked networks in his radical days."

"All right." Rosalind nodded. "Call him. We have to tell him about this anyway. Maybe he'll know some way to deal with it. I hope to god he does. I certainly don't."

Invitation

The documents outlined a vision: an entire new generation of military technology, intelligent, programmable, mass-producible in huge quantities for a fraction of the cost of training and deploying a conventional army. Divisions would engage the enemy without need for human participation on the battlefront. Medical services and food supplies would be eliminated. Lives would be saved; dollars would be saved; messy little conflicts would be settled cleanly, efficiently, and simply.

Alone in his cubicle on the thirty-fifth floor of the Federal Building, Bayley scanned the neatly printed pages, each one embellished with the North Industries logo and a SECRET classification. This was the official history of LifeScan, faxed to him from Ellis Horton's office less than an hour ago, and the more of it he read, the less he believed.

Here and there among the tech-speak he found fragments of hard data, actual test results hidden in footnotes and appendixes. And taken as a whole, the numbers told a very different story: of a program that had blundered from one failure to another, never even coming close to its goals. LifeScan had successfully simulated the neural net of a flatworm, the humblest of lab animals. But even that small achievement was hedged with adjectives such as *preliminary* and *tentative,* suggesting that the simulation was still riddled with bugs.

In which case, Bayley asked himself, how had the project survived?

Funding was listed in a separate section. He saw that there had been some cutbacks, especially ten years ago when North Industries had surrendered to government ownership. But *some* money had always come through. Adding it up, over a period of three decades, LifeScan had managed to spend twenty billion new dollars without a single substantial achievement to justify its existence.

Bayley stared at the pages, feeling baffled. Here was yet another mystery on top of all the others. He turned to his microdisc player. He'd already listened once to the recording he'd made outside Rosalind French's laboratory. Now that he'd read the history of LifeScan, he needed to hear it again. He put on his headphones and closed his eyes, concentrating.

At first there was silence, then a rustle and a thump, the sound of the miniaturized microphone being pressed against the window in the laboratory door. Sensing-circuits compensated for the attenuating effect of the glass pane, and voices came into focus:

". . . last thing we need right now is an audit." Rosalind French's voice.

"Yes, when we are so near the end." That was Hans Voss speaking.

"Oh, but you know how slowly they move. By the time they get an audit rolling, we'll be done and gone." A lazy, laconic voice; by elimination, it had to be Michael Butterworth.

"Mike has a point. . . ."

More rustling noises, a click, and then the rest was blank.

Bayley took off the headphones. Only fifteen seconds of conversation, but the message was clear: French and her scientists were getting ready to quit. Because they were being fired? Because the project was a failure? No; they sounded complacent, satisfied, as if they'd fulfilled all their goals. In which case, what did they know that their employers didn't know? Had they withheld some of their results? And if so, how and why?

"Internal mail." The voice came from the entrance to Bayley's cubicle.

He turned and found a young woman offering him a sealed evidence packet and a plain white envelope. He signed the delivery form, then ripped the packet open and checked the contents. The electronic handgun was in there together with the scrap of stainless steel that he'd filched from Voss's workbench that morning.

He opened the white envelope. It contained a one-page report from the FBI's own forensic laboratory. Based on their analysis of crystalline structure and trace impurities in the scrap of metal and the casing of the gun, it was 99 percent probable that the two samples had come from the same original stock.

Bayley massaged his temples. He had taken the metal sample illicitly, which meant that strictly speaking it was stolen property, inadmissible as evidence. It had confirmed his private suspicions, though: there was no further doubt where the handguns came from. If this was any normal case he should now get a scarch warrant, tell the defense contractor to seal the laboratory, and place all LifeScan personnel under arrest.

And yet if he did that, French and her colleagues would be charged with a relatively minor offense, conspiring to make and sell illegal weapons, maybe stealing some company property. They'd be released on bail, and then, if they were involved in something bigger as he suspected they were, they might well disappear.

Meanwhile Bayley would be assigned to another case, and he'd never learn anything more about LifeScan. No one else would, either, because no one else would know enough to ask about it. If North Industries believed its own negative data, it might just junk the whole thing without bothering to take a closer look.

Bayley slowly shook his head. He had to follow his own track a while longer. He had to find someone who would answer some of the questions.

He stood up and walked out of his cubicle. It was a Friday, near the end of the business day, but there might be enough time for what he had in mind. He walked down the row of adjoining cubicles, past plain gray acoustic partitions, people sitting and talking into computers, transcribing reports, cataloging evidence, preparing statements. He stopped at a doorway at the end of the line and rapped his knuckles on the metal frame. "Norm," he said, "do you have a moment?"

The man behind the desk was broad-shouldered, overweight, with a fat, jowly face and thinning black hair brushed straight back. He'd taken his jacket off, opened his shirt collar, and rolled up his sleeves, and he was lounging in his chair with a sugar croissant in one hand, a container of coffee in the other.

"Jimmy," he said, with a big grin. "Come on in. Siddown. What you been doing with yourself?"

Norm Harris was the only person in the office who called Bayley "Jimmy." Dealing with Harris was always an ordeal, but sometimes it was unavoidable. The man was a walking Rolodex; he always knew someone who knew someone.

Bayley sat on the edge of the chair opposite the desk. The cubicle was a foot larger than anyone else's on the thirty-fifth floor, for reasons that Bayley had never been able to discover. The extra space enabled Harris to keep a spare chair for visitors. "I'm sorry to bother you, Norm, but—"

"No bother, no bother. I was just celebrating." He grinned some more, obviously waiting for Bayley to ask what was the happy occasion.

"What's the happy occasion, Norm?"

"Just closed the book on a case. Judge gave the guy twenty years, no parole." Harris laughed cheerfully.

Bayley was finding it hard to appear interested. Nothing interested him, right now, beyond his current investigation. But he knew from experience that if he wanted anything from Harris, he had to play along. "Congratulations," he said. "What was the charge?"

"Making false statements to an employee of the Federal Bureau of Investigation." He leaned forward. "See, this guy had been one of my little pigeons. But he started getting greedy. I had to teach him a lesson."

Harris was a bully. He smiled a lot, he acted friendly, he never forgot your name, he'd buy you a drink and ask after your wife and kids. But that didn't mean he liked you. It meant he expected you to give him something in return, some gossip, maybe a personal secret that he could file away in case it might come in handy sometime. As a small boy, Bayley had been mistreated and betrayed by kids like Harris. He had learned to avoid them.

"So what's up, Jimmy?" The fat man finished the last of his croissant and wiped his fingers on a paper napkin.

Bayley suppressed his distaste at having to ask for help. "I'm . . . trying to find someone. A man named Leo Gottbaum. He probably lives somewhere in California, but I don't know where. His phone and address aren't in the usual databases.

He's a retired computer scientist. He may have taken steps to conceal his location. Have you ever heard of him?"

"Gottbaum." Harris narrowed his eyes, testing the name like a gourmet cook sampling a new dish. "Nope."

"He won a Nobel prize and he used to work at North Industries, in Long Beach."

"So you come to see me looking for a phone number, is that right? You figure to ask Norm, 'cause Norm always knows someone who knows someone."

"Well, yes."

Harris grinned again, as if he enjoyed having Bayley sitting in front of him. "Jimmy, I'm always happy to be of assistance. I'll take care of it. No problem."

"Thanks." Bayley stood up. "Shall I—"

"I'll come find you."

"Thanks," he said again, and left.

Back in his own cubicle he shuffled the LifeScan documents into sequence, clipped them in their binder, and stowed it in his briefcase beside his compad. After a moment's hesitation he added the gun, the scrap of metal, and the lab report. The microdisc he erased; its recording had been obtained illegally, and as such, it incriminated him as much as his suspects.

He unblanked his office window and sat for a moment staring down at the view. The white obelisk of city hall stood a dozen blocks away, looking like a kid's toy from this perspective. He wondered if Sharon was in there, doing her interview with the councilman. He wished he could see her, better still, be with her. Dealing with Harris reminded him how out of place he sometimes felt in the bureau.

When he'd been new on the job he'd accepted an invitation from Harris to hang out with a few of the guys after work at a local bar. They went there every Friday, watching baseball, telling stories, laughing loudly, drinking beer, flirting with the waitresses, doing the whole jock number. Bayley had felt embarrassed, and by the end of the evening they were kidding him about it. There'd been a couple of unfunny jokes implying he wasn't, so to speak, a red-blooded all-American boy.

"Here you go, Jimmy."

He turned quickly and found Harris standing in the entrance to the cubicle.

"Already?" he said.

"Yep. I got Gottbaum's private line at his retirement hide-away. Good enough?" He held out a piece of paper.

"Well, thanks." Bayley put out his hand.

"Although, on second thought—" Harris grinned. He flipped the paper out of reach. "What you got for me in return?"

Bayley felt a surge of irritation. "Norm—"

Harris laughed loudly. He threw the paper down on Bayley's desk. "Take it. A gift. I'll collect from you later, right?" He gave Bayley a meaning look, then winked and walked away.

So now he was indebted to Harris, and without a doubt he wouldn't be allowed to forget it. He flexed his hand, opening and closing his fist, looking for an outlet for his frustration. One day, Harris would make him mad enough to do something really destructive. Maybe break into the fat man's legendary database of informers, whores, and drinking buddies, and create a little mischief. Transpose some records or reduce them to garbage. Cracking it would be trivial; the password was bound to be something dumb, like Harris's birth date or even his own name. Bayley could probably take care of the whole job during a ten-minute coffee break.

It was petty to think in these terms, but it made him feel better all the same. He looked down at the number on the piece of paper. A 408 area code; that was near San Jose. He told his phone to connect him.

A man's voice answered. "Gottbaum speaking."

"Dr. Leo Gottbaum?"

"This is he. Who is this?"

Bayley paused, trying to restore his usual orderly sense of purpose. "This is Richard Wilson, Dr. Gottbaum. I'm with North Industries, security division, in San Diego. We're conducting a preliminary audit of the LifeScan program, and there are some points about its past history that aren't quite clear to me. Since you were in charge of it for so many years I thought I'd give you a call."

The line was silent for a long moment. "What do you need to know?" Gottbaum's tone had shifted, no longer sounding quite so offhand.

"Well," Bayley said, "I have a summary of the project here,

but, frankly, Dr. Gottbaum, I'm unclear about what, exactly, has been achieved. I was wondering—"

"May I make a suggestion?" Gottbaum interrupted. "This is not a good moment for me to talk. But I have a lot of free time tomorrow. Would you be interested in coming up here? I don't get many visitors, and I'd be glad to discuss LifeScan. It's an endeavor that's always been dear to my heart, and I can assure you there are excellent reasons for its continuation, which I could demonstrate if we met in person. Also, you'd probably enjoy the trip; this is one of the most unspoiled areas on the coast. It's quite exceptional."

Bayley thought for a moment. "Tomorrow's Saturday," he said. Wasn't there something he was supposed to do? Yes, shopping with Sharon for new living-room drapes.

"I fully realize it's the weekend," Gottbaum was saying. "That's why I thought you might like to get out of the city."

Bayley made his choice. "All right."

"Very good." He showed just a hint, now, of satisfaction. "Shall I transmit a map of my location?"

"No," Bayley said quickly. "We're having problems with our data lines here. Tell me how to find you, and I'll write it down."

Gottbaum supplied the directions and added a pathfinder number for Bayley to call when he was within range. "Any time in the afternoon is acceptable," he said. "I'll be pleased to meet you, Mr. Wilson."

Bayley hung up. He spent a minute sitting quietly, replaying the conversation in his head. Gottbaum's invitation had been unexpected; but a retired scientist living in isolation might naturally enjoy receiving visitors once in a while. It was natural, too, that he'd want to talk about a project that had meant a lot to him, especially if there was a chance to save it from being axed.

Cautiously, Bayley allowed himself to feel some satisfaction. Even the thought of Norm Harris didn't irritate him anymore. He grabbed his briefcase and walked out.

Thinking Machines

That evening he sat on a stool in the kitchen, using the counter as a workbench while he tested the components of Talking Teddy. On the other side of the counter, in the living room, he could see Sharon watching the wallscreen, sitting on the couch with Damon.

An anchorman was in closeup. "Angry demonstrators outside city hall today demanded the resignation of councilman Max Daniels, citing his alleged involvement in last month's conspiracy to sell contaminated drinking water to residents throughout the San Fernando Valley. With more on this, here's Sharon Blake reporting from city hall."

Suddenly Sharon herself was on the screen, life-size. In the background demonstrators were carrying signs and chanting.

"Mommy!" Damon shouted. "Mommy on television!"

Bayley watched as TV-Sharon gave a recap of the scandal. Then there was a clip of the accused councilman making an uneasy denial.

"Whether Daniels will be called as a witness is not yet known." TV-Sharon wrapped it up. "But observers believe his chances for reelection have been severely damaged by this highly embarrassing scandal."

She jumped up off the couch and came into the kitchen. "Was it okay? Did it look right?"

"It looked totally professional." He pulled her close and hugged her.

"So are you proud to be married to a glamorous TV news reporter?"

"I'm—I'm knocked out. Delighted." And he was.

"What about Talking Teddy?" said Damon, standing in the doorway, giving them a suspicious look.

Bayley disentangled himself from his wife. "I guess we have to remember our priorities." He turned to Damon. "I think I fixed it." He mated the halves of the bear's body, snapped them together, checked the fit, then squeezed, activating the pressure switch.

"Hi, Damon," said Talking Teddy. "How are you?"

"Yay!" Damon stopped pouting. He ran forward and reached up.

Bayley handed him the toy. "There was a loose connector on the main board."

"Shall I tell you a story?" said Talking Teddy.

"Yes," said Damon, carrying it back into the living room. "But not 'The Three Bears' again."

"How about 'Little Red Riding Hood'?"

"All right, into bed, both of you," said Sharon. She glanced at Bayley. "Did you set its timer?"

He nodded. "Talking Teddy will be singing a lullaby at eight, and will then shut down till tomorrow morning."

Later, sitting on the couch with her, he described his visit to North Industries, the history they'd sent him of the LifeScan program, the fragment of conversation that he'd monitored, his phone call to Gottbaum.

"You really think there's something important going on," she said when he'd finished.

"Yes. I do."

She drew her knees up under her chin, clasped her hands around her legs, and gave him a quizzical look. "But why should the old guy know anything about it?"

"Maybe he doesn't. But he's the only lead I have left. And he seemed ready enough to talk. He probably wants to tell me how LifeScan is going to make this country great again. A benefit to mankind."

She looked at him shrewdly. "Which you think it isn't."

Bayley kicked off his shoes and rested his feet on the coffee table. "Let's deal with that. Let's suppose for a moment that this seemingly useless research achieved what it set out to do: create an intelligent computer."

"We already have intelligent computers," she objected.

"Not really. That's still the holy grail of AI. We have special-purpose computers that do one task very, very well, like the dedicated chips inside that DVI system, creating a 3-D landscape and allowing you to walk through it. Or, we have general-purpose gadgets that *imitate* intelligent behavior, like Talking Teddy. But that's just a set of preprogrammed responses. There are no systems that can think in the broadest sense, using judgment, drawing inferences, making decisions in the real world."

She mulled that over. "So maybe it does make sense to copy the way nature does it."

"Sure, it's a valid approach, although the complexity of the task is almost inconceivable. The real point, though, is that bioscience has come such a long way in the past thirty years, it's a better bet now than LifeScan, for military purposes. They can already interface quantum-electronic devices with individual nerves. In a couple of years they'll be able to take a dog's brain and use it to control anything they want: a robot, a jet plane, a tank. True, that brain will grow old; but when that happens, they can unplug it, throw it out, and plug in a new one. There's no shortage of dogs, and they're cheaper and more reliable than exotic computers running complicated software."

"Yuk," said Sharon.

"I agree, it's distasteful, but that's how it's going to be. So logically, LifeScan should have been cancelled. Even if it worked, it's the wrong approach for what they have in mind. And it doesn't work. It may never work." He shook his head in exasperation. "It's absorbed billions in public money. And for no reason! It doesn't make any sense!"

"So you'll ask him about it," she said, leaning forward, ruffling his hair with the palm of her hand. "Calm down!"

He realized he'd been raising his voice, getting excited. "Sorry."

"The only thing that bothers me," she went on, "is your cover story. I mean, it would be easy for Gottbaum to check. All he has to do is call the security department at North Industries and ask to speak to this Richard Wilson."

He paused a moment, concentrating on her question. "Okay, you're right, but here's how it seems to me. First, Gottbaum had very little time to call anyone, because I spoke to him late today, a Friday afternoon. Second, if he did decide to place a call, he'd be more likely to contact his old colleague Horton to ask what's happening, and Horton would have to maintain my cover, otherwise he'd be obstructing justice. Third, even if Gottbaum does find out who I am, he'll still feel motivated to answer my questions. The only thing I don't like is that if he tells the LifeScan team there's an FBI investigation, they might try to destroy some evidence, or just conceivably abscond. But I think that's extremely unlikely. Whatever these people are involved in, they're still basically scientists, not criminals."

She gave him a shy, worried look, as if she was embarrassed by her own anxieties. "You don't think they'd do something more . . . drastic, to protect themselves?"

"Like what?"

Her voice dropped to a lower pitch. "Like . . . something to you?" Her forehead creased and a little furrow appeared between her eyebrows.

He laughed. "What do you think they are, hit men? You're talking like a TV drama."

She sighed. "All right, I know I worry too much. But when are you going to see this Gottbaum?"

"Well, he invited me up tomorrow. Saturday."

"Tomorrow?" She drew back, and her worried expression turned into a vexed look. "Jim, you agreed—"

"I know, I know, the drapes. Sharon, I'm sorry, but this is more important than drapes. It really is." He looked at her, hoping there wasn't going to be an argument, and she would tell him she understood.

Finally, she shrugged and her face relaxed. "All I can say is, you'd better be reasonable about it if I have to cancel a plan of yours sometime. Like if the station ever wants me to cover a weekend assignment." She prodded him with her finger. "Right?"

"Right. I promise."

She stood and held out her hand. "But I think you should make it up to me, all the same."

He allowed himself to be pulled up off the couch. "Make it up to you? How?"

She tilted her head. "Come in the bedroom. Maybe I can think of something."

Echoes

The little winding highway traced a contour between forest and ocean: steep hillsides green with pines, waves crashing over tumbled rocks, sun casting rainbows in the spray. The air smelled of brine and pine needles. Above the hum of the car's motor and the mutter of tires on gravel, he heard birds calling to each other, crickets singing in the grass.

The sky was blue, the sunshine warm and bright. It was so perfect, so seductive, it made him uneasy.

Sharon had planted a little dark seed of doubt when he'd left the apartment that morning. "Be careful," she'd said, looking up at him with troubled eyes. "I still don't like the sound of this Gottbaum."

Bayley wasn't superstitious, and he'd teased her for being full of doom and gloom, but he couldn't block her warning entirely out of his mind. On a brief straight section of the highway he pulled his compad out of his briefcase, linked it with the accessory jack of his phone, and dialed through to a public-access database. "Searching for Gottbaum, Leo," he said, and spelled the names. "Career summary and personality profile."

For the next couple of miles the compad recited the downloaded data. Much of the career summary Bayley knew already, but the profile contained some surprises. Gottbaum had evidently been a minor media personality in the 1980s and 1990s, propounding radical views and challenging his colleagues to prove him wrong. He believed Asians were more intelligent than whites, and whites were smarter than blacks, and he claimed he could prove it. He wanted to end all government supervision of research. He lobbied Congress to remove controls from experiments with recombinant DNA. He advocated unilateral nuclear disarmament but believed that everyone over eighteen should be trained in the use of conventional weapons. The networks had used him in talk shows and interviews—probably more for entertainment value than anything else—but eventually he seemed to have offended one sponsor too many, and they dropped him.

Then, in the twenty-first century, he did an about-face and

became a recluse. He complained there had been a decline in intelligence and ambition among average Americans and said he was disgusted by the way people wanted the government to take care of them. In his final press conference he stated that he would devote the rest of his life to pure research, and he wanted nothing further to do with the general public.

This, then, was the man who had invited Bayley to drop in for a friendly visit.

The road looped inland through a small town that lay abandoned, windows boarded up, paint peeling, front yards waist-high in weeds. Tourism had sustained this part of the coast thirty years ago, but rising fuel prices and a falling birth rate had changed all that. As the highway veered toward the ocean again Bayley wondered where he would be able to buy food and recharge the car.

Eventually he came to a general store, a homemade plywood shack with two rusty gas pumps outside, Texaco signs bleached pink by the sun. An ancient Dodge van was standing nearby under the trees, side panels hand-painted with pictures of knives, hearts, and lightning bolts, the rear bumper held up by an old piece of gray nylon rope. In the rear window was a sticker, ragged at the edges: Van Halen Lives!

Bayley parked his car and went into the store. The place was crammed with supplies: frozen food, sacks of rice, auto parts, all-weather hiking gear, boxes of ammunition. An elderly man in a black T-shirt with the arms ripped off stood leaning against the wall by the cash register, smoking a cigarette. He had a sagging beer belly, long, stringy gray hair brushed back behind his shoulders, and he looked close to seventy. His face was ravaged by sun, age, and drug abuse.

Bayley selected a couple of homemade snack packs from a freezer with a cracked glass door and took them to the counter. "Do you have fuel cells?"

The man nodded. He dropped his cigarette and stepped on it. "Not much call for 'em, but we got 'em." He stooped down, rooted around in a closet at the back, hauled out a cell, and hoisted the forty-pound load onto his shoulder, refusing Bayley's offer of help. "Got to stay in shape," he said, grinning, showing rotten teeth.

Outside, he set down the new cell, opened the hood of Bayley's car, and removed the old one. "Most folks around here still use gasoline." He dropped the new cell into place, slit the federal inspection seal, and snapped the circlips over the terminals. "I'd go electric myself, 'cept the government don't let us do no recharging here, 'cause we don't meet the safety regulations. We got to send cells back to San Jose for chargin', you believe that?" He shook his head. "We used to think the oil companies was bad, but the feds—"

"I'm looking for a man who lives somewhere around here," Bayley interrupted. "Leo Gottbaum."

"Gottbaum?" He nodded. "Sure, you go just a half-mile further on, there's a dirt road. You got a pathfinder in your car, you'll be in range. All you got to do is say, 'Beam me up, Scottie.' " He gave a short, loud laugh.

Bayley didn't get the joke, but he didn't bother to ask what it meant. "Thanks for your help," he said, wanting to get away. There was something morbid, here, not just backwoods primitivism but a sense of loss, failure and poverty, dying echoes from a bygone century.

Prophet

He found the dirt road and dialed the number that Gottbaum had given him. The pathfinder screen lit up with a highlighted route, a flashing cursor pointing the way.

Soon he found himself climbing a steep grade through a tunnel of green. Small creatures scampered out of the way of the car, and somewhere nearby a stream was trickling. It was so peaceful, so verdant, he felt like a pilgrim rediscovering Eden.

He passed the row of mailboxes, rounded the last couple of sharp bends, and saw the dome ahead. But as he emerged from the forest his trained eye noted the squat concrete pillars among the trees, cameras tracking his approach. The car rumbled over a grating; when he looked down he saw that the grid was retractable with a deep concrete trench beneath.

So much for Eden. Feeling more like a moving target than a pilgrim now, he parked in a graveled area and set the brake.

From his open briefcase he selected what he might need: the history of LifeScan and his compad, which still contained Gottbaum's biography and profile. The rest of the stuff relating to his investigation—the electronic handgun, especially—was best left in the car. He closed the briefcase, locked it, and set it on the floor.

He got out and paused for a moment, shading his eyes against the afternoon sun. A warm breeze ruffled the tall grass. Beyond the trees rimming the hillside, in the far distance away and below, sailboats were tiny black flecks in the haze-blue crescent of the sea.

"Are you Wilson?"

Bayley turned and saw a white-haired man standing in the entrance to the dome. "Dr. Gottbaum?"

Gottbaum stepped out and the door slid shut behind him. He came over to Bayley and gave his hand a perfunctory clasp, obviously not much interested in formalities. "I was just stepping out to do a little maintenance," he said. "It'll only take ten minutes. Come along."

Bayley nodded, feeling disconcerted by the man's abrupt manner. Gottbaum stood tall and moved quickly, despite his age. His eyes didn't seem to miss much; there was a grim watchfulness about them, accentuated by the deep lines in his face, humorless and severe. He walked around the dome, and Bayley fell into step beside him.

"So you've come to ask me some questions." The voice was dispassionate, matter-of-fact. Bayley had heard corporate CEOs and high-level government administrators speak like that, getting straight to the point as if business was all that mattered and personalities were irrelevant.

If he was going to draw Gottbaum out, he would have to establish some sort of link with the man. "It's true I have a few questions," he said. "But I'd also like it if we could just sit and talk for a while." He tried to make it sound amiable.

"If you wish," said Gottbaum. He started down the south side of the hill, placing his feet with methodical caution as the slope steepened. "In the meantime, though, I assume you want to know two things: first, why the LifeScan program should have been funded for thirty years without producing much in the way of results, and second, why it should be allowed to continue. Correct?"

Small talk and pleasantries obviously weren't in the man's vocabulary, and he seemed determined to control the parameters of the conversation. "Actually, my interests aren't quite as cut-and-dried as that," said Bayley.

"If I omit anything, I expect you'll say so." He reached the edge of the solar-panel array, a mosaic of black squares amid a flat white area of concrete. He unlocked a door in a tall metal box, checked some digital readouts, then picked his way to a panel near the center of the area. "The LifeScan program has survived," he said, taking a small screwdriver out of his pocket, "because I put the right administrator in charge of it." He bent down and made an adjustment, realigning the panel. "When North Industries was taken over by the government ten years or so ago, they were compelled to ask me to retire. I'd just turned seventy, you see, and it was federal policy." He grimaced as if he tasted something sour. "My work was unfinished and I didn't want it wasted. So I picked Horton to supervise and mediate with the Pentagon. He had a bunch of old buddies there; they owed him favors. The usual bureaucratic bullshit."

"You're . . . very candid," said Bayley.

Gottbaum put the screwdriver back in his pocket and straightened up. He touched his back, his face showing a flicker of discomfort, but it was quickly erased. Bayley guessed he had little tolerance for weakness, in himself or others. "I've never seen the sense in beating around the bush. It's a waste of time. People who speak plainly to one another generally show respect for one another, don't you agree?"

"Of course," Bayley said, although he didn't believe a word of it. Gottbaum was a man who had surrounded his retreat with automatic weapons in remote-controlled silos. His openness obviously had severe limits.

"Do you generate all your own power?" Bayley asked, gesturing toward the solar array.

"There's a municipal supply. But it's unreliable. I supplement it with wind power, solar power, and a geothermal generator that I installed under the dome just this year. There's a shaft that goes down a thousand feet. I use the heat differential between the bottom and the top to run a turbine."

"I'm familiar with the system," Bayley said.

"Technical background?" Gottbaum gave him a quick, evaluating glance.

"Some."

Gottbaum grunted. "Well, it's good of you to come all the way up here, Wilson. Must have been a long drive from San Diego. That's where you live, is it?"

"In that area."

Gottbaum smiled faintly. "So let's go inside."

The heavy steel door slid aside when Gottbaum touched a sensitized panel, and Bayley found himself in a semicircular living area whose floor was paved with slabs of raw gray slate. Old Bauhaus chrome-and-leather armchairs were submerged under stacks of scientific journals. A deep shelf at waist height ran all the way around the dome's perimeter, loaded with expensive equipment: black metal cabinets, high-definition displays, power lights glowing, cooling fans murmuring. More hardware cluttered the floor amid snarls of cable.

Gottbaum picked his way to a redwood table beneath windows overlooking the forest and the ocean beyond. A young woman was sitting there, engrossed in a book. When she sensed Gottbaum standing over her she glanced up with an uncertain, startled expression. She had Asian eyes and a demure Japanese mouth, but her skin was almost as fair as his.

"My daughter, Yumi." He indicated her with a stiff, awkward gesture. "Yumi, this man has come up from the lab to talk to me." He stood looking down at her, clearly waiting for her to leave.

Bayley moved between them. "Good afternoon," he said. "I'm Richard Wilson. Pleased to meet you."

She stood up. She was wearing a white peasant blouse and a handmade, ankle-length cotton skirt. She plucked absently at the fabric, and Bayley noticed that her nails were bitten short. "Hello," she said, in a small voice.

"I hope I'm not disturbing your afternoon."

"No. Not at all." She looked quickly from Bayley to Gottbaum, and back again. "Is this a private meeting, or—"

"Yes, please, Yumi." Gottbaum's lips were compressed. He made no attempt to conceal his impatience.

"Maybe I'll see you later," Bayley said to her. He felt oddly struck by her, not just by her face, which had a demure, child-like beauty, but by her presence. She was shy, and she obviously deferred to her father, yet at the same time some part of her seemed detached, steadfastly maintaining a separate identity.

She gathered a couple of paper plates from the table and ducked her head as she turned and disappeared through a doorway. There was the brief sound of running water, then a door closing, then silence.

Gottbaum gestured to the chair Yumi had been using. "Sit down. Have I answered your first question satisfactorily?"

Bayley sat in the chair and laid his compad and the LifeScan history on the table in front of him. He wished Gottbaum would stop forcing the pace. "As I understand you," he said, "you're saying that Horton has so many friends at the Pentagon, the program hasn't had to produce any results in thirty years. I guess I find that a bit hard to believe."

The old man laughed without any humor. "Come on, Wilson, results don't mean diddlyshit. Ever since the premillennial depression and the environmental crises of this century, it's been the Roosevelt years all over again. Bailouts and buyouts. Progress has been snail-paced at best, and expectations have declined accordingly. Private industry barely exists anymore, and defense is no exception. It's one big government bureaucracy, with all the stupidities of a bureaucracy, and a man like Horton knows exactly how to exploit them."

Bayley nodded slowly, beginning to understand, now, what Gottbaum was really about. He gestured to the compad. "I downloaded some biographical notes on the way here," he said. He selected text mode, and the screen lit up. "Do you mind if I just take a moment?"

Gottbaum shrugged. He waited.

Bayley scrolled the text. "You were born in 1950, so I guess you were a teenager in the 1960s. A student radical?"

Gottbaum grunted. "Something like that." He leaned back in his chair. "We occupied the campus for a few days, threw a few rocks and bottles. Is it relevant?"

"I'm just trying to get the picture," said Bayley. "You see, from a modern perspective, to someone of my generation, those times sound like anarchy."

Gottbaum's eyes narrowed. "Not anarchy, no. There was a bit more freedom, but that's all."

"Really? Well, after you got your Ph.D. in 1975—"

"Do I assume you're going to ask about my computer virus?"

"Well, yes. I gather it incapacitated a whole network of the mainframes they used to use back then."

"Just a prank," said Gottbaum, sounding a little testy now. "It didn't do any damage, didn't trash any files, didn't corrupt any data. The network could actually have stayed up and running, except some sysop panicked."

"That prank of yours would be a federal offense today," Bayley pointed out. "But I guess back then, there were no laws to cover it. So, let's see, in 1985 you started your own microcomputer business, and you became a millionaire."

Gottbaum didn't look any more friendly than before. He laced his long, bony fingers together on the table in front of him. "You left out a few years of intense research that beat out all our competitors, both here and in Japan, but otherwise you're correct. What's your point?"

"My point is this. You grew up in a time of institutionalized lawlessness. People routinely broke the rules, got away with it, and even got rich in the process. Today, centralized government and a planned economy have brought things back under control, so that greed doesn't dominate society as it used to, and everyone is properly cared for. But to you, because of your background, it's nothing but a big, stupid bureaucracy."

Gottbaum's face twitched. His mouth made tiny motions as if he wanted to respond. But whatever he was thinking, he evidently chose to suppress it. "I've long since learned," he said, "not to bother debating these issues." His voice sounded dismissive.

Bayley felt disappointed. For a moment, there, he sensed he had almost got the old man to open up. "That's too bad," he said.

Gottbaum stood up. "Let's get back to business. Over here a moment, if you please." He walked to a beige steel cabinet that had a glossy, dustless finish, as if it had just been uncrated. "You know what this is?"

Bayley followed him. "It looks like a Pollenz T-five-twelve."

"Quite right. Inside this small box are thirty-two thousand, seven hundred sixty-eight coprocessors and five hundred twelve terabytes of molecular memory. That's *half a quadrillion* addresses."

"I don't quite see—"

"I'm about to answer your second question," Gottbaum said impatiently, as if it should have been obvious. "You see, Wilson, despite all the regulations and protectionism, an entire generation of computing equipment is still being developed every fifteen years. And we keep rebuilding from the ground up. Gallium arsenide replaced silicon, and quantum electronics is replacing that. And this is something that *nature cannot do*. Nature is evolutionary. It has to live with its mistakes. We, however, can strip everything down and start over. We can be *revolutionary*."

Bayley recalled something about this in the LifeScan history. "You're saying that once we develop true artificial intelligence —possibly by replicating a brain—we can then make revolutionary improvements?"

"I'm saying *only* we can do that. See, Wilson, people doing bioscience are always stuck with the same old shit. They fiddle around with base-pair sequences, variations on a theme, but the theme's always the same: DNA. But in the physical sciences we can invent any new shit we want. Once we've modeled intelligence as a bit pattern, we can decode it, enhance it, transform it, maybe even program it to transform itself. The military applications are just a convenient way to get it funded. I'm talking about something that can change the whole goddam world." He lowered his head slightly, staring directly at Bayley. "Surely, you must see the possibilities."

This, evidently, was what Gottbaum lived for. His eyes were wide, very compelling. He had an intense presence. He was like a prophet trying to enroll Bayley as a believer.

"The trouble is, though," Bayley said, choosing to ignore the intellectual bait being dangled in front of him, "it's been thirty years, and according to the official summary, the LifeScan program still hasn't managed to make a model of anything."

Gottbaum dropped his hands by his sides. "It will. If it isn't cancelled. If they don't keep cutting the funding." He turned away. "I have some work to do now, if you'll excuse me."

88 CHARLES PLATT

Bayley found himself watching the old man's back as he walked away to a terminal whose screen was filled with text. "That's . . . all?" he said.

"Yes, that's all I have time for." He sat down and pulled a keyboard onto his knees.

"I was hoping to have more opportunity to talk."

"In that case, I regret I must disappoint you."

"Did I cause offense?"

"You didn't, but if you continue to trespass on my hospitality, you certainly will."

Bayley felt his surprise giving way to annoyance. "I thought you were concerned about the future of LifeScan," he said. "I thought you wanted to tell me—"

"I don't think anything I say to you is going to make any difference," Gottbaum interrupted. "I'd be wasting my breath. Go on back to San Diego; do whatever you want."

"Well, all right." Bayley nodded. "Thanks for sparing some of your valuable time." He picked his way across the tangle of cables and walked back to the door where he'd come in. It slid aside in front of him, and he was back outside again, in the sunshine.

Go-Between

He stood for a few moments, disoriented, trying to analyze what had happened. Maybe he'd pushed too hard. Maybe he hadn't pushed hard enough. Maybe he should have seemed more receptive to Gottbaum's visionary spiel.

He noticed Yumi sitting cross-legged in the grass, staring at her book in her lap. Her black hair gleamed in the sun.

He walked over to her. "Excuse me," he said.

She squinted up at him. "Yes?"

"May I talk to you, for just a moment?"

"What about?"

He gestured vaguely. "I—think I irritated your father."

She tilted her head to one side, looking contemplative. "Why would you think that?"

"Because . . . hell, he just threw me out." He laughed, seeing the humor of the situation: he'd come up here feeling haunted by Sharon's gloomy premonition, and he'd been met, basically, with indifference.

Yumi seemed more relaxed out here than she had been in the dome. She shrugged. "He always throws people out," she said. "Some of them last longer than others, but in the end, he gets bored and tells them to go away."

"Nice guy." Bayley still felt annoyed—at Gottbaum for being such a prima donna, and at himself for not handling it better. But maybe he could salvage something even now. He crouched down in the grass opposite Yumi. "You sound as if you've seen a lot of people come and go."

"Yes, in my childhood, when I still lived here. Journalists, congressmen, graduate students." She stopped abruptly as if it had occurred to her that she was speaking too freely to a stranger.

"May I ask where you live now?"

"Hawaii." The word barely escaped her. Her face had become composed, cautious.

He wondered how he might draw her out. "It can't have been easy, being the daughter of a genius."

"Two geniuses. Before she died, my mother was a brilliant biologist." She closed her book but kept her finger in it, marking her place. "So, you're leaving now?"

Bayley raised his eyebrows. "Are you throwing me out too?"

She quickly shook her head. "No, I was going to ask if you might give me a ride down to the bottom of the hill. To the general store."

"Oh. Well, sure."

She stood up and brushed fragments of grass off her long skirt. "You see, I never learned to drive."

He felt tantalized by her. She spoke in short, direct sentences, just like her father, and her eyes were equally intent and watchful. At the same time, there was a vulnerability to her; a gentleness. And she was wary of him, maybe wary of men in general.

They got into his car. He started it and headed back down the track. "So what prompted you to come here on this visit?" he asked her.

She gave him a quick, sidelong glance, which he guessed he wasn't supposed to notice. "Did my father say anything to you about his . . . plans, next week?"

"No." One of the wheels jolted into a deep rut, the car lurched, and he had to wrestle with the steering. "All we talked about was the LifeScan program."

"Oh. That." She said it in a disparaging tone. "Are you part of that?" She sounded as if she hoped he wasn't.

"I work for the security department in North Industries." For some reason he felt bad about lying. Something about Yumi seemed very trusting, despite her cautiousness. "I told your father that LifeScan seems pretty much a failure. That was when he threw me out."

She sat looking straight ahead, her hands folded in her lap. She was doll-like, poised, perfect. "A failure," she said.

"Doesn't it seem that way to you?"

She looked as if she was trying to decide what to say. "I—don't know much about it."

Bayley was driving slowly, but they had already covered half the distance down the track to the coast road. He wouldn't have much more time with her; he had to get to the point. "I almost had the feeling," he said, "your father might be keeping something secret."

"Probably." She gave a little shrug. "He is a very secretive man."

Her seeming candor was disconcerting. He wished he knew how to tap it. "Do you get to know what his secrets are?"

"No, I don't." Now she seemed deliberately discouraging. "Even if I did, I would suggest you should ask him, not me."

They reached the end of the dirt track. Bayley turned onto the highway and allowed the car to pick up speed. He let the silence drag out, hoping it might prompt her to say something more. But she sat without speaking.

Maybe, he decided, the direct approach would be better, and he should simply tell her what was on his mind. "Here's what really concerns me," he said, as the general store came into view. "I get the feeling that the LifeScan team may have stumbled on something important. So important, they haven't even told management about it. You know, scientists can be seduced by their own power. The work becomes an end in itself, they ignore the potential side effects, and anyone who tries to exert some control over them is seen as an irritation or even as an enemy. That can be very dangerous."

His words seemed to affect her. She looked down at her hands in her lap and picked at the side of her thumbnail, tearing the skin. She flinched. "That's very true," she said, in a small voice.

He stopped the car opposite the store. "I think your father may have maintained regular contact with the people at the lab. He may still be involved in the research. He's a formidable man, and he has a history of taking things into his own hands. That's why I'm concerned."

She was silent for a long time. Finally, she seemed to reach a decision. "I'm sorry, Mr. Wilson, but I really prefer to keep out of my father's affairs."

Bayley reached for the notepad he kept by the car phone, wrote some digits on a page, and handed it to her. "If you ever feel like getting in touch, this is my home number. If I'm not there and someone else answers, just say you have a message for Jim. That's . . . my middle name."

She looked at the paper as if she didn't want to accept it. Then, impulsively, she slipped it into the book she had been reading. "I will keep it," she said. "But I doubt you'll hear from me." She reached for the door release.

He took her hand. Her skin was very soft and her touch was gentle. "Thanks for talking to me. It's probably best if you don't mention any of this to your father."

She gave him a quick, startled glance, then turned her head, hiding her face as she got out of the car and walked away. He sat and watched her till she disappeared into the little store. Then, reluctantly, he started back toward Los Angeles.

Betrayal

She walked back to the dome and found her father doing what she'd seen him do so often over the years: sitting at a desk, staring at a screen. Discreetly, she left him there. She went outside and read her book till the sun set and the sky dimmed from blue to purple. Then she went back in again and found him still in the same chair, still typing on the same keyboard.

She walked over and stood at his elbow, knowing he could never work while someone was watching him. She waited silently, and after a moment he looked up. "Yes?" He seemed to have trouble focusing on her. "What is it, Yumi?"

"I'm going to eat," she said. "Are you interested?"

"Um, yes. I'll be done in a few minutes."

She had learned long ago that that could mean anything from an hour to a day. She stayed where she was, refusing, just for once, to be dismissed. To confront him made her stomach clench, and sometimes it even made her hands tremble. But if she gave in to him, she would feel angry with herself and ashamed, which was worse. "You know," she said, "it seems to me, if you're really going in to the hospital on Monday, you might want to take a little time just to talk. I mean, you did say that was why you asked me to come here."

He looked up at her again and seemed genuinely puzzled. "Certainly, we can talk. I just have to get this done first." He gestured at the screen. "It's extremely important."

They stared at each other, baffled by each other, as if they were animals of two different species. "Are you working on the LifeScan thing?" she asked. It was unlike her to question him;

but her conversation in Richard Wilson's car had stirred something in her.

"Yes, as it happens."

She kept her face composed, presenting him with the demure, innocent facade she'd learned from her mother. "You've spent so much time on that project, for so many years. You must feel disappointed that it was a failure."

He pulled his hands back from the keyboard. The movement was so abrupt, it reminded her of a cowboy reaching for his guns. "Who told you it was a failure?" His tone was sharp now, and she saw the muscles tighten in his face. She felt as if she had just poked a ferocious animal with a stick.

"The person who was here this afternoon, Mr. Wilson, said something about it. When he gave me a ride down to the general store."

"Wilson." Gottbaum gave a short, sharp laugh.

"He said the managers at North Industries—"

"They don't know what's going on. And with good reason. LifeScan has dangerous potential for abuse. And it certainly is *not* a failure."

So Wilson had been correct, and there was some sort of cover-up. Her father made it sound ethical, of course; he was so self-righteous, he believed he knew what was best for everyone. What surprised her was that he had told her anything about it. The words had emerged like a reflex, as if she'd knocked his knee and he couldn't stop himself from kicking out.

She wondered how much more he might be willing to say. "You know," she said, still demure and diffident, "I've never really understood what LifeScan is all about."

He gave her a suspicious look, and she saw the barriers fall back into place. "No need to go into that." He paused as if he was replaying his previous statement and regretting it. "This is something that you shouldn't be involved in. Do you understand?" He gave her a hard look.

"Of course, Father." She inclined her head respectfully, the dutiful woman deferring to the wise man. She wondered if it reminded him of his one-time bride, who had seemed so naive and submissive yet turned out, in reality, to be as ruthless as he was. She had been the only one who'd ever managed to sneak past his defenses and steal things away from him: his affection, his time, his genes—even, ultimately, some of his money.

He turned back to the screen. "If you don't mind," he said, "I really do have to finish this."

"Certainly, Father." She took a step back.

As she went to the kitchen, she passed the dining table. There was a plain black folder lying on it together with another item no bigger than a man's wallet. A compad, she realized, with its keyboard folded flat against its postcard-sized screen. She paused, wondering where it had come from, and then realized: Richard Wilson must have left his things there when her father had ordered him out of the house.

Yumi glanced over her shoulder. He was already submerged in his work again. Quietly, she picked up Wilson's possessions, then crept out of the living area. She retreated to her bedroom and shut the door.

She sat cross-legged on a patchwork quilt that she had stitched herself, fifteen years ago. She examined the compad, hesitated, then set it aside, unwilling to snoop into Wilson's personal notes. The black folder, however, was another matter. She opened it and looked at the title page.

For a moment she felt dazed. Here in her hands was the answer that her father had refused to give her. She had heard passing references to LifeScan all her life, but never before had there been any way for her to make sense of what she'd heard.

The SECRET stamp didn't bother her; she'd grown up in a home where classified documents were routinely left lying around. And so, she began reading.

Two hours later, when she finally finished, she understood for the first time the real dimensions of her father's grandiose obsession. The goals described in the summary were surely just the beginning, as far as he was concerned. Knowing him as she did, she was able to extrapolate from the official summary and guess what he really had in mind.

She closed her eyes for a moment. Goosebumps rose on her arms and she shivered, feeling very alone and frightened. She wished, now, she had trusted Wilson and confided in him. She should get on the phone to him immediately, except that there was no safe way to do so. Her father's monitoring system routinely recorded all calls to and from the dome. None of her neighbors had phones in their cabins. The general store on the coast highway closed at sunset, eliminating access to its pay phone. And she had never learned how to drive.

Tomorrow morning, as soon as the store opened, she would walk down there and make the call. It would be a betrayal, of course, and it was scary to imagine her father's rage if he ever discovered that she had crossed him. But by then, if her assumptions were correct, it should be out of his hands.

For the first time in her life, she realized, she had real power over him.

Rendezvous

His shoulders ached and his head felt muzzy and he missed Sharon—missed her a lot, because they always spent Saturdays together, and when he'd tried to call her from his car during the long drive back to Los Angeles he'd been unable to get through. There'd been a circuit-busy message, there'd been strange noises in the line, and when he'd tried to go via an operator he'd been told his home phone was out of service. So he'd asked the operator to try his other number, at which point he'd been told that that was out of service too.

But he was almost home, now. Soon he'd be hugging her, sitting with her and Damon, eating a meal with them, and his long drive up the coast and his futile meeting with Gottbaum wouldn't matter anymore.

He reached his street and started along it, past the jacaranda trees shedding their blossoms, the tall palms silhouetted against the last dim light of evening. He imagined families inside the little Spanish-style houses either side of the street, people eating dinner, playing with their kids, gossiping or laughing or maybe making love. Me too, he thought. Give me all of the above.

He pressed the button on the dashboard and swung his car onto the concrete ramp leading down to the basement garage. The headlight beams lit up the entrance—and showed the garage door still tightly shut.

Bayley stopped his car. He pressed the button again. Still nothing happened. He cursed his own laziness; he should have done the maintenance on the door weeks ago.

Well, maybe he could move it manually. He got out, walked down the ramp, and leaned on it, trying to slide it open.

It still didn't budge.

He considered his options. He could walk around to the building lobby, let himself in with his key, go down the stairs to the garage, and try opening the door from inside. He had a feeling, though, that that wouldn't work either.

So he'd have to park his car on the street. No big deal; it wasn't a high-crime neighborhood.

Tired and irritable, he walked back, got in, and reached for the drive selector.

There was a sound behind him. A rustle of clothing. An arm grabbed him around the neck. He grunted and flinched from the sudden shock of physical contact. Cold metal pressed against the side of his forehead, and he made a little noise of surprise. Instinctively, he grabbed at the arm. Then reason took over and he groped inside his jacket, reaching for his gun.

"No!" The voice behind him was female, high-pitched, very loud.

Bayley froze. "What do you want?" His skin prickled. He felt his pulse accelerate. He cursed himself for leaving his car unattended, allowing someone to slip into it. Then he realized the whole thing had been a setup: the garage door had been sabotaged to lure him outside. "You want money," he said, "I'll give you money." He looked in the mirror, but the face behind him was invisible, shrouded in shadow.

"Back the car onto the street," the woman said, her lips close to his ear, her breath on his neck. "Drive around the corner." She sounded very tense, possibly unstable.

The panicky ones were always the most dangerous. "Sure," he said, "just take it easy. I'll do what you say." He hoped she wasn't on drugs, hoped he could unwind her a little. At the same time, he realized there was something familiar about her voice. She wasn't off the street. White, middle-class— "Rosalind French," he said suddenly. Without any real reason, he felt a wave of relief. "Jesus Christ, you scared the shit out of me." He started to turn his head.

"Do what I tell you!" She sounded right on the edge. "I mean it!" The cold metal pressed harder against him, trembling. "This will kill you instantly. You know that."

He had a horribly clear vision, as if he was looking down from above, watching himself sitting in his car with the electronic handgun pressed against his head. It would be an instant, silent, painless death. He would simply be found an hour from now, or maybe tomorrow morning, with no brain function.

He moved his eyes, looking left and right, trying to see along the street. The sidewalks were empty; no one had any reason to go strolling after dark. No cars, either; it was a family neighborhood where people stayed home on Saturday nights. In any case, here inside his car, in the darkness, there was no way anyone could see what was happening to him.

"What do you want?" he asked, speaking with difficulty, as his own anxiety increased and tightened his throat. He could understand how they might have figured out that he wasn't Richard Wilson, but his real identity and his home address should have been impossible for them to discover. It seemed impossible that they should have breached FBI security. But how else had they found him? "Tell me what you want," he said. "There's no need for this."

"Do what I say! Just do what I say! Drive around the corner!"

"All right," he said. "I'm shifting into reverse. You see?" He reached slowly for the lever and moved it one notch. "I'm taking hold of the steering. Okay?"

"Good. Back up slowly. Don't look around."

His mind was checking off the possibilities. He couldn't reach his gun unobtrusively. His one-shot backup pistol, snug against his left leg, was even less accessible. What were his other options? Knock the phone with his knee and hit the autodial button for his home number, but dammit, his home number was out of service. Push his elbow against the car horn and attract some attention—but it would take too long, far too long, for anyone to come and see what the fuss was about. Jam his foot down hard and hope that the surge of power would throw her into the back seat—but that was too chancy. He felt anger along with his fear. After all the genuinely dangerous work he'd done in the past, it was outrageous to be trapped like this by a woman scientist playing at street crime.

But the only thing to do, right now, was follow her instructions. Take it a step at a time, try and calm her, talk to her as much as possible, and wait for an opportunity. That was what he'd been trained to do in situations like this, and his training was correct.

He shifted into forward gear and started along the street—slowly, slowly. "Which way?" he asked her.

"Turn right."

He did so.

"Stop behind the car parked there. In front of the empty building."

It was a house that had been left vacant during some kind of dispute over property rights. In front of it he saw a vehicle at the curb, its reflectors and its license plate glowing in his headlight beams. The number on the plate looked familiar. He had a memory for numbers. He realized he'd seen it just a couple of days ago on the car belonging to the masked figure he'd run into in Little Asia. So, it was Rosalind French's car. And there were two silhouettes inside it: her associates, waiting for him.

"I guess I should congratulate you," he said, making himself sound calm. "You did a good job figuring out who I was and where to find me."

"We had some help. Stop here."

He did as she said. And then it slipped into place. "Help from Gottbaum?"

"Just be quiet!" The gun still pressed hard against his temple, and her hand was still trembling.

Bayley was beginning to realized the degree to which he'd underestimated them. They were scientists, not hit men. Wasn't that what he'd told Sharon? He'd been so sure of himself, laughing at her for worrying about him. But he'd been wrong. He'd betrayed Sharon with his overconfidence. That was the hardest fact to deal with: that in some way he might have let her down.

Still, they *were* scientists, they *weren't* hit men. He could sense Rosalind French's fear as she pressed the gun against his head. If he could seize his opportunity—

One of the figures in the car ahead of him turned around, opened the door, and got out.

Bayley realized that whatever he was going to do, it would be a whole lot easier to do it while there was still only one person to contend with. "Dr. French." He made it sound commanding. "I work for the FBI. Assaulting an FBI agent is a very serious federal offense. Kidnapping him is worse. It could mean thirty years without parole. You're obviously in trouble. You should tell me what the trouble is. I'm not necessarily your adversary. I can help you."

"I told you before, just be quiet." She still sounded unstable.

"I'm going to turn around," he said, ignoring her. "You'll put down your weapon—"

"Hold your hands up in the air! Press them against the roof!"

He heard the shrillness in her voice, and the gun jammed harder against his head. For a moment, he hesitated. Then he did as she said.

The door opened beside him. From the corner of his eye, he saw a figure outside in the night. "Rosalind." The voice was mature, measured. "Everything is okay?" A faint East European accent. Hans Voss's voice.

"Be careful, Hans." Her voice was a little less tense. She obviously felt grateful to have some assistance.

Voss slid his hands around Bayley's chest. In the dim reflected glow from the headlights he was calm and expressionless. He searched methodically, found Bayley's shoulder holster, reached inside, and took out the 9mm automatic. But he didn't check any further, didn't find the second weapon. "Now, your hands behind your back, please," he said.

"No," said Bayley. "This is as far as it goes. I'm going to get out of this car, understand me? I'm going to walk back to my building—"

"We will kill you," said Voss, dispassionate and deliberate. He showed no trace of French's anxiety; he made it sound as simple as stepping on a bug. "I have served in the armed forces. I have killed people in the past, when it has been necessary. So, you will do what I say, now."

Bayley felt a pang of genuine fear. He tried to judge if he had room to hit Voss in the throat and roll out of the car. But the man was now covering Bayley with his own gun, and French had hers. There was little doubt that one of them would hit him. He thought of his briefcase, resting on the floor, containing the electronic weapon that he'd been holding as evidence. But there was no way he could reach it. And sitting with his legs under the instrument panel, there was still no easy way he could get to his backup pistol, either. "Okay," he said, trying to sound reasonable. "Let's talk about this. Tell me what you want."

"There is nothing to talk about." Voss sounded impatient. "Hands behind you. I will not ask again."

Slowly, Bayley obeyed. He felt his wrists being tied with adhesive tape. Here in the darkness in front of the empty building there was still no one to see what was going on. The cool night air wafted in through the open door, and he heard the distant hum of traffic on the freeway a dozen blocks away. A gentle breeze ruffled the fronds of a nearby palm tree.

Then Bayley heard something rustling. Plastic—a plastic bag. "No!" he shouted as Voss brought the bag down over his head and pulled it tight around his neck.

The bag was black and it plunged him into total darkness. He started struggling. He couldn't breathe.

"Hold still." Rosalind French's voice came to him faintly through the plastic. "We're not trying to suffocate you."

Her sharp fingernail ripped a hole in the bag close to his mouth. He took a deep, urgent breath. "Goddam it, what the hell do you people think you're doing?"

A rag was stuffed between his teeth. More tape was wound around his head, holding the rag in place.

He was hauled out of the driving seat, the rear door was opened, and he was pushed into the back. Strangely, he wasn't scared now. He only felt his anger, and his frustration. He had no more options; everything was out of his control.

Someone got into the back beside him and held his arm. Doors slammed. The motor of his car whined, tires crunched over gravel, and they moved away along the street.

Prisoner

The journey lasted at least an hour, mostly along freeways so far as he could tell. Bayley tried to plan, but the situation didn't allow much room for it. What worried him most of all was that French and Voss hadn't tried to disguise themselves. They obviously weren't worried about the future possibility of his testifying against them. And yet, they didn't want him to know where he was being taken. That didn't make sense.

He thought of Sharon. He imagined her sitting at home with Damon, wondering what had happened to him. The thought made him feel sick with guilt.

The rhythm of the car changed as it drove down a street where the surface seemed cracked and broken. Vegetation scraped past on either side. The car bumped and lurched. He imagined they must be up in the hills somewhere, on a dirt road. Then the car slowed, turned, edged forward a little farther, and stopped.

Bayley heard French get out. She opened the back door, and he smelled plants moist with dew, night-blooming jasmine, the faint tang of the ocean.

"Take him inside, Jeremy."

So Porter was here, too. He would have been the third one, following behind in French's car.

Bayley felt himself pulled out and up. His limbs were stiff; he could barely walk as they hustled him through waist-high undergrowth into some sort of building. A door slammed behind him and he smelled damp plaster and old, dusty carpet. There was the sound of a lock turning, hinges squeaking.

"Careful with him down the stairs. Don't let him fall."

They were concerned about his welfare?

He picked his way carefully, into a basement, he guessed. The floor here was solid and unyielding. Concrete. "Incredible," he heard someone say. "You actually did it."

"Shut up, Michael." French's voice. She hustled Bayley across the room, and he felt a seat behind his knees. He fell into it with a jolt that clicked his teeth together.

"Hans, tape his wrists and ankles there," she said.

Bayley considered making a grab for the little pistol still nestling undiscovered against his left leg. But it was only good for one shot, and before he could use it, he'd have to rip the bag off his head. His eyes had adjusted to darkness; he'd be dazzled by normal room lighting. Someone could still be covering him with a weapon; he wouldn't even know, for sure, till it was too late.

Meanwhile, Voss had cut the tape securing Bayley's wrists

and was quickly binding them to metal armrests mounted on either side of the chair in which Bayley was sitting. He moved down, then, and took hold of Bayley's ankle.

Bayley grunted behind his gag and tried to jerk his leg free from Voss's grasp. But the man was tenacious. His fingers closed—and found the little one-shot. He pulled it free. "It is fortunate I discovered this," he said.

"Christ." Bayley heard French's voice nearby. "Do you think he has anything else hidden away?"

"I will check." Voss finished securing both of Bayley's ankles to the legs of the chair, then searched methodically while Bayley sat there, unable to see, unable to resist.

Finally, after satisfying himself, Voss slit the black plastic bag and pulled it off Bayley's head.

The light dazzled him, and he blinked at four fuzzy silhouettes. Someone bent close and cut the tape holding the rag in his mouth. He spat it out, worked his jaw muscles, and swallowed, wincing.

His vision gradually adjusted and he recognized them all: Rosalind French, still very nervous, wide-eyed, her lips thin and pale; Jeremy Porter, standing self-consciously, trying to avoid looking Bayley in the eye; Hans Voss, calm and impassive, the ex-soldier taking refuge in old routines and discipline; and Michael Butterworth, his face full of wonder.

French turned away from Bayley. "Jeremy," she said, "here's the recording of his voice." She held out a small cartridge. "I hope it's enough."

"I'll see what I can do." Porter took it, obviously grateful for the opportunity to retreat.

Bayley checked his surroundings. White concrete floor, walls, and ceiling. Stacks of equipment, expensive equipment. Maybe that was another reason why French had traded handguns in Little Asia: to pay for this stuff.

He looked down at the chair he was in. It was metal—aluminum sheets bent and bolted together. He looked up. There was some kind of hemispherical cap hanging above his head, lined with sensors and electrodes, wires running from it to a large piece of equipment that he couldn't identify. Something about it looked medical, as if it belonged in a hospital. Homemade surgical gear. He felt a coldness in his abdomen, spreading lower, sucking at his groin.

"We're going to call your wife," Rosalind French was saying. "Jeremy has a gadget. He talks into it, and someone else's voice comes out, synthesized from a sample. You talked a lot while I had you in your car, which gave us the sample." She gave him a tight, brave smile and brushed her hair back from her face. He could see that she was rebuilding her confidence, her self-control. "We're going to tell your wife that your car broke down on the coast road. We'll say that you're staying the night in a motel, and tomorrow you'll try to find a garage. So you see, no one will suspect anything, and no one will start searching for you."

"My home phone is out of service," he said.

Another little smile. Some of the color was returning to her cheeks. "No, it isn't. Not anymore. Leo saw to that."

"Gottbaum?" Bayley forced a laugh. "What, he works for the phone company?"

French started to answer, but Voss stepped forward and held up his hand. "Rosalind, if you please. This man is encouraging you to talk, trying to establish a relationship between him and us. He knows that this will make it harder for us to do . . . whatever we have to do. Please remember to treat him dispassionately, as our prisoner."

Conflicting emotions showed briefly in Rosalind French's face. Bayley could see that she didn't like being corrected by Voss; but she held back her irritation. "You're quite right, Hans." She turned away.

"Where were you trained, Hans?" said Bayley.

"I fought in the Lithuanian Liberation Army." Then his mouth snapped shut and he turned away. "Michael, for the first part of your procedure, does our prisoner need to be conscious?"

"Makes no difference," said Butterworth. His face still showed a childlike wonder as if he was uninvolved, watching the whole scene on video.

"Administer some Demerol," said Voss. "We can bring him around when we need him, yes?"

"Sure, any time." Butterworth wandered over to his drug cabinet. He pulled out a vapor syringe.

"Just tell me what this equipment is for, all right?" Bayley said. He realized he was starting to lose it. Fear was showing in his voice, although maybe that was to his advantage. Voss was tough, but the others didn't seem to be. French, in particular. The more scared he sounded, the more he might be able to get through to her emotionally. "Are you going to kill me, or torture me, or what?"

"No, man," said Butterworth. "Not kill you. Just the opposite." He smiled. There was something strange in that smile. It was serene, mystic. "We're going to start with some tests. There won't be any pain." He rolled up Bayley's sleeve and touched the syringe to his arm. "Trust me," he said, as he pressed the button.

Signals

The drug erased all fear. He felt himself drifting. He forgot where he was—remembered, with a start—and forgot again. People moved around him. He knew who they were, but he didn't much care. He told himself he needed to care. He had to get the hell out.

He remembered Sharon. He thought about the first time he saw her, in the college cafeteria. She was sitting in one corner, wearing a lime-green T-shirt and white pants, reading a book about wildflowers. He'd sat at the next table and leaned across and asked her if she was studying botany. "No," she'd said, looking surprised. "I just happened to pick this up. I read all kinds of different stuff." They'd looked at each other, and that's how it had all started.

A sudden bright light in Bayley's eyes. A big fluorescent panel that Voss was holding in front of him. It started changing color and Voss recited some numbers. Bayley realized the hemispherical helmet that he'd seen dangling above him had been lowered. Tiny filaments tickled his scalp. "Getting a real good signal." Butterworth's voice, far away.

Bayley heard himself talking. "Car trouble," his voice said. Something about a motel. Dimly he realized it was Porter, speaking through his synth gadget to Sharon. Bayley stirred, trying to pull free. He needed to talk to Sharon. "Let go of me," he muttered.

"Tell me when you see pure white," a voice said in his ear. "It's very important. Concentrate on the color."

Bayley lost track. He stared at the glowing panel. "White," he said. He remembered what Sharon had been wearing. The lime-green T-shirt, the white pants. She still had those clothes somewhere, stored away. Sentimental value.

Bayley summoned his strength. He struggled. "Let me go."

"Give him another shot," said Voss.

Patterning

He was asleep for a while. At least, he thought he was. He dreamed he was in a room full of machines, people moving around him calling out numbers, equipment touching his head. A needle prick by the corner of his left eye, then his right. Sudden flowering patterns, kaleidoscopic fragments that were very beautiful, very intense. Then a ringing sound. A sweep of noise, from deep bass to a pure high whistle, off the end of the scale. The taste of cloves. His body felt covered with fur. Then very, very cold. He seemed to be drinking barbecue sauce; he was burning up inside. "Water," he muttered.

Later, when he woke, it was very sudden. He looked down and saw another syringe being taken away from his arm. Reality hit him hard, bright, and loud. He was still sitting in the chair. It was unyielding beneath the base of his spine. He ached.

"Good," said Voss, straightening up and turning away.

"Yeah, it really brings 'em back fast," said Butterworth.

Bayley tried to turn his head but it was clamped, rigid. The metal helmet was still in place, and there were probes in his skin near his eyes. He was still in the basement. Air hissed through a vent. Wires trailed around him. "What are you doing?" He heard his own voice, tight, confused, and apprehensive.

Butterworth glanced at Voss. Voss nodded.

"I've been monitoring the areas of your brain that process signals from your sense receptors," Butterworth said.

Bayley instinctively tried to look at him. His head was still clamped. He winced. "Meaning what?"

"We are mapping the functions of your brain," said Voss.

Bayley turned his eyes from one of them to the other, and back again. He was afraid he knew, now. Maybe he'd known as soon as he'd seen the probes and sensors. But he still couldn't bring himself to put it into words. "Why do you . . . want this information?"

"So we can make a computer model of your intelligence," said Butterworth. "Why else?"

Infomorph

When he started screaming for help, they gagged him again. French and her team obviously didn't enjoy the noise.

They gave him some kind of mild intravenous tranquilizer. Valium, he guessed. Then she came and sat down in front of him. "There's very little time." She was calm and businesslike, now, showing no emotion, the same as he remembered her from his visit to her laboratory. "I have to explain everything to you. It will be much easier if you cooperate voluntarily, and you're more likely to do so when you understand the situation."

Bayley watched her face. She wasn't really as calm as she seemed. But he was still gagged, and without being able to talk there was no way for him to exploit her anxieties.

"I gather you received the official LifeScan history," she said. "As you may have realized by now, that history is inaccurate. We succeeded in modeling the intelligence of small mammals eight years ago, but we decided not to share these results with our employers. They would have started interfering in our research, pushing it in a direction we didn't want to go. We have no interest in military applications."

Very moral, Bayley thought to himself. He was glad to know he was dealing with people of high ethical principles.

"Our biggest problem," she went on, "turned out to be the electromechanical process of reading neuron states and mapping their interconnections without introducing errors. We tried a number of noninvasive, nondestructive techniques. But none of them was reliable. The only system that works is a destructive system, literally peeling the brain in layers."

So there it was. Dispassionate, inhuman, horrific. He shivered and closed his eyes.

"Hans and Michael finally perfected a reliable technique, working on samples cooled to low temperatures. Fortunately Leo Gottbaum has contacts in cryonics who were willing to participate with us in this area. Meanwhile, Jeremy designed and built a system with appropriate architecture to hold the uploaded intelligence. We have successfully scanned and stored the brain of a dog, and so far as we can tell, none of its functions is impaired. Its intelligence is still alive, supported by computer hardware instead of biological cells. We were preparing to do our first scan of a human brain next week. Leo Gottbaum had volunteered to be the first subject."

Bayley felt a dull sense of surprise. But then he realized Gottbaum's motivation. With routine maintenance, a computer memory could last forever. Maybe that had been Gottbaum's interest in LifeScan all along. Twenty billion new dollars of public money, so the great man could make himself immortal.

"So far as we can tell," French was saying, "an intelligence in computer memory functions no differently from an intelligence composed of neurons, providing the copy is made accurately. And the intelligence should also experience total realism if we feed the brain an accurate imitation of the nerve impulses that it's accustomed to receiving. Just as an amputee may feel he has a 'phantom limb,' an electronic intelligence should be able to experience a 'phantom body.' Leo was willing to take that risk, as were the rest of us. But it had to be done covertly. If the public knew what we were doing, there'd be an outcry. There'd be regulations to restrict it or ban it outright."

"You see now," said Voss, "why it was necessary to stop your investigation. To protect this crucial research."

"Not just the research," said French. "The whole human future."

She said it straight-faced, totally serious. Hubris, Bayley thought to himself. They honestly believed they were molding destiny.

"Leo invited you to his home because he thought there might be a chance of persuading you to drop your investigation," French went on. "But after talking to you, he decided it wasn't an option."

"But please understand, we are not in the habit of killing innocent people," said Voss.

More ethical principles. They had to believe they were humanitarians.

"We could have held you as a long-term prisoner," said French. "But sooner or later, people would have started to look for you. They would get suspicious. Our work would still be in jeopardy. So, the alternative was clear. We will, in due course, create an automobile accident to explain your death. Your body will be found, but by then your mind will have been copied and stored. We have sufficient storage for eight infomorphs. There is room for you."

"An infomorph is what we call intelligence held in computer memory," Butterworth put in. "Like an information entity."

"Even though your physical form will have died," Voss went on calmly, "your intelligence will survive indefinitely."

"Yeah." Butterworth gave his strange, detached smile. "Just so long as no one pulls the plug."

Receptors

They left him alone for a little while. Rosalind French disappeared upstairs. Butterworth and Voss started calibrating a piece of equipment that was outside Bayley's field of view. Jeremy Porter was nowhere to be seen, though Bayley heard the intermittent tapping of fingers on a keyboard somewhere behind him.

He felt dazed, psychologically unable to accept what he'd

been told. But he saw the risks they had already taken, and he was forced to believe how serious they were. Computer scientists tended to be alienated misfits to begin with; this little team had been working together for ten years, out of contact with the outside world, sharing their own private reality, which had been based, in turn, on one man's obsession. To them, the abnormal would seem normal.

Butterworth seemed the only possible exception. His ironic detachment suggested that he might be less committed to the cause that the others seemed to believe in. If there was any real hope, Bayley decided, it lay with him.

Voss came over, wiping oil off his hands with a paper towel soaked in alcohol. "I will remove the gag now," he said. "You must realize that if you make more noise, it cannot be heard outside and it will slow our work. If we do not do our work properly, your future as an infomorph will be defective." He pulled the wad of cloth from Bayley's mouth.

Bayley coughed. He grimaced. "You expect me to believe in this—this electronic afterlife?"

Voss gave him a steady, thoughtful look. "You will remember, please, Dr. Gottbaum planned to submit to it. Indeed, he still plans to. You will agree, he is an intelligent man."

"What about you, Voss? Are you going to be scanned and stored?"

He nodded slowly. "Of course. Eventually we will be neighbors, you and I, yes? Now, if you please. In order to simulate physical sensations accurately after your intelligence is coded, we must first obtain a lot of sensory data. We took baseline readings while you were anesthetized. We need to refine them. We will begin with vision. Are you ready to cooperate?"

He looked at Voss's face. Voss looked back at him, implacable, unyielding.

As the time dragged on they showed him grids, color charts, geometric patterns, printed text, dot mosaics. They made him look up, down, near, and far. They explained that they were monitoring impulses from his optic nerves, feeding them into some sort of analysis unit. Once they'd digitized the nerve impulses, they could imitate them. They'd be able to feed the signal for "green" back into the brain area that normally processed his visual input, and he'd see green even though he didn't have eyes anymore. They could deal with his other senses in the same way, and build an entire artificial environment for him a piece at a time. It would look, sound, taste, smell, and feel authentic in every way.

The tests seemed to continue for hours. He had no idea of the time.

Rosalind French reappeared during the long night—or was it morning, now? She brought with her an array of glass droppers. Each contained a synthetic flavor to be applied to his tongue, then washed away. They needed to map his taste receptors. Even after he was an infomorph, the sensations of eating would still be available to him.

Finally, they injected him with a hypnotic, and he fell into a restless sleep, still sitting in the chair, the probes in place, now monitoring his dreams.

Link

Yumi read the number off the creased piece of paper, angling it toward sunlight filtering through a cobwebbed window beside the pay phone. Behind her the store owner was mopping the floor, shuffling around, whistling some old forgotten rock song. She turned her back to him, watching her reflection in the chrome faceplate of the phone as she keyed in the digits. Her cheeks looked pale, her eyes dark and intense.

A woman's sleepy voice answered. For a moment Yumi felt unable to speak. She hadn't necessarily assumed that Richard Wilson was single; she hadn't really thought about it at all. And yet, she felt surprised. "Hello," she said. "I would like to speak to . . . Jim."

"He's not here right now." The woman stifled a yawn. "Who's this?"

"My name is Yumi. He told me to call if I had anything to tell him. And now there is something, very important." She heard herself sounding so grim and serious, and she wished she wasn't having to go through this.

"I'm afraid I don't know when Jim will be here. He called last night to say he had car trouble. He's staying somewhere on the road till he can get it fixed." A pause. "Can I help? He shares most of his business with me."

"Are you his wife?" She couldn't hold back her curiosity.

"Yes. I am." She didn't sound offended by the question. She sounded gently amused as if, to her, curiosity was a very natural human trait.

Yumi tried to decide what to do. "I guess I'll call again

later," she said. "Tell him that Yumi called, but please tell him not to call me back. That's very important."

"All right."

"May I ask your name?"

"Sharon."

"Okay, thank you Sharon. I'll try again this afternoon."

Shutdown

Placing the phone call had made her anxious, and she felt more anxious still as she headed back up the hill. There was nothing rational about the feeling: it materialized inside her from nowhere, tightening its grip as she approached the dome.

She walked in and found her father throwing documents into a suitcase. A shaft of morning sun angled across the living area, golden dust motes billowing into it as he sorted through papers, dumping most of them, selecting a few. She stood watching him, wondering what he was doing and why the dome seemed so quiet. Then she realized that almost all the computer systems had been turned off.

He became aware of her and looked up, sharp and suspicious. "Yumi! Where have you been?"

Immediately she felt guilty, as if he'd read her mind or somehow listened in to her call. He was so omniscient, sometimes anything seemed possible. "I went down to the store," she said, maintaining her demure, neutral facade, carefully hiding her feelings.

"Why?" He was still staring at her.

Feeling foolish, she realized she hadn't remembered to buy anything. She was standing in front of him empty-handed. "I just felt like taking a walk."

"Well, I'm glad you're back. We have to leave." He threw some clothes in on top of the documents and snapped the case shut. "Something has come up. I've been in touch with my friends at Cryonic Life. I have to check into the hospital in Los Angeles today instead of tomorrow. If we leave here in fifteen minutes there'll be just enough time for me to drop you at the airport along the way. There's a flight leaving for Hawaii at seven this evening, and I've reserved a seat on it for you."

She looked at him blankly. No matter how often she tried to anticipate his moods and his demands, he always managed to do something that left her feeling startled and numb. "What happened?" she asked. "Is—the cancer getting worse?"

"The cancer?" He looked baffled. Then he shook his head impatiently. "No, no, it's something else entirely."

"Something to do with the work they're doing at the lab?" Even though it was a Sunday, she knew the people down there kept odd hours.

He waved his hand. "There isn't time to talk about it. I'm sorry." He turned to the one computer system that was still running and started shutting it down. "Please pack your things right away," he said, over his shoulder.

She sat down on a heap of documents on one of the black leather chairs. She saw why she still felt like a child when she was around him. He always treated her like a child. "What if I'm not ready to leave?"

He turned slowly, rerunning her words through his head, trying to make sense of them. "This is my home," he said, laying the words out one by one, looking at her as if she was stupid. "You are my guest here, Yumi. You signed a document yesterday in which you surrendered all interest to the property. You have absolutely no justification for staying here after I leave."

She made a little sound of disgust. "Well, of course, you're right. I don't have any justification, as you put it. It's your place, your life, your decision, and whatever I want is irrelevant." She stood up and headed for her room. "So don't worry, I'll get ready. I couldn't bear it, Father, if I ever kept you waiting."

Unloading Zone

They drove in silence. The silence ate away at her, made her stomach cramp, made her head ache, made her want to do something drastic: kick her father, scream, throw open the door and jump out of the moving car. But she held it all in and she sat staring out at the scenery, not really seeing anything, trying not to think of anything.

If the silence bothered Gottbaum, he didn't show it. He drove quickly, efficiently, following the schedule he'd obviously mapped out for himself. By midafternoon they reached LAX.

He stopped in an unloading zone, set the brake, and looked at her, and she thought, very briefly, she actually saw something in his eyes—an unresolved emotion, maybe even a moment of regret. "I'm sorry the visit wasn't more pleasant for you," he said.

She studied his face a moment longer, trying to confirm that he was actually feeling something. But under the pressure of her attention he seemed to retreat back into himself. The stern wrinkles deepened, and he looked away from her, glancing at the clock on the car's dashboard.

So that was that. He had finished with her, and he wanted to go. "I guess I won't ever see you again," she said, finding it hard to speak. "Although I still can't quite believe you're really going to—to do what you said."

He shrugged. "You will see my obituary in the news by the end of the coming week."

She fingered the fabric of her dress. "Are you going to come into the terminal to see me off?" She knew he would refuse, but she had to hear him say it.

"I'm sorry," he said, "I can't."

She reached for her bag on the back seat, pulled it onto her knees, and cradled it in her arms. She imagined suddenly shouting at him, "Get out of the fucking car like any normal human being, and hug me and kiss me good-bye, you bastard!"

She opened the door. "Good-bye, father."

"Good-bye, Yumi." His hand moved to the gearshift.

She got out and slammed the door, hard. She stood and glared at him as he moved the little car out from the curb. Would he really drive away? Just like that?

The car moved into the flow of traffic. Within ten seconds, it was out of sight.

Reasonable Doubts

She walked into the air terminal taking long, angry strides, her face pale, her teeth clenched tight. She stopped at the first pay phone she came to and dialed with fierce little stabs of her finger. Before, she had felt some misgivings. Not anymore.

"Sharon Wilson?" she asked, when a woman answered.

There was an uncertain pause. "No. This is Sharon Bayley."

Yumi steadied herself, resting her forehead against the cool metal panel at the side of the phone booth. "But you are Jim's wife. I recognize your voice. I called you earlier."

Another pause. "Who is this?"

"This is Yumi." And then she realized what must have happened. "Your husband told me his name was Wilson, maybe because he needed to keep his real identity secret. He works in security, isn't that right? But please tell him I'm calling. I'm sure he'll want to talk to me."

The woman laughed nervously. "Oh, I see."

"Is he there?"

Another pause. "No. He called again. He's somewhere on the coast highway, still trying to get his car fixed. Look, I'm sorry, but if this is . . . security business, I don't think I should be getting involved in it."

Yumi had been brought up always to respect the other person's wishes, so as not to impose or cause offense. Her mother had advised it as a courtesy; her father had demanded it as his right. But standing by the pay phone, Yumi realized she felt so hurt, so angry, she couldn't defer to other people anymore. "When I called earlier," she said, "you told me your husband shares the details of his business with you."

"Well, sometimes." Sharon said it reluctantly.

"Did Jim tell you he was visiting Dr. Leo Gottbaum? I am Yumi Gottbaum, his daughter."

"Oh. I see."

"Your husband was interested in my father's research. The LifeScan program. I now have the information about it that he wanted. Please tell me how to get in touch with him."

Another long pause at the other end of the line. "There isn't any way to reach him. He called me from a pay phone and said his car phone had stopped working, and he can't find a garage to get his car fixed because it's a Sunday, and he may even have to stay over another night and come home tomorrow."

Yumi stared out of the windows of the terminal feeling deeply uneasy. Should she trust her intuition? Yes; she'd learned it could be quite reasonable to expect the worst of her father. "I just drove all the way down the coast highway," she said quietly. "We passed several garages that were open. If your husband was able to call you from a pay phone, he must have been able to call a towing service. Tell me, are you sure it was his voice when he called?"

"It . . . sounded like him." Sharon sounded anxious, now. "What are you getting at?"

"I don't know. I just have a bad feeling." She thought a little more. Part of her wanted to hang up and forget this whole situation, go back home to Hawaii, and settle into her relaxed everyday routines. But when she thought about the way her father had abandoned her out there on the sidewalk, she felt, again, her determination. "I realize you have never met me," she said, "and I'm asking a big favor, but I don't know what else to do. Can I come to your home? There are some things belonging to your husband that I should return to him. And if he calls again, I have to be there to speak to him."

Sharon started to reply, then stopped herself. Yumi waited patiently, ignoring the air terminal around her, the flight announcements, people walking across the concourse. "No, I really don't think you should come here," Sharon said finally. "It's Jim's rule never to give out our home address to anyone connected with a case."

"Then perhaps you could come to me," said Yumi. "You surely have a portable phone? Your calls can be forwarded to it from your home."

"You're very persistent." She laughed nervously.

"I am not normally like this. I live a very quiet life making jewelry and selling it to tourists. This is an extremely unusual situation for me. I am trying hard to do what is right. Please, can you help?"

Sharon sighed. "All right. All right, where are you?"

Yumi allowed herself a moment of quiet satisfaction. She had done something she would normally have considered impossible. "I'm at Los Angeles International Airport," she said. "I'll describe myself. I'm half Japanese, I'm carrying a white canvas bag, and I am wearing a long skirt and a white cotton blouse. I will be waiting outside the Federal Airlines Building, on the upper level."

Threats

It took Sharon ninety minutes to show up at the airport. When she arrived, she was driving a little red electric Fiat with a dented fender, a bent antenna, and a broken headlight. She stopped at the curb, leaned across, and opened the passenger door. "Hi," she said, a pretty young woman with lively eyes and a shy smile. "You must be Yumi. Sorry I took so long; I had to get a baby-sitter."

"That's quite all right. I'm pleased to meet you, Sharon." She got into the car, feeling less sure of herself now that they were face-to-face. Being bold had been easier on the phone.

Sharon gave her a quick searching glance. She seemed to relax a little. "I guess it sounds dumb, but I was afraid you were . . . I don't know, somebody different from who you said you were."

"I am the daughter of a famous man who thinks he is above the law," said Yumi. "And . . . I want to help your husband." She felt embarrassed at the way it sounded, so stern and humorless. She looked down at her knees and straightened her skirt. The car was as funky inside as it was outside, she noticed. There were gas-station receipts lying on the floor, a child's toy truck, a crumpled road map. The glove compartment was held shut with some Scotch tape. Maybe in her professional life Sharon presented a chic image to the outside world, but privately, she obviously didn't care that much about keeping everything squeaky-clean. Instinctively, Yumi liked her.

"So, do you want to talk?" Sharon asked.

"Definitely. I have four hours before my plane takes off. I picked up my ticket while I was waiting for you."

"I guess we should go someplace. How about on the sea wall, at Venice? That's close."

Yumi shrugged. "Fine."

A little later, after they parked the car, they climbed steps up the side of the white concrete wall. It stood twenty feet high, ten feet wide, overshadowing the condos, bars, and restaurants that had once looked out onto the ocean. On top of it, a promenade was busy with bike riders, couples out strolling, kids flying kites, old people sitting on benches.

"You know, I still remember the beach," Sharon said, as she walked beside Yumi, looking at the waves as they foamed across breakwaters and lapped at the foot of the wall itself. "My dad used to bring me here sometimes when I was little."

"Did you swim?"

She shook her head. "It was much too polluted back then."

They stopped at a restaurant cantilevered out over the water, tables scattered across a semicircular patio under a yellow sunscreen. Almost all the customers were in their sixties and seventies, sipping beer or coffee, reading old-fashioned newspapers or paperback books, quietly enjoying the afternoon.

A serving robot came gliding over as Sharon and Yumi found chairs at an empty table. "Hi there, how are you? My name's Frank. May I take your order?"

"God, I wish they wouldn't give robots names," said Sharon.

"Do you have iced green tea?" Yumi asked.

"Yes, we have iced green tea. Would you like iced green tea?"

"Yes, please."

"One iced green tea," said the robot.

"I need a drink," said Sharon. "White rum and soda on the rocks."

"One white rum and soda on the rocks." The robot's infrared scanner turned, checking for other customers at the table. "Will that be all?"

"Yes, that's all."

"Thank you for your order. I'll be right back."

"I came here once with Jim," said Sharon, "back when it first opened, a few years ago. He had a thing about the ocean. He felt there was a sort of mysterious quality to it, because so much was hidden beneath the surface. He could spend hours looking at the waves." She seemed to subside momentarily into her memories, then dragged herself back to the present. "So," she said, "can you please try to tell me what all this is about?"

Yumi placed her hands on the table in front of her, covering one with the other. She looked at Sharon. The woman had a pleasing face: honest, open, genuinely concerned. Yumi normally found it hard to make friends, harder still to trust people, but in this case she didn't have time to be cautious. "I will tell you the story from the beginning," she said.

Sharon was a good listener. She sat attentively as Yumi described her father, his work, his sudden request to see her, and everything that had happened since then. The serving robot brought their drinks; Yumi ignored hers as she went on talking, explaining what she now knew about the LifeScan program. "There is no doubt in my mind," she said, "that my father is not just interested in scanning and storing the intelligence of laboratory animals for military purposes. The obvious application from his point of view would be to scan and store the human brain. It would provide a form of immortality. It might also give him a position of power."

Sharon had already drained her glass. She sat opposite Yumi, leaning forward on one elbow, resting her chin in her hand, studying her intently. "I don't know a lot about computers," she said, "but storing someone's intelligence sounds impossible."

Yumi shook her head solemnly. "When I was a child, my father once said that computers even then were big enough to store one person's memories. He said there were only two real problems: scanning the neurons, and imitating the way they are connected with one another."

"But when Jim talked to me about the LifeScan thing a couple of nights ago, he said it had been a total failure."

"My father revealed to me, almost inadvertently, that it is a success. He has hidden this from your husband's employers at North Industries."

Sharon smiled faintly. "I guess I might as well tell you, Jim doesn't work there. He's employed by the FBI."

Yumi stopped short. "Oh. Now I see." She nodded slowly to herself. "Now I understand." She thought back to the few minutes she had spent with Bayley in his car. "You know, I think he wanted to tell me the truth about himself, when he gave me his real first name and his phone number."

Sharon nodded quickly. "Absolutely. The fact that he had given you our number was what made me agree to come and meet you. He must have judged that you were sympathetic and trustworthy."

"So is he involved in a big police investigation?"

Sharon laughed. "God, no. He stumbled into this whole thing entirely on his own. He hasn't even filed a report."

"Oh." Yumi bit her lip. "That concerns me," she said. "Suppose, for a minute, that my father has learned your husband's identity somehow. If he knows there is only one man, posing a threat to his research . . ." She trailed off.

"Well, now, hold on a minute." Sharon started picking at the paper napkin under her glass, tearing little scraps off one corner. "Your father's not a criminal. And these people working at North Industries, they're respectable scientists." The way she said it, it sounded more like a question than a statement. She looked at Yumi for reassurance.

Yumi shook her head. "Imagine you have dedicated yourself for thirty years. You really believe you can cheat death. You believe, in addition, your research can change the whole world. And then, in the last few days, someone threatens everything you have achieved. And you are a man who only cares, really, for two things: science, and personal survival."

Sharon looked down, saw the mess she had made of the napkin, and grimaced. She started to speak, stopped herself, and rubbed her eyes. "This is all a bit hard to take."

"Can I get you anything else?" The serving robot came gliding around again.

"No," Yumi snapped in a sudden burst of anger. "Nothing else."

"Here, let me get this," said Sharon, obviously glad of the distraction. She fished her credit disk out of her purse, dropped it in the robot's reader, and waited till it was ejected with a paper receipt.

"Thanks," said the robot. "Come back again soon."

"I hope I am not alarming you unnecessarily," Yumi said. "But I do believe there is a real danger. And I feel responsible.

If I had confided in your husband, when he asked for my help yesterday—"

Sharon forced a smile. She took a deep breath, getting herself back under control. "It's not your responsibility. Jim takes his own risks."

Yumi shrugged. "I still feel an obligation to help."

Sharon studied her for a moment. "But is Jim really the only reason? It seems to me, maybe you're mad at your father. Do you want some sort of revenge?"

The question caught Yumi by surprise. She felt her cheeks redden. "You are a very perceptive woman."

"I'm a journalist. I guess it's part of my job. But I should get busy." She pushed back her chair, seeming stronger now that she had learned the worst.

"What are you planning to do?"

"I'll call Jim's supervisor, if I can reach him on a Sunday. Or I'll go to the local police, file a missing-person report, and ask them to find the hospital where your father has admitted himself. Tomorrow, first thing, I'll contact North Industries—"

"No!" Yumi slapped her palms down on the table. The impact was sudden and loud, and she felt surprised at herself for being so demonstrative. But it seemed so vital to get through to Sharon and make her understand. "If you call the police over regular phone lines, or if the police themselves use regular radio transmissions, it's quite possible that my father or his coworkers will learn what you are doing. They will feel more threatened, and they will be more dangerous—to your husband, and to you."

Sharon looked disconcerted. "I really don't see how they could possibly—"

Yumi seized Sharon's hand. "Please believe me! Your husband underestimated my father. You must not make the same mistake. Leo Gottbaum was cracking security codes and invading databases fifty years ago. He has systems that I'm sure can monitor thousands of calls automatically, listening for key words. I don't know the details, because I'm not an expert, and I don't involve myself with computers. But I grew up with him and I know what he can do, and I know he would have no compunction about doing it."

Sharon laughed uneasily. "You're really convinced about all this, aren't you?"

Yumi looked down. "I'm sorry, I didn't mean to shout." She saw her wristwatch and realized how much time had passed. "I'm afraid we must start back. I still have to catch my flight." Clumsily, she pushed back her chair and stood up. "But please, Sharon, so long as it's possible that your husband is still alive, don't do anything that might alert my father or his team."

A little later they were back in the car, heading toward the airport. Sharon drove in silence, staring straight ahead, deep in thought.

"You mentioned you are a journalist," Yumi said.

Sharon nodded slowly, still self-absorbed. "That's right. I work for a local TV station."

"Good. Then you know how to gather information and how to distribute it. Publicity could be a powerful weapon against my father." Yumi pulled the LifeScan history and Bayley's compad out of her bag. "Your husband accidentally left these things at my father's house. I assume this compad contains his notes. I have not looked at them, but they may be of some help. This binder contains the history of the LifeScan program. When you read it, remember that my father admitted privately to me that the program has actually succeeded in all its goals." She turned and put the two items on the back seat.

Sharon took the ramp to the Federal Airlines Building and found a spot at the curb. She set the brake, leaned back in her seat, and rubbed her hands across her face. "I have to thank you," she said, sounding subdued. "I just hope you're wrong about what . . . may have happened."

"Of course I may be wrong. Your husband may be at some motel on the coast highway. It's quite possible."

"Perhaps I should go looking for him myself. That couldn't do any harm."

Yumi thought it over. She shook her head. "If he is all right, he will obviously get in touch with you. If, on the other hand, something bad has happened, my father will do something to divert your suspicions. I realize it's hard to wait, but either way, I am sure you will hear something soon." She glanced at her watch, then opened the car door. "I'm afraid I have to go. I feel I should stay and help you, but if my father checks the passenger list and finds I never got on the plane, he'll know that something is wrong."

Sharon stared at her hands on the steering. Impulsively, then, she turned and opened her door. She got out and walked quickly around to the passenger side as Yumi stepped onto the sidewalk. Sharon took her arm. "You've done more than your duty. I'm very grateful." Unexpectedly, she hugged her.

Yumi was too surprised to react as Sharon clutched her tight, then released her, staring into her eyes with clear, obvious gratitude. It was so spontaneous, it left her not knowing what to feel or what to say.

"Can I call you and tell you how things work out?" Sharon asked.

"Yes, yes, please do." Yumi searched clumsily in her bag, glad for the diversion. She scribbled her number on a piece of paper. "Call any time. Although, until this is all resolved, you should be careful not to refer to the things I've told you." She pressed the paper into Sharon's hand. And then, afraid of the emotions that were suddenly rising up inside her, she turned and hurried into the air terminal.

Last Rites

His head was painful, feeling bruised all over, and his mouth tasted sour. He winced and blinked, trying to focus. It was dark and he seemed to be moving . . . in a car? His body jostled against the seat. He tried to free his arm and found his wrists were tied once again with tape. And there was something over his head. Another black plastic bag. Was that what it was? He moved his head. Yes, plastic against his face, tight around his neck.

It didn't bother him much. He was very, very drowsy. Whenever he tried to concentrate his thoughts slipped away, wandering into darkness. *Still drugged,* he realized dully. He swallowed and tried to moisten his lips. "Where am I going?" He heard himself talking, and it sounded strange, loud inside his head.

"I'm taking you to visit some associates of mine."

Bayley tried to concentrate. He tried again. Who—Gottbaum, it was Gottbaum, beside him. "Are we going back to the dome?"

"No. We are in greater Los Angeles, Mr. Bayley. You are my responsibility now. Dr. French wanted it that way."

"I want to see out. Can I see out?"

"Sorry. It's best that you don't see where you are being taken. My friends agreed to help on condition of anonymity."

Bayley laughed. The laugh hurt his head and made him cough, which hurt more. He struggled feebly. He hated not being able to see. "You're going to kill me. What does it matter what I see?"

"Not kill you, deanimate you," Gottbaum corrected him.

"But if everything goes as it should—and I believe it will—you will retain all your faculties. Including your memory."

"An infomorph." It didn't really seem to matter. Nothing did.

"You'll be an infomorph, yes." Gottbaum's voice sounded remote, uninvolved.

Bayley tried to think clearly, despite the drug. "If you let me go," he said, struggling with the logic of it, "if you let me go, I won't say anything. I won't hassle you. You see, I never filed a report on the case."

"I'm pleased to hear that," said Gottbaum. "Thank you for confirming it. But the stakes are too high for us to release you on good faith."

Bayley squirmed around. He realized, vaguely, he was in the front passenger seat, with Gottbaum beside him doing the driving. Maybe he could smash his head out through the window, crawl out, fall into the road; someone would see, rescue him. He didn't want to go where he was being taken. He was scared. He was drugged, so he couldn't think right, but he knew he was scared. Maybe he could smash his head out through—

The car stopped. Gottbaum tapped the horn once, twice. "We have arrived," he said.

They carried him into a room that smelled of chemicals. It was cold. They laid him out flat on a hard surface and strapped him down, then pulled the bag off his head. He squinted and blinked. He swallowed. He was hungry. Why hadn't they fed him, and where was he now? Electronic equipment in racks on one wall, a couple of devices with tubes coming out of them, two people in green masks and gowns. What was happening here?

A third figure appeared. It was Gottbaum. He, too, was wearing a face mask, a cap, and a sterile gown. "I assure you," he said to Bayley, "it will be relatively painless."

"Painless?" He turned his head slowly, trying to understand.

"Scanning takes a while, Bayley. It's a long, delicate business. We need to bring your brain down to a low temperature to stabilize it. But my friends, here, are experts in cryonics. They believe in our research and are quite confident of its outcome."

Bayley grimaced. "Don't," he said feebly. "I don't want you to do this."

"We're ready to start the perfusion, Dr. Gottbaum," said one of the gowned figures. Above his surgical mask he had pale blue eyes, a small pink birthmark on the side of his forehead. His voice sounded reluctant, as if this wasn't something he felt very happy about.

A memory reached Bayley through the haze. Instinctively, he tried to sit up. "Where's Butterworth?"

"Michael Butterworth is with the rest of the team, over at North Industries, preparing the scanning equipment for you. Fortunately it's a Sunday, so we can proceed without having to worry too much about interruptions. Butterworth will be doing the brain section. He's the only person at this time who possesses the necessary skill."

Bayley groaned feebly. The man he'd wanted to trust was the one who was going to—to cut him apart. "Just let me go," he said. "You leave me alone, and I'll leave you alone."

"Dr. Gottbaum?" The man with the birthmark was holding something. "I think you should be the one, who—"

"Yes. It's my responsibility." He looked down at Bayley. "This will counteract the sedative you were given earlier. You will suddenly find yourself feeling extremely alert and aware. We will then begin perfusion—replacing your blood with agents to protect the cells from freezing damage—and you will quickly lose consciousness. It will feel as if you are fainting." He injected something into Bayley's arm as he spoke.

Fuzziness crystallized into sharp focus. It was like walking out of a murky overheated room into a dazzling, ice-cold winter day. Bayley's pulse rate doubled. He found himself strapped to an operating table. They switched on an enormous light directly overhead, blinding him. There were steel instruments laid out on a tray beside his head. They were going to kill him.

"No!" he shouted. "Oh my god. Sharon!"

A tube was jammed into his arm. It hurt, badly. Bayley screamed. A machine started chugging. His arm turned ice-cold and began to throb and burn.

"Stop!" he jerked with all his strength at the straps tying him down. "You bastards, goddam you—"

"Two liters," said a voice.

Everything started to recede from him. His thudding pulse changed pitch till it was nothing but a rapid tapping sound in his ears. The table seemed to be sinking under him, into the floor. The men in the gowns were dolls drifting up around the glaring white light.

"Sharon!" he gasped.

And then he was gone.

FBI AGENT DIES IN CAR BLAZE

A Granada Hills man employed by the FBI plunged to his death in the early hours of Monday morning when his car smashed through a guard rail near Cayucos, on Highway One, and burst into flames.

Firefighters called to the scene were unable to rescue James Bayley, aged 33, from the inferno that incinerated him in his vehicle. According to local fire chief Larry McGregor, the impact of the car on the rocky seashore ruptured its electric fuel cell, releasing hydrogen gas that contributed to the blaze. Remains of the driver were so charred, identification had to be done by DNA sampling.

Bruce Taylor, whose restaurant the Fisherman's Inn is located less than 500 feet from the accident, told investigators he heard a squeal of tires followed by a crash and a loud explosion around 5:00 A.M. "It made the windows rattle," he said. "I got down there as quick as I could, but the guy inside looked like he was already burned up."

FBI sources stated that although Bayley was a special agent in the Department of Technology-Related Crime, he was off-duty at the time of the accident.

Local police discounted the possibility that a mechanical fault might have caused the car to go off the highway. "I figure he just didn't see the curve in the road," said Sergeant George Turner of the Cayucos Police Department. "We put up a steel barrier and a warning sign after the last guy went over the edge there. It looks to me like this one just fell asleep at the wheel."

Bayley is survived by his wife, Sharon, and four-year-old son, Damon.

PART
TWO

The Arena

Sheets of jagged color flashed and dazzled him, spawning purple after images that swam across a sudden field of black. A humming sound began, growing louder—so loud, it made his teeth hurt. And then everything was eerily silent, and he felt himself turning slowly, head over heels, as if he was underwater. There was a horrible bitter taste in his mouth, and he felt hung over, weak and dizzy, his temples throbbing. Something bad was happening and he wanted to shout, but his lips seemed to be stuck together, and he couldn't breathe—

Bayley found himself lying on his back with his eyes closed, a gentle breeze caressing his face, sunlight warming his body. He groaned and rolled onto his side. God, he thought, what a terrible dream.

He opened his eyes and found himself on flat white concrete under a pure blue sky. He squinted in the glare. He seemed to be in the center of some kind of gigantic circular plaza, a high wall marking its perimeter. Suddenly, then, he remembered.

Panic surged up inside him and he scrambled onto his knees, glancing quickly around. His last moments of consciousness on the operating table were vivid in his mind, and he could almost hear the echoes of his final shout for help. Where the hell was he?

He dropped forward onto his hands and felt the concrete, rough and solid and warm from the sun. He rubbed his palms across it, feeling little grains of dirt digging into his skin. He smacked his hand against it, and his skin tingled from the blow.

He sat back on his heels, closed his eyes for a moment,

pressed his fingers to his ears, and took a deep breath. He heard the air rush into his lungs. He heard his heart thumping.

He got up onto his feet and looked down at his body. He was wearing the same clothes as when he'd visited Gottbaum: white shirt, brown pants, sandals. He still had his watch and his wedding ring. He raised his hands and inspected them closely. Tiny particles of grit were still clinging to his skin. He brushed them off and watched them drift down to the ground.

Had the experiment failed? Had Gottbaum and his people been placed under arrest before they could scan him? Had he been revived, somehow, somewhere?

He turned slowly, trying to be methodical, trying not to lose control. The concrete plaza extended away from him on all sides, flat and featureless. He shouted, and his voice was loud in his own ears, and there was a faint returning echo from the wall at the perimeter. He stamped his foot; the slap of his sandal echoed, and he felt a little twinge of pain from the impact of his heel against the ground.

His clothes were itchy against his skin. The wind was colder than it had seemed at first. And, he realized, he was hungry.

He started walking, trying to follow a straight path across the plaza. After a few minutes he paused and looked over his shoulder. The wall behind him had receded slightly; the wall ahead had come slightly closer.

He walked on. The wind blew hard, cutting through his thin shirt, making him shiver. The hunger in his stomach became a persistent, hollow pain, and he felt increasingly weak. How long had he been unconscious? days? years? He touched his jaw and found himself clean-shaven. That didn't make sense. Toward the end, he had had two days' growth of stubble. Either someone had shaved him while he was unconscious, or—

There was a loud noise behind him. He turned quickly, scared, instinctively drawing his arms up against his chest. His nerves were shot. Adrenaline washed through his system, making him tremble. He stared across the plaza, searching for the source of the sound.

It came to him again, a wild, mournful, moaning noise. There was a faint black speck in the distance, growing gradually larger. Some sort of animal—a dog?

Bayley decided there was no advantage in waiting to see if the creature was friendly. Instinctively, he ran.

The straps of his sandals cut into his skin as he pounded across the hard concrete. His lungs ached. His vision wavered. He glanced behind him and saw the creature gaining on him—a big black shape, its mouth hanging open. It howled again, and the noise echoed around him.

By the time he reached the perimeter wall the animal was less than twenty feet away. It was like nothing he'd ever seen, as big as he was, covered in thick black fur, a cross between a wolf and a bear.

The wall ahead was featureless, white, high and smooth and impossible to climb, but there were arches in it at regular intervals. He ran through the nearest one, found a flight of stone steps directly ahead, and started up them two at a time. He was so exhausted, his legs were buckling under him. He reached a turn in the stairs and hesitated, finding a plain white door set in the stone wall in front of him.

He tried the handle. The door opened and he fell through it, slamming it behind him just as the animal came bounding up the stairs.

He found himself in a small square room lit by a single fluorescent ceiling panel. There was a narrow bed at one side, a sink, a stove, and a refrigerator. Everything was white: the walls, the floor, the bedcover, the kitchen equipment.

Bayley sank down onto the bed gasping for breath and lay there hugging himself, waiting for his pulse to return to normal. Something about the room reassured him. The kitchen facilities could have come from any low-income suburban home. The fluorescent panel reminded him of the lights in his office. Everything was displaced yet familiar.

After a minute he sat up, then stood up. His chest was aching and he felt dizzy, but he still needed to make sense of his surroundings and find out where he was. At the same time, he was desperately hungry. He went to the refrigerator and pulled the door open.

Inside, on the top shelf, was a large round chocolate cake.

The cake was on a circular white plate. Bayley slid his hands under it, lifted it, and carried it to the counter beside the sink. He searched for a drawer or a cupboard that might contain dishes and flatware, but there didn't seem to be any. Tentatively, he touched the frosting of the cake with his finger. He scooped a blob of it and raised it to his mouth.

He was light-headed, salivating wildly, as if he had gone for days without food. He closed his lips around his finger, sucked the frosting into his mouth—and started to choke.

It tasted foul, like rotten meat or rancid cheese. The flavor filled his mouth and made his stomach heave.

He grabbed the faucet and turned it on. Water splashed into the sink. He cupped some in his hands and drank, desperate to wash the taste away.

The water burned his mouth like acid. Some of it trickled down his throat, and he felt as if he was being eaten from within. He screamed and staggered back from the sink, clutching his hands to his neck.

As he fell back onto the bed, the room turned, and the light dimmed to black.

Maphis

He woke up in a large, wide bed. Linen sheets were cool against his skin. His head was resting against a soft, deep pillow.

Bayley groaned. He looked around apprehensively, half expecting to find himself still in the little white room. Instead, he saw antique furniture, maroon wallpaper, a fine, old rolltop desk against one wall, glass-fronted shelves of leather-bound books, a window framed with red velvet drapes.

He swallowed tentatively, afraid his throat would still hurt—but it felt normal. He was no longer exhausted, no longer hungry, cold, or scared. "What the hell is going on?" He spoke aloud for the reassurance of hearing his own voice.

You are in your new home.

The answer seemed to emanate from inside his own head. He flinched, startled. It sounded characterless, impersonal. A machine voice.

"You actually did it," he said. "Goddam you." He rubbed

his hands over his face, massaged his scalp with his fingers, pressed his palms against his forehead. Then he grabbed the sheets, dragged them up, and bit into them. They were soft yet firm between his teeth. They even tasted like real linen, freshly laundered and bleached.

I did nothing, the voice in his head said.

Bayley threw the sheets back. He stared at his own nakedness, then slid his hands down his chest to his belly, touching and probing. The skin, the hairs, everything looked and felt as it always did. "Get out of my head!" he shouted.

I do not understand. I cannot parse that command.

"Am I talking to a computer? An AI? Is anything real, here?"

I am a very large data-processing system. My acronym is MAPHIS: Memory Array and Processors for Human Intelligence Storage. Nothing that you see here is real. Everything is a simulation fed to your sense receptors. Your sense receptors themselves, and all other components of your brain, have been replicated inside my hardware.

Bayley swung his legs around and sat on the edge of the bed. He rested his elbows on his knees and held his head between his hands. "Just shut up till I ask you another question," he muttered.

Obligingly, the voice fell silent.

His body still felt the same. His memories still seemed the same. He thought of his childhood, his parents, the kids he'd known at school, the summer job he'd taken in his first year at college. He remembered Sharon, the day he'd met her, when she'd been in the cafeteria. What had she been wearing? The lime-green T-shirt, the white pants—

That was too painful to think about.

He stood up. The carpet was thick and it tickled the undersides of his bare feet. Once again, he surveyed the room. It was large and opulent, sunlight streaming through the windows, gleaming on the polished wood of the antique furniture. There were contemporary touches here and there, too: an entertainment center in the wall opposite the bed, a computer keyboard in the rolltop desk, a portable phone on the satin bedcover. A door stood half-open revealing a modern bathroom beyond.

Could all of this really be a computer simulation? Every detail seemed so realistic. The floor felt solid under his feet, and as he shifted his weight he heard the faint creak of old-fashioned wooden boards.

"So what are you going to do to me now?" Bayley asked. "More poisoned food and drink? Something else to scare the shit out of me?"

Nothing will happen without your permission.

He slapped his hand to his forehead. "MAPHIS, make your voice come from somewhere other than my own brain."

Is this better? The voice emanated from the loudspeakers built into the entertainment center.

"Yes." He paused, trying to steady himself, trying to come to terms with what had happened. But there was no way to cope with it; it was too much to deal with. And since it felt so much like the real world, he found himself automatically responding as if it were, in fact, real.

"So why was I in that concrete plaza, with that thing chasing me?"

It was necessary, to perform initial calibration of basic physical and emotional responses. Exposure, hunger, threat, pursuit, shelter, sustenance. There were some data conversion errors, but I have now corrected the inverted taste senses. You should not experience any further discomfort. If you need any sensory inputs to be adjusted, I am online at all times and available to help. Simply speak your instructions. The nerve commands that would normally go to your larynx are rerouted to an interpreter and parsed by my natural-language processor.

He nodded to himself. The computer-literate part of his mind understood and even respected the technical achievements involved. At the same time, though, he felt dazed, displaced, and horribly alone. Worst of all, he was very conscious of his vulnerability. If his mind had been remade inside a large and complex computer that was managed by an artificial intelligence, he had absolutely no way to defend himself—from painful sensory experiences, programming errors, or power interruptions.

He sat back down on the bed. The cover was smooth and slippery, just the way satin should feel. He scraped his fingernails over it, and that didn't feel quite right. His nails didn't dig into the stitching the way he expected. There were limits to the accuracy of the simulation after all.

Is the room satisfactory?

"Satisfactory? It seems comfortable."

Is your mood satisfactory? Would you like to feel happier or more confident?

"Jesus Christ. You can control that too?"

Partially.

"Explain that to me, MAPHIS. I want to understand how things work in here."

Your mind now resides as a pattern inside a very large computer. I can transmit into your mind an accurate imitation of the nerve impulses you would normally receive as a result of being in various environments. I have a catalog of places and things, which I can add to at your request. I can also modify the stimuli you receive, in any way you want, or I can use direct access, via a low-level interpreter, to areas of your brain such as the hypothalamus, where a change in voltage can manipulate your mood in much the same way that drugs can affect a human brain.

"Does that mean you can mess with my memories, as well?" He was beginning to feel as if nothing belonged to him anymore.

No. Your memories were copied into the computer from your biological brain, but no one understands, at this point, how memories are encoded. Therefore, I have no control over your memories. Nor can I extract any information from them.

"You mean Gottbaum and his people copied my brain without knowing how some of it really works?"

Yes. By analogy, an audio recorder can store and play a piece of music without understanding harmony and composition. All that matters is that the copy is accurate.

"I'm glad there's something that you can't mess with. And as for my mood, it's fine the way it is, thanks."

I attempted to create baseline-normal emotions.

So that explained why he wasn't feeling the same kind of panic that had gripped him in the previous scenario. He glanced around the room again, trying to decide, now, what he should do. In one sense there was no need to do anything; as an infomorph, he would not need to eat, drink, sleep, or work. But he didn't *feel* like an infomorph. He felt like a person, James

Bayley, flesh and blood, full of the same old needs for human company, intellectual fulfillment, and physical safety.

"I'd like some clothes," he said. "Clothes should help me feel more normal. Just my everyday clothes. Is that possible?"

Of course. Garments sprang into being out of nowhere, draped across the chair that stood directly in front of him.

Bayley gave a little shout of surprise and flinched as if a blow had been aimed at his head. Hesitantly, then, he reached out and touched the fabric of the shirt. It was as solid and as real as the bed under him. "Don't—do that," he said. "Don't violate the normal laws of space and time. It's very disorienting. I mean, I understand, intellectually, that everything I see is a simulation, and can be altered. But it seems real, and the only way I'm going to cope with it is by letting myself assume that it *is* real."

I am not sure I comprehend. My knowledge of physical laws and constraints is limited. You must tell me specifically how alterations in your environment should occur. Everything is being managed on an experimental basis.

"Because I'm the first infomorph? There aren't any others in here with me?"

Not yet.

"Isn't anyone in the outside world monitoring this?"

I am not permitted to provide that information.

Bayley shook his head. It was too much to think about. He started pulling on the garments. "I suppose you aren't going to tell me where the hardware of MAPHIS is located, either," he said.

I am not permitted to provide that information.

He glanced at the phone lying on the bed. Impulsively, he picked it up. But there was no dial tone. "Doesn't this thing work?"

It can only simulate contact with the outside world at this time.

He imagined a synthetic version of Sharon's voice. The idea was repugnant, and extremely sad. He threw the phone back on the bed. "No. I want genuine, realtime contact. I want to speak to my wife."

That feature is not yet implemented.

"Maybe in version 1.1?"

I do not understand.

"Forget it. A joke." He paced across the room, then back again. His clothes moved as he moved, touching his skin. When he concentrated on the sensations, they didn't seem exactly right; the fabric felt a little stiff, somehow artificial. But if he hadn't thought about it, he wouldn't have noticed.

He poked his head into the bathroom and checked out the washbasin, the tub, the toilet, and the bidet, all in solid white enamel, sparkling and immaculate. Then he went to a door of polished, paneled wood, opened it, and found himself looking out onto a landing at the top of a flight of carpeted stairs. "MAPHIS, where is this meant to be, this house I'm in?"

Anywhere you want it to be. The house is modeled on a real building in the eastern United States. Your current scenario assumes you are a man of wealth and power.

The voice was still emanating from the speakers in the bedroom, so Bayley walked back in there. He looked out of the window and saw an immaculate lawn, a stone fountain, pine trees bordering a graveled drive. "Very nice," he said. "Although it's not my idea of paradise."

Other scenarios are available. I have a variety of environments and features stored into my catalog. You can retrieve any of them, at any time. Or, if the environment of your choice is not available, we can construct it piece by piece and adjust it to suit your requirements.

"Too good to be true," said Bayley. Now that he was beginning to understand the possibilities, the responsiveness of this synthetic world, he had an ominous sense of being set up. He remembered the perfect day when he'd driven up the coast to see Gottbaum. It felt like that.

On the other hand, if MAPHIS was telling the truth, and he could really adjust his environment to please himself, without any unexpected tricks or traps, where would that lead? It was an absolute power fantasy. And absolute power tended to corrupt absolutely.

He wandered over to the bookshelves and scanned the titles. Most of them were classics. He pulled down a copy of *Moby Dick*, opened it—and found that all the pages were blank.

The contents of that book are not in my catalog. If you wish, I can download it from the Library of Congress.

"All right. Why not."

Almost instantly, the white paper was covered with text. Bayley riffled the pages; magically, they had all been filled.

Is the typeface satisfactory?

"Sure." He laughed grimly. "It's just fine." He closed the book, feeling as if he were living inside Aladdin's lamp, and set it down on the corner of a nearby chest of drawers. But he was still feeling confused, and his coordination was poor. The book nudged an ornamental glass paperweight and toppled it. It hit the floor and smashed.

"Damn." He stood and stared at the glass fragments.

Shall I restore the paperweight?

"Yes. Please."

The pieces gathered themselves together and became a seamless whole.

Bayley bent down and picked it up. He felt the heft of it, the cool, smooth curve of the glass. A pink crystalline flower lay at the center. He stared at it and saw it as an analog of himself, trapped in a private universe, isolated and unreachable.

He carefully put the ornament back on the chest, then turned and sat on the bed again. What else could he ask for? "Can you make the wallpaper a different color? Green, for instance?"

Certainly. And instantly, the walls changed. *Is that tint satisfactory?*

Bayley blinked, startled by the sudden transformation even though he'd been expecting it. "It's fine. And . . . what about the view from the window? Can you change that? From day to night, for instance?"

Of course. The sun faded as if storm clouds were gathering. Electric lights inside the room came to life as the sky outside turned black.

Bayley felt like a magician. And yet, there was no real point to these tricks. He should ask for something more substantial. What did he really want?

To be back in his everyday world, he realized. In his own home, with Damon and Sharon. When he contemplated the permanence of his exile, here, he felt a sense of dull futility.

I sense you are unhappy.

"I'm lonely. For my wife."

Do you want companionship?

"You said I'm the only infomorph in here."

Yes. But a variety of human simulations are on file. We call them pseudomorphs. Shall I select one?

He shrugged. "Go ahead."

Someone knocked on the bedroom door almost before he had finished speaking. He looked up, startled. A figure was standing there. A nurse in a crisp, clean uniform: white shoes, white pants, a white jacket, a white cap. "Sorry," she said. "Did I startle you, Mr. Bayley?"

He nodded dumbly.

"May I come in?"

"Sure."

He sat and watched as she entered the room. She was pretty and very young, with blue eyes, a turned-up nose, generous lips, long, wavy blond hair escaping from under her cap and flowing to her shoulders. Her uniform was tight around her body, which was slim but big-breasted. She gave him a smile as she came over and sat beside him on the bed.

Bayley went on staring at her. She was an adolescent fantasy brought to life.

"So, are you feeling better?" she asked.

Like everything else around him, she seemed totally real. But she was a creation of MAPHIS, and MAPHIS had promised to adjust his environment in any way he wanted. Did that mean she was under his control?

"Is there anything I can do for you?" she asked. The way she looked at him, and her tone of voice, made it clear that there were no limits; none at all.

He could smell her perfume. He reached out, slid his hand around behind her neck, and felt her hair and her soft, perfect skin.

She laughed. "That tickles." She tilted her head to one side. "Do you want me to undress for you?"

Bayley nodded dumbly. "Sure."

She unbuttoned her jacket, and opened it. She was naked underneath. Her breasts were large and round and heavy with small, pink upturned nipples. Centerfold breasts, Bayley thought, staring at them.

"Just tell me what you want," she said. She parted her lips, moistened them with her tongue.

He suddenly saw himself sitting on the couch beside Sharon, at home in their living room, talking about his day or hers, feeling that deep, special bond that came from so many shared experiences and ideas and emotions. They would end up cuddling, he would end up kissing her, or she would kiss him, and they'd make love, sometimes right there on the couch, the mental and physical closeness blending seamlessly. Afterward, they would lie together for a while, sometimes without saying anything at all, because nothing needed to be said.

He stood up, turning to face the wall. "I don't want this."

"Are you sure?" Her voice, behind him, sounded soft and sexy.

"MAPHIS, take her away. I don't want her. I'm not interested in—in pseudomorphs, and I don't want any of this." He gestured at the opulent room. "It's juvenile wish fulfillment. Who programmed it—Gottbaum? Porter?" He closed his eyes. "I want to be back in my own life," he said, feeling a sudden wave of self-pity. "Can you manage that? Can you fake it so well that I can't tell the difference?"

I will try, said MAPHIS.

Everything went black.

Replicas

The darkness was only momentary. The lights came on again after just a couple of seconds, and he found himself standing in an entirely different place. The ceiling and the floor were a featureless dull gray, and so were all the walls except one, which glowed white, illuminating the little room. There was a stool in the center, and on the stool lay something that looked like a pen, blunt at one end, pointed at the other.

Was the transition between environments acceptable?

"I guess." He was turning around, checking his new surroundings, trying to readjust. "It would be better, maybe, if I could walk out of one space, through a doorway, into another. That would seem more natural."

I will arrange that next time. Are you ready to begin?

"What do I do?"

Please observe the white wall. As MAPHIS spoke, the wall became a screen displaying a life-size, full-color picture. It showed Bayley's street in Granada Hills, his apartment building in the background. *Is this your home?*

He nodded slowly. "Yes. It is." He felt a twist of nostalgia. Even though he had been there just two days ago, it felt infinitely far away in time and space.

Do you want to make any improvements? You can describe them to me, or use the stylus to indicate your revisions.

He laughed without much humor. "You don't understand. I don't want to change anything. That's the whole point."

The building is completely satisfactory?

"Yes." He said it impatiently. "Where did you get the picture, anyway?"

It has been modeled from architects' records downloaded from the city planning office. Here is the side elevation. The picture on the screen slowly rotated, as if Bayley were gliding around the building, across lawns, through shrubbery.

"The jacaranda trees should be taller," he said. "I guess they've grown since the plans were filed."

The trees on the screen extended themselves upward and outward. *Like this?*

He looked carefully. The view seemed correct now in every detail, yet it still had a synthetic quality, like a computer simulation. Well, that was exactly what it was. "Can we go inside?"

MAPHIS showed him the lobby. Bayley corrected some details: the color of the paint, a missing ornamental plant. Since MAPHIS didn't understand how his memories were stored, there was no way for the computer to obtain this information directly from his mind.

The scene changed in front of him, showing a view of his own apartment. The rooms were completely bare; he had to set about furnishing them. He became engrossed in the task, describing furniture that MAPHIS then displayed for him on the wallscreen so that he could modify it, upholster it in his choice of fabric, and shift it into the positions he remembered from real life.

Subjectively, an hour passed. Bayley realized he had been using all his concentration, working hard, and yet he wasn't tired. There was no nagging ache from his neck and shoulders, no eye strain, no need to take a break or stop for a snack, because he was no longer relying on his body to feed nutrients to his brain. He might feel a need to pause and reflect, once in a while, but physical exhaustion had been eliminated forever.

Eventually, he had the interior of the apartment looking exactly the way he remembered it. He began to feel a sense of anticipation. The task had been easier, and more successful, than he'd expected.

Do you want to walk into it?

"Yes, that would be good."

The picture of his living room disappeared as the wall in front of him returned to its former state, glowing featureless white. *If you exit through the door behind you, you will find yourself on the street where you live.*

"All right." He turned and found the door. Tentatively, he turned the handle, opened it a crack, and peered out.

Mellow afternoon sunlight slanted in. Birds were singing. Jacaranda blossoms drifted down.

Bayley stood there for a long moment, staring. Now that the details of the scene were being fed directly into his electronic eyes and ears, everything felt entirely real. Maybe some of the colors were a fraction wrong; maybe the trees still weren't exactly the right size, and when he squinted up at them he saw a fractal artificiality, a vagueness in the fine detail at the tips of the branches. And yet, as he stepped out into the world he'd created, the sidewalk felt solid underfoot, and the breeze felt warm on his face.

He took a couple of steps, turned, and looked back. The little gray room had gone. The illusion was now perfect: this was his street, and in front of him was his apartment building.

He started toward it. It was so eerily authentic, he could almost believe that he was back in the real world and all the other events had been hallucinatory. He hurried up the path, past the wild roses and the cacti, to the lobby entrance. He pulled the door open, and it didn't make the little squeaking sound that he remembered. Good, he thought, someone finally got around to oiling the hinges. And then he realized, foolishly, that no one had gotten around to doing anything. The only reason the hinges didn't squeak was because MAPHIS didn't know they were supposed to squeak.

He ran up the stairs and approached his apartment door. "The door should open when the mechanism recognizes me," he said.

Like this? The voice was disembodied; it came from somewhere vaguely above him.

The door swung open.

"Yes. Like that."

He walked forward—and was inside his apartment. He went from room to room, feeling a growing sense of relief. He rearranged the cushions on the couch, and they felt the way they were supposed to feel. He went into the kitchen and ran his hands over the cupboards, the stove, the sink.

In the living room, he stopped in front of the DVI system, staring at the big blank screen, suddenly remembering Damon exploring the interactive video of Old Macdonald's Farm. The whole apartment was like Old Macdonald's Farm, now, and he was like Damon, stumbling around in a world that didn't really exist.

Is everything satisfactory? The voice came from the speakers either side of the blank screen.

"Yes," he said, some of his enthusiasm fading. "Yes, it's fine." Except that Old Macdonald's Farm had been full of lovable singing animals, and his apartment was silent and empty. He could almost imagine that Sharon and Damon had just gone down to the store, and they'd be back any minute, running up the stairs, tumbling in through the front door, Damon racing Sharon, and Sharon letting him win.

He steeled himself for the task ahead. "I guess I'm ready to start on the—the simulation of my wife and child."

You mean you wish to create your own pseudomorphs?

"I guess that's what I mean, yes." He pulled a chair over and sank into it. "Can we do it on the DVI screen here?"

Of course.

"So—how do we begin?"

Ideally, I should start from a digitized photograph.

Bayley thought for a moment. "There's no way to get you a picture of Damon. But Sharon's photograph should be on file in the employee records of the City of Los Angeles, Department of Media. Can you access them? She works for KUSA, the state-owned TV channel. Her first name is Sharon. She uses Blake, her maiden name, professionally."

One moment.

Bayley waited. He felt nervous, now. The apartment had been fun to create, just an exercise in computer-aided design. He and Sharon had done much the same thing in real life when they'd moved in.

Now, however, he was getting involved in something very different. Replicating a person—the person whom he knew best and cared for most—made him a latter-day Frankenstein. True, everything he was experiencing was merely a pattern of electrons. He was not creating life, he was imitating life; but it made him apprehensive nonetheless. Apart from anything else, he doubted it could be done.

Her picture appeared on the screen in front of him. She seemed to be smiling at him from the screen, her eyes alive, her expression a little mischievous. She was very photogenic, and he felt a pang of longing for her. He told himself to be strong; that he might be able to satisfy his longing if he could deal with this challenge objectively enough.

He started working with MAPHIS, first replicating Sharon's face as it should look from the side, then developing a three-quarter profile, then constructing views from above and below and in between. It was difficult for him, and several times he had to break off, wrestling with his emotions. Nor was the job over quickly; even after the views had been established, he still had to specify different facial expressions, tiny alterations of mouth and eyes that he had come to know over the years as vital, almost subliminal, cues to her feelings.

Lastly, MAPHIS depicted a generic female body, and Bayley managed to adopt sufficient clinical detachment to adjust the dimensions, the subtle curves, to match his memory of his wife.

A lot of time passed. When the task was finally complete he sat staring at the screen, wondering whether the effort had been wasted. The process of recreating her image had merely made him want her more.

Shall I animate the image on the screen?

"Yes," he said. His voice was quiet. He watched, not really hoping for very much.

The view of the figure shifted, rotating first left, then right. The arms and legs moved experimentally, like a marionette. The face went through a variety of expressions. The eyes closed and opened.

Satisfactory?

He drew a shaky breath. "As far as it goes, yes." It was not pleasant watching such a parody of her.

Before we continue to the next stage, are there any features you wish to improve?

"I've told you before—" He broke off. He was remembering, once, he and Sharon had talked about a person's physical self-image. They had agreed that everyone, no matter how beautiful, was always conscious of some feature that she or he would like to change. In Bayley's case, he had always wanted to be a couple of inches taller. Sharon, meanwhile, had told him she hated her ankles. They were thick, she said, "like a peasant's ankles."

"Make the ankles slightly thinner," he said. He felt as if he was doing it for her, not him. She would have wanted them that way.

MAPHIS obliged. *Any other modifications? Do you wish to remove any body hair?*

Bayley sighed. Now he had started, where should he stop? "All right," he said. "She didn't like the hairs on her arms. And her legs." And in truth, nor had he, although it was something he had never had any trouble living with. But if you had the option to change something, painlessly, instantly—was there really anything wrong with that?

Do you wish to remove armpit hair?

"No." He said it sharply—because he already felt guilty for modifying her. "No, leave it."

Improve any facial features?

"No! Leave her the way she is!"

Improve her body? A slimmer waist? Firmer breasts?

He couldn't help thinking that if her mind was what he had always been in love with, why would it hurt to change her body a little? And he couldn't help remembering the body of the pseudomorph nurse that MAPHIS had created. But if that was all he wanted, he should have settled for the teenage fantasy instead of taking all this trouble to replicate his wife as he remembered her.

"No changes," he said firmly.

All right. We must now develop the personality.

"How?" He leaned forward, contemplating the task that still lay ahead. "How can you possibly hope to do that?"

I will animate her image, speaking various common English phrases. I will ask you to advise me on pitch, intonation, gesture, expression, and timing.

Bayley's first thought was that this could take all night. But, he realized, he had all night, and all the next day, the next week, as much time as he needed, to get the job done right. Time was no longer a factor.

"Let's get started," he said.

Do you wish to do this via the screen, or do you want to use a solid physical model?

"The screen."

"Hello," said the screen image. "My name is Sharon."

The smile looked real, the eyes were right, but the voice grated on his nerves and the speech sounded stilted and clumsy. "I'll do an imitation of how it should go," he said. He closed his eyes, imagined Sharon's distinctive speech rhythms, and tried to mimic her.

For the next few hours, that was how it went. It was like trying to teach a student the finer points of a foreign language: all the little details that distinguished a native from an outsider. The process was painful at first, because the version on the screen was such a caricature. But MAPHIS learned fast, and Sharon gradually began to seem less like a marionette, more like a video recording.

Eventually they reached a point where no further improvement seemed possible. There was still something off-key about her, but he couldn't pin it down. Part of the problem, he realized, was that he had spent so long staring at Sharon on the screen, the image was beginning to displace his memories of the real person.

Lastly, I need to know Sharon's typical vocabulary. Sentence structures, commonly used terms and phrases, and endearments.

That was much easier. He stretched out on the couch, closed his eyes, thought back to all the times he had sat here with her, and started recreating the conversations in his head, speaking her part aloud. There were some bad memories among the good: fights over money, in the early days, and disagreements about when to start a family. But the more he remembered, the more nostalgic he became.

Eventually, MAPHIS interrupted him. *Mr. Bayley, you are starting to repeat yourself. I have enough data now.*

Bayley blinked, jolted out of his reverie. He swung his legs down and sat up. "You're . . . ready?" He noticed that the screen had blanked.

I am ready. Are you?

"Yes." He said it quickly, before he could find an excuse to postpone the moment. If a convincing replica of Sharon could exist here, he reminded himself, the experience of being stranded outside of reality might become at least halfway bearable.

The front door opened, and there she was, walking into the room. "Hi, honey." She looked down at him, smiling.

He stared at her, studying her. She looked like Sharon. She really did. He laughed, a strange, uncertain sound, not sure of her, of himself, of what he wanted to happen next. "It's really you," he said, trying to make himself believe it.

"Of course it's me." She shut the door. "How are you?" She sat down on the opposite end of the couch and clasped her hands in her lap. She raised her eyebrows a fraction, looking at him inquiringly. It was all exactly the way he remembered.

"I'm fine," he said reflexively. "I mean . . . well, I'm doing okay, I guess, considering—" He broke off. That wasn't what he wanted. What he wanted was to be back in his old life, wasn't that right? "It was a long day. I've missed you," he said. He felt as if he was playing a role, imitating the life he had lived just a little while ago.

She blinked. She didn't say anything.

He reached out and took her hand. It startled him with its solidity and warmth. "So—how was your day?" Under the circumstances, it was a dumb question, but it was what he always said, and habit was addictive.

"Not bad." She shrugged and smiled some more. And what else could she do? She wasn't a person, she was a construct controlled by MAPHIS, and MAPHIS didn't know what sort of day Sharon Bayley had had. MAPHIS didn't understand anything about TV journalism, personality conflicts on the job, promotions, turf battles, rewrites, video edits, voice-overs, all the everyday details of Sharon's work. MAPHIS probably didn't know much about daily suburban routines, either: commuting on a freeway, shopping, inviting friends over for dinner, washing the car, fixing things around the house. It was a mass of trivia that human beings took for granted, yet it rested on a foundation of complex physical and mechanical interactions, power relationships, social rituals, human desires, and other concepts that a computer was ill-equipped to disassemble. That was the eternal problem with artificial intelligence: it had to be programmed with a lifetime of common knowledge that people accumulated by growing up, moving around, interacting with other people, doing all the things that a human being did.

In a moment of awful clarity, Bayley saw the blunder he had made. He had imagined recreating his home life as a world through which he could move. MAPHIS could achieve this for him with relative ease, but when he needed to *interact* with that world and the people in it and have them respond to him authentically, that was another matter. It was a task, in fact, beyond the capabilities of the system.

And yet, Sharon looked so real, so loving and lovable. And MAPHIS could obviously cope with low-level dialogue. Some sort of conversation should be possible. "It was warm today," he said. It sounded lame, but it was a start.

"What was warm today?" She tilted her head to one side, just the way he remembered it. She frowned at him.

"The weather. The weather was warm."

"Oh, I see. The weather."

"It's almost June. I guess we'll have to start using the air conditioning."

She nodded seriously. "You're right, we'll have to."

"Do you still want to take your vacation in July?" He said that without thinking. It was something he'd been meaning to mention to her, before—before.

She looked uncertain. "I don't know." And how could she know? Suppose that MAPHIS understood what a vacation was, and what a job was, and what a month was. Suppose MAPHIS knew that "taking" a vacation didn't mean stealing it, or swallowing it like a pill, or capturing it like a chess piece, or enrolling in it like a college class. Even assuming all that, there was no way for MAPHIS to know the pros and cons of a vacation in July rather than August.

He sighed. "You're looking very pretty today," he said, just going through the motions, now, feeling lost.

"You're looking very handsome." Her smile was beginning to look fixed and unreal.

"Do you know who you remind me of?" he said.

She shook her head, making her black hair bob to and fro. "No. Who do I remind you of?"

"Talking Teddy." There it was: the truth.

She tilted her head to one side, as if she'd forgotten that she'd done that just a moment before. "Who's Talking Teddy?"

"Never mind. It doesn't matter." He stood up.

She looked up at him. She looked so real, so right. It was unbearably tantalizing. He reached out his hand. "Give me a kiss good-bye."

She grasped his hand and he pulled her up beside him. "Are you going somewhere?" she said.

"Just for a while. Do I get my kiss?"

"You always get a kiss." That was something Sharon had liked to say. MAPHIS knew that, because he had told MAPHIS.

He hugged her to him. She felt good. The shapes, the curves were the way he remembered them. He looked into her upturned face, then touched his lips to hers before he could think too much about what was happening.

The kiss felt strange and wrong. How could MAPHIS know how it had felt to kiss Sharon? And how could he ever hope to describe it?

He let go of her and looked away. "When I walk out of the door," he said, "I want to find myself in a hotel room. Something totally ordinary and anonymous."

He turned back to Sharon, then. He gave her hand a squeeze. "Good-bye," he said.

Pleasure Centers

It was a modular room, mass-manufactured with a foam-plastic carpet and imitation 1950s antique furniture. There was a narrow bed, a flat-screen TV, a tiny bathroom molded in one piece out of glass fiber. The view from the window was of a wall of cinderblocks ten feet away, painted brown.

Bayley locked the door and blanked the window. He found a control panel and fiddled with it till he managed to dim the glow panel in the wall above the bed. He kicked his shoes off, doubled the pillow behind his head, and lay on his back with his arms folded across his chest, staring up at the featureless ceiling.

Sharon's face kept swimming to the surface of his memories. He willed it away, telling himself that he could no longer allow himself to think about his past life.

The hotel room provided solace in its anonymity. There were no sensory cues, here; no links with the world he had known. It was a good place in which to plan how he should continue.

But did he really want to continue? He could never again be with the people he loved. His working life was over, at least as he had known it. His physical body and his physical brain no longer existed. He was in exile in MAPHIS, not just for his natural lifetime but forever.

Would the system obey him if he asked for his life as an infomorph to be terminated? It would surely be simple enough to do—merely a matter of erasing an area of computer memory. He toyed with the idea, but set it aside, at least until he had explored his remaining options.

"When will other infomorphs be in here with me?" he asked.

I am not authorized to give you that information. The voice came from the speaker in the TV opposite.

"Why not?"

I am not authorized to give you that information.

Well, it didn't matter, anyway. The only people who were likely to join him would be Gottbaum, French, and her team. He had no desire to deal with the people who had done this to him.

"Is there no possibility of speaking to someone on the outside?" he asked. "You obviously have the capability to access external information networks. Why can't I be patched through to the telephone system?"

It is not permitted.

Which left him with—what? He could design any environment he wanted. He could act out fantasies with simulated people—pseudomorphs—whom MAPHIS retrieved from its catalog or built to Bayley's specifications. And that seemed to be all.

He thought back to his former existence. Love, work, procreation: those were the three human functions that had seemed most meaningful in the long term. None of them was available to him anymore.

Still, there was always physical sensation. "You said you have control over my hypothalamus?"

Yes.

"Does that mean you can provide me with pleasure?"

Yes.

Bayley remembered an old experiment in which laboratory rats had been given one button to press for food, another for water, and a third that gave them a jolt hardwired into their pleasure centers. They had quickly lost interest in the food and water and had pressed the pleasure button till they died from exhaustion. Maybe it wasn't such a bad way to go—especially since, within MAPHIS, he was effectively immortal. "So give me some pure pleasure," he said.

His body started tingling. His face felt flushed. Exquisite sensations started pulsing from his groin. His penis became erect. Tension grew like a weight in his lower abdomen, making him groan and arch his back, his muscles straining. Without warning, then, he climaxed. But it was no normal orgasm; it lasted twenty seconds, thirty, forty, gripping him, eclipsing all other sensations. "Enough!" he cried out finally, feeling as if he were drowning, losing all ability to think.

The pleasure subsided. He lay limp and dazed, breathing heavily. As his perceptions gradually returned to normal he focused once again on his surroundings, and found that the little room looked grimmer, more austere than before.

Maybe if he asked MAPHIS for pleasure at a less intense

level he could erase his angst yet still remain functional. And yet, wouldn't that be like perpetual masturbation? or drug addiction?

Either way, it still wasn't what he wanted.

"Do you have the parameters of any external environments stored in your catalog?"

I have sixty-four predefined environments.

"Any cities?"

Selected areas in New York, London, Los Angeles, Tokyo, and others.

So if nothing else, he could see the world. "London," he said. "When I leave this room, I want to find myself in London."

All right. You will find yourself in London.

Bayley got up off the bed. He went to the door, opened it, and walked out.

Crash

He found himself descending two stone steps into a tiny street of old-fashioned row houses. There was a crowd of people facing him: journalists with cameras, British uniformed police holding them back. Video lights came to life, pinning him in their glare. People were shouting. He flinched from the sudden light and noise.

"This way, sir." Someone took his arm, guiding him toward a black limousine waiting at the curb, its rear door standing open.

Bayley glanced over his shoulder. He saw a black wooden door with white numerals on it. Number 10. Inside, he glimpsed a hallway, an antique table lamp, an Edwardian umbrella stand. No trace of the little hotel room he had been in a moment before.

"MAPHIS, what is this?"

"Can we have a statement, Prime Minister?" A journalist was leaning forward, almost breaking through the police cordon, pushing a microphone toward Bayley.

"Quickly, sir." The man at his elbow hustled him toward the waiting limo. "They're waiting for you at the House."

"Will there be a formal declaration of war?" another journalist shouted.

"MAPHIS," said Bayley, "whatever this is, I don't want it. Get me back to the hotel room, immediately."

The aide beside him stared at him blankly. "Sir, they're waiting for you at the House."

The journalists were pressing forward and the police were losing ground. Bayley remembered his experience in the white concrete plaza. He could be hurt as an infomorph. He ducked his head, ran through the mob, and threw himself into the rear seat of the limo.

His aide joined him, slammed the door, and the car pulled away along Downing Street, turning right onto Whitehall. Culture shock, Bayley thought to himself, feeling dazed. Instant, massive culture shock. Worse than that: identity shock. He had been dumped into some predefined scenario. "MAPHIS! Get me out of this!"

His aide, beside him, gave him a worried look. "Sir?"

Bayley looked back at the man. He was dressed in an old-fashioned three-piece suit and bowler hat, a fat leather briefcase on the seat beside him. Outside, the streets of London moved by; but everything looked antique. There were no modern buildings. Even the car he was in, he realized, was ancient. Mahogany paneling, seats of pleated brown leather, the roof lined with beige felt. A glass panel separated the rear of the vehicle from the chauffeur. Up ahead Bayley saw the Houses of Parliament coming into view.

"Your speech, sir," said the bowler-hatted aide. He handed Bayley some typewritten pages.

Bayley took them. They were dated September 3, 1939. He had been dropped into a reenactment of World War II. Who was he meant to be, Churchill? But Churchill hadn't come to power till later. There were other things wrong, also: too much traffic on the street, and the video lights that had dazzled him a moment ago. Whoever had programmed the simulation had been historically illiterate.

Bayley didn't want to be stuck in a second-rate fantasy for the next five years, refighting a long, grim, ugly war in a country that had almost starved to death. But if his command link with MAPHIS was down, did that mean he had no choice?

The limo stopped at a traffic light at Parliament Square. Impulsively, Bayley threw open the door. He jumped out onto the sidewalk and started running.

There were confused shouts from behind him, but he ignored them. He turned a corner and started up a narrow side street, past old buildings stained with soot and grime. He turned another corner . . . and collided with an invisible barrier.

There was no pain, no sense of hitting something. He felt as if he had been abruptly frozen in time. He tried to press forward, but his muscles were paralyzed, and the street looked like a photograph. All sound had cut off. Nothing was moving.

He tried to speak, and found that it was impossible.

Fear welled up inside him. It could be either a hardware failure or a programming error. His mind was still alive, but the vast, complex program that simulated his sensory inputs had crashed. No, not crashed. If that had happened, everything would surely have gone black. This seemed more like the system was running an endless loop. He could still feel the breath in his lungs, waiting to be exhaled; his weight on one foot, his other foot poised in midstride. Maybe he'd precipitated the failure by doing something so unexpected, jumping out of the car and running into an area of town for which MAPHIS might not have sufficient data. And yet there'd been something wrong at the start, when he'd addressed commands to the system and it hadn't responded.

He strained to move, but he couldn't even blink. He was stuck on the sidewalk, staring straight ahead, a couple of pedestrians frozen motionless farther down the block, cars standing in the middle of the street, exhaust fumes hanging behind them.

And then, one by one, the elements in the scenario started winking out. The pedestrians faded away. The traffic disappeared.

With a sense of dread, Bayley wondered if he would be next. Suddenly he wanted very much to stay alive, even if life was merely a simulation.

The white line down the center of the road started dissolving, as if it were being absorbed by the road itself. The cracks between paving stones in the sidewalk were suddenly gone. All around him, details were vanishing: reflections in store windows, clouds in the sky, street signs, the lines between bricks in a building opposite. The scene was gradually simplifying to a set of sterile, abstract planes: the black street, the gray sidewalk, dirty red facades of the buildings, white-framed windows.

Then the windows disappeared. He was stuck in a minimalist abstract painting: a half-dozen big blocks of featureless color.

The sidewalk disappeared from under his feet, leaving a dark gray void. The buildings started winking out one by one, revealing a featureless gray plane stretching to a flat horizon. The road, then, began to disappear.

Lastly, the sky. It gradually darkened till it became the same nondescript tone as the plane below it, and there was no longer anything to focus on, just grayness filling his vision.

For god's sake, get me out of this, he thought. Get me out, take me away, anywhere, back home, back—where?

His fear intensified as he realized he couldn't remember the name of the neighborhood where he used to live. It was in—in that big city on the West Coast, in the state of—of what?

Quickly, he started probing his memories. Before he had become an infomorph, he had been an investigator. Yes, he definitely remembered that. He had worked for—some sort of agency. The national agency of—no, that was wrong. Everything was evaporating from his mind. Think, he told himself. Think hard. Your wife, her name was . . . Sheryl? And your son, David. No, Donald. And you drove a car to work, along . . . a road, it was called a runway. A byway? To a place, a tall place, a thing made of, of shiny stuff. There were people, some of them were nice people, some of them were not nice. They gave you, something. Food, you took the food to your home, you ate the food, you went to sleep. You had bad dreams sometimes and when you woke up, there was a nice woman who took care of you.

I want to go home, he thought. I want—I want what? I want someone, someone who loves me. Someone who takes care of me and knows my name, my—

What was his name?

That was his last coherent thought as the grayness slowly darkened, a warm fuzziness crept over his body, and a hissing sound filled his ears. His mental functions faltered. Consciousness was like the picture on the cathode-ray tube of an antique TV, suddenly shrinking to a bright point that faded into nothing.

Wreckage

The car lay on the beach, twisted and blackened, stinking of soot and burned rubber. The windows had shattered in the heat, and some of the rocks nearby were sticky with residues from chemicals that the fire department had sprayed over the blaze.

"Came through the guard rail up there," said the tall, skinny cop who'd been detailed to guard the area. He was in his early twenties; his uniform looked baggy on him, and his voice was too loud, as if he was trying to use volume to make up for what he lacked in depth. "See where I mean?"

"Yes," said Sharon, too distraught to pay much attention. She ducked under the temporary police barrier and scrambled over rocks streaked with seaweed and crusted with barnacles. The tide had come in, and waves were breaking just below, tossing spray into the wind. The sun was a couple of hours from setting, laying a swatch of gold across the ocean.

There was a tightness in her chest as she came close to the car. Even though she knew that her husband's body had been removed earlier that day, she felt as if she was approaching his final resting place—or, worse than that, the device that had murdered him. Murder was what had happened here, she no longer had any doubt about that. They had decided he was too much of a danger to their research, and they had put him in his car and crashed it and killed him in such a way that it looked like an accident. After everything Yumi had told her, she was sure of it.

"You best be careful on those rocks," the cop called down to her. "They can be kind of slippery, you know?" He paused. "What you looking for, anyhow?"

"Mr. Bayley had a briefcase with him in the car," she said. He laughed. "Hell, there won't be much left of that."

"The case had a metal frame. That should still be here, even if the rest got burned up." Not to mention the homemade handgun that had been inside it. She stopped where rescue workers had forced open the door on the driver's side, and peered in. The entire interior was crusted with soot. She saw blackened seat springs, skeletal remains of the instrument panel. The floor was covered in ash, puddled with congealed plastic. There was no sign of the case, either in the front or the back.

She scrambled around to the rear of the car and pried at the trunk lid with her fingernails.

"Hey, you're not supposed to interfere with that." The cop started picking his way down toward her. "I know you told me like you're a journalist, but this is being held as evidence."

She ignored him and rummaged in her purse for the spare set of keys that she always carried.

"You hear me?" The cop was coming closer.

She found the right key and jiggled it in the lock. There was a scraping sound, then the trunk lid sprang open shedding flakes of scorched paint.

She stood for a moment, staring. There had been less heat from the blaze, here. She saw a rubber ball that Damon used to play with—partially melted, but still recognizable. An old beach blanket that she had sat on with Jim. A picnic chest, a pair of sunglasses. She felt herself swaying, and gripped the edge of the trunk for support.

The cop came around the car to her. "Hey, how'd you open that?"

There was no briefcase. Sharon dumped her keys back in her purse. She slammed the trunk lid and turned away.

She ignored the cop, walked back up to the highway, and went to her own car, parked at the curb. For a while she sat in it and stared out blankly at the ocean.

She remembered, clearly, seeing the contents of Jim's brief-case before he had left the apartment: the handgun, the scrap of metal he'd taken from the laboratory, the photocomposite of

Rosalind French, together with his compad and the LifeScan history. Evidently he had taken the last two items into Gottbaum's house; that was how they had subsequently come into Yumi's possession. Sharon was sure, though, he would have left the rest of the things in his case in the car rather than risk Gottbaum's seeing them.

And so it was clear enough: Gottbaum and his people had intercepted Jim on his way home, had removed the briefcase from the car, then arranged the "accident." She clenched her fists, making the nails bite into her palms. Then she realized what she was doing and carefully placed her hands flat on her knees. But as she calmed herself her emotions seesawed from anger to deep, bitter grief.

It had been a mistake to come here. She'd imagined that taking some sort of action would make her feel better; instead, it just showed her how helpless she was.

With unsteady hands she started her car, U-turned, and drove back toward Los Angeles.

Wish List

Much later, back in her apartment, when Damon was asleep and the baby-sitter had gone, Sharon sat at the dining table staring at the blank page of a yellow legal pad. Jim had always laughed at her for using a pen and paper. He said it was an anachronism, very twentieth-century, and sometimes he called her "the last of the literates." But there was something therapeutic about filling the lines with handwriting, feeling the ballpoint roll across the paper, seeing the text take shape.

Looking at the page, she relived the last twenty-four hours. Yesterday, Sunday, after she'd left Yumi at the airport, she'd come home and received another call from Jim, or from a voice that sounded just like him. He'd told her that his car was finally being repaired but had taken longer than he'd expected, and he felt too tired to start back to Granada Hills. He'd decided to stay one more night at a motel and head for home early Monday morning.

Tormented by the doubts that Yumi had created, Sharon had wanted to drive out to see him. No, he'd told her; that made no sense. "At least tell me where you're staying," she'd said. "What's the phone number?"

He'd started to answer, but the line had gone dead. Her phone had completely ceased to function; she couldn't dial out, and no further calls had come through until the police had contacted her early today, Monday, notifying her that they'd found a wrecked car registered in her husband's name. Identification of the driver had been impossible, and they wouldn't know who he was until they got the DNA sample back from the lab tomorrow. But there had been no doubt in Sharon's mind: the body in the car, the body that was now in their morgue, was of her husband.

She'd had nothing to lose, at that point, so she'd called Jim's squad supervisor, but he'd been out sick, and she'd spoken to Norm Harris, one of the agents Jim used to work with. Jim had told her about Harris once, and she knew they didn't get along. But she had no authority to ask to speak to someone else. And she didn't know who else to ask for, anyway: Jim hadn't been particularly close to anyone at the office.

Harris had said he would tell the local police to guard the car and not move it until someone from the FBI could get over there and check it out. He'd also made an appointment to see Sharon at his office tomorrow; but she could tell he had mentally classified her as a hysterical woman who was inventing conspiracy theories because she couldn't accept the fact that her husband had simply driven his car off the road.

At that point she'd called in sick to her own job, then gone out to look at the wreck herself. But the journey had achieved nothing. Could she hope to do any better in the days to come? She started writing on the legal pad:

> *Because he was incinerated in the fire, no way to determine whether Jim was murdered.*
> *The people who killed him were probably smart enough not to have left any evidence that his car was tampered with.*
> *Briefcase missing, must have been taken before the car was wrecked.*
> *Jim's own suspicions about Gottbaum, French, etc. were not*

properly supported by evidence, and the little evidence he did have was in the briefcase, which is now gone. He never got around to filing a report on LifeScan with the FBI.

Gottbaum is missing, perhaps will soon be dead, and therefore cannot be questioned.

Even if someone from FBI questions scientists at North Industries, they can simply deny everything. Why should anyone believe they would kill a federal agent? They are respectable people, not criminals.

How can I find out what they were really doing? Some way of investigating their equipment there, even though the work is all classified?

She stared at the list. It looked hopeless. She turned to a fresh page.

Number-one objective: find the people who killed Jim and bring them to justice.

Turn over to the FBI the documents and notes that Yumi gave me. Maybe this will help to convince them to investigate.

Check all hospitals for Gottbaum.

Try to contact North Industries and speak to French or her team.

Try to gain access to people caretaking Gottbaum's home, despite defense system Yumi says has been installed.

Try to convince KUSA staff there is a story here and I should be assigned to it on company time and pay.

And finally, on another page:

Funeral arrangements.

Where is Jim's will? Call attorney.

Close joint bank account.

Notify all friends. Send announcements.

Call life-insurance company.

Ask for a week off work.

Deal with Jim's possessions.

*Arrange daytime care for Damon and try to explain to him
what has happened.*

This was the worst list of all. She stared at it and felt herself
crying. Looking at the words through her tears, there was no
escape from the reality. Her husband was dead, and she was on
her own.

She went and lay on the couch, where she'd sat with him so
often. She cried for a long time, till all the tears were gone.
When there was nothing left and she felt empty and dead inside, she gradually fell asleep.

Police Procedure

The next day, at noon, she waited on a wooden chair in a
small, utilitarian lobby without any windows. A receptionist sat
in a cubicle behind a thick panel of armor glass, chatting on the
phone. Cool air trickled through a ceiling vent. Time passed
slowly.

When the access door to the offices opened and a big man in
a baggy suit came striding toward her, Sharon knew instinctively that he was Norm Harris. "Mrs. Bayley?" He came over
to her, looking busy and preoccupied but forcing a smile, as if
he really didn't have time for this but he was going to go
through the motions because he was a nice guy. "Real shame
about your husband. All of us here are kind of shook up about
it." He extended his hand to her.

She grasped it briefly. "Where can we talk?" she asked.

"Right this way. We use this room for taking statements. It's
soundproof, bugproof, who knows, it's probably waterproof as
well." He chuckled and gave her a grin as if to make it clear he
was sympathizing with her, trying to use a little humor to
lighten her burden. But she saw something in his eyes, a pruri-
ent interest, that made his big-buddy act look like a lie. He had
no real concern, she decided. There was a callousness about
him.

He ushered her into a room ten feet square, with walls

painted grubby beige, the floor covered in thin brown carpet.
Four chairs were positioned around a wooden table. She took
one and Harris sat down opposite her. "You know, it's too bad
we never got a chance to meet before," he was saying. "Terrible
thing to have to meet under these tragic circumstances. But you
know something? Your husband, he was always kind of a loner.
Didn't like to mix business and pleasure, family and business."
Harris shrugged. "His choice, right? I can respect that."

And yet, Sharon decided, Harris didn't respect it at all. What
was he telling her? That Jim hadn't been one of the guys, so
now he was gone, she shouldn't expect the guys to go out of
their way for her?

"I was really hoping your squad supervisor—" she began.

"Not back till next week," said Harris. He spread his hands,
then placed them palms-down on the table. "So all you got is
me. But believe me, Mrs. Bayley—it's Sharon, isn't it?—believe
me, Sharon, I'll do everything I can to help."

Maybe she was being unnecessarily paranoid, letting her
imagination run away with her, but she didn't believe him. And
yet, he was still a federal agent, wasn't he? It was his job to
conduct investigations. If she could convince him that there
were suspicious circumstances surrounding Jim's death, he
would have to file a report.

She laid Jim's compad on the table, and the binder containing the history of the LifeScan program. "I don't know if
you're aware of the case Jim was working on—"

"I looked it up." Harris gave her a cautious glance. "He told
you about it?"

"Yes. Everything."

Harris sighed and shook his head. "That's a violation of regulations right there. Our Jim, he never did it by the book. Used
to say he liked to follow his own track."

"Yes," said Sharon, repressing the emotions that came along
with the memories. "That's exactly what he said. But it
achieved good results, didn't it?"

"Sure! Sure it did! Don't get me wrong, the guy was very,
very talented. The work he did, I admired it. Some of it was
just incredible."

Sharon thought Harris more likely felt envy than admiration,
but she wasn't going to pursue that. "So let me tell you what

Jim had found out," she said. "I know you won't have looked any of *that* up, because he decided not to file his report till he had more material." And she started describing, step by step, the sequence of events from Little Asia to North Industries to Gottbaum's home.

Harris listened attentively, or seemed to. He didn't interrupt and he didn't hurry her. At the end of it he sat back in his chair, clasped his hands in front of his broad belly, and slowly shook his head. "What you've just told me," he said, "is what I call a string of suppositions in search of a theory. You say he got positive ID of this scientist, this Rosalind French?"

"That's what he told me."

"So where is it? Like you say, we don't have it. Not a damn thing."

She stared at him blankly. "He had the evidence in his briefcase, which was in his car, and is now missing. That in itself is further evidence that the wreck was not an accident."

"Well, all right, maybe so. But how do I know that? You see what I'm saying?"

She placed Jim's compad on the table. "All his notes are here. You'll find they confirm everything I've said."

Harris glanced at the compad but made no move to pick it up. "I don't have to tell you, Mrs. Bayley, electronic data of that kind is worthless as evidence. Anyone could have typed it into that unit. You could have. I could have."

She'd expected him to be skeptical, but she hadn't expected this. She felt as if everything was being taken away from her—all her hopes, her sense of justice. "Are you suggesting I'm making all this up?"

"Making it up? Hell, no!" Harris leaned forward. He reached out and patted one of her hands with his. "You're a sincere lady, Sharon. I can see that."

She fought the urge to pull away. Even though he was only touching the back of her hand, she felt as if she was being molested by him. She had to remind herself how much she needed his help. "So what are you saying?"

"I'm just saying, we're talking police procedure, here. We got to have evidence. We can't just go running with a bunch of wild ideas, hauling people in for questioning, arresting them on charges that don't make sense. You really think these people, these scientists, killed your husband? I mean, where's the motive?"

Grateful for an excuse to remove her hand from under his, she picked up the LifeScan report and slid it toward him. "This is the history of their research. If you read it carefully, and you bear in mind that they have succeeded in their aims while concealing this from their employers, you'll see that they have a strong motive to protect their work."

Harris opened the report. "Now, wait a minute. This is classified."

"Yes." She frowned at him. "You don't have a security clearance?"

"Sure, *I* do." He closed the folder, slapping his fat hand on the cover. "But Sharon, *you* sure as hell don't. Do you realize the penalties for unauthorized possession of classified military documents? Jesus Christ, we're talking espionage, here!"

She realized, finally, what was going on. She stood up, pushing her chair back, scraping its legs across the floor. "So arrest me." She clenched her fists and pushed her wrists out toward him as if she was ready for handcuffs. "If I'm a criminal, you should place me under arrest."

For the first time, Harris looked disconcerted by her. He laughed uneasily. "Now, that's not what I meant, Sharon. You know that."

"If you didn't mean it," she said, giving him a patronizing smile, "then why did you say it?" She felt the anger rising up, all the rage at what had happened to Jim suddenly focusing itself on the fat man sitting opposite her. She knew it wasn't in her interest, but she didn't care anymore. "Do you get some sort of pleasure from seeing a woman in a helpless position? Do you get off on tormenting her?"

Harris lumbered to his feet. He was no longer grinning. "Now, look, I know you've been under a whole lot of stress. But you don't have any right, Sharon——"

"You don't like it when someone calls it the way it is, do you?" she snapped. "Because you have no interest in the truth. It doesn't matter to you, what really happened or didn't happen. You're just interested in what's good for Norm Harris."

Muscles twitched in his face. With satisfaction, Sharon saw

that she had made him mad. "See here, I took time out of a busy day—"

"You resented having to take the time to see me, so you got your own back by watching me beg for help and toying with me a little. Well, the entertainment is over. Are you going to do anything with what I've told you, or not?" She clenched her jaw, feeling herself trembling. She folded her arms under her breasts so that he wouldn't see her hands shaking.

He grabbed the folder and shoved it under one arm. "I'll file a report."

"Will you send someone to question Rosalind French?"

"No, I don't think that's necessary." He stared at her, waiting for a reaction.

Sharon tried her best not to give him that satisfaction. "Are you going to have Jim's car checked for sabotage?"

He gave her a nasty little smile. "We already did that. Through the local PD. They called this morning, just before you arrived. Didn't find a damn thing."

So that was that. She hadn't expected them to, but it was a blow, nonetheless—assuming Harris was telling the truth. Without a word, she walked around the opposite side of the table and reached to open the door.

"Hey. Don't you want this?" He picked up the compad. "You could hang onto it, like for sentimental value."

She heard the sarcasm in his voice. "If you were such a buddy of Jim's," she snapped at him, "if you respected him so much, maybe you'd like to keep it yourself."

Dismissively, he threw the compad into a wastepaper bin in the corner.

She turned without a word, opened the door, and strode out.

Solace

Sharon could still remember when the window displays had been so big and bright that every weekend in the shopping mall had seemed like Christmas. She'd been a dreamy-eyed five-year-old, trailing behind her parents, staring up with an expression of wonder at the colors, the animated signs, the sales-point videos, the pyramids of food and consumer electronics. Walking into the mall had been like walking into a giant toy store.

The place had changed since then. There were still a few electric billboards and 3-D videos, still some high-tech gadgets, but ever since the premillennial depression the street level of the mall had been taken over by state-owned food and clothing outlets: giant stores like stripped-down K-Marts, drab aisles stocked with generic necessities. Meanwhile, on the second level, the little boutiques and gourmet snack stores had mostly turned into family businesses selling home-grown food and homemade clothes, and the multiscreen movie theater had become a lotto hall where Chicano women wagered their federal assistance checks to win Canadian vacations.

Yet Sharon still liked coming here, especially when she was feeling stressed. Wandering among the crowds, lost in her thoughts, looking at the stores without quite focusing on anything, she found a kind of numb tranquillity.

She bought a soyburger and sat in a little plaza under an ornamental glass canopy. Mostly old people hung out here these days, reading, gossiping, stuck in habits from forty or fifty years ago. A uniformed guard wandered around, chatting with the regulars.

The wood-grain Formica of Sharon's table was worn and chipped at the edges, and the floor was sticky underfoot, but she didn't really care. The mall had a mainly nostalgic appeal, and in any case, it was like background music: she could absorb it without really noticing it.

After a while she didn't feel angry with Norm Harris anymore. The main thing was to move forward rather than agonize over the past. She dragged her legal pad out of her bag, set it down beside her plate, and crossed one of the options off her list. She had taken her evidence to the FBI; that was now a dead issue.

But the remaining objectives no longer seemed to make much sense. Suppose, for instance, she actually found the hospital where Gottbaum was, or she located Rosalind French, or even gained access to Gottbaum's house. What could she possibly achieve if the FBI didn't believe her and there was insufficient evidence to arrest anyone?

She closed her eyes and imagined herself describing the situation to Jim. What would he tell her? To define her goals, most likely. She could be sharp-witted and precise critiquing other people's ideas, but when it came to her own she was distracted by all the possibilities. Sometimes she was still a little kid wandering around, staring at the world with wide-eyed wonder.

She turned to a new page. *Goals,* she wrote as a heading at the top. And then: *I wish to bring to justice the people responsible for Jim's death.*

But what did she really mean by *justice?*

I want them in jail.

Purely for revenge? Well, that was part of it. When she allowed herself to think about what had happened she felt a rage that was so intense, it seized control of her entire body. A group of people had stolen the greatest source of happiness she had ever known. Instinctively, she wanted to punish them, to destroy them for what they had done.

She tried to see past her emotions and look at the situation dispassionately. Did she have a rational imperative too? Yes. Other people should be protected from the fanaticism that had killed her husband. Whatever Gottbaum and his team were into, they should be stopped.

But how, if law-enforcement authorities were unwilling or unable to help?

Yumi had already given her the answer. Sharon was a journalist; she knew the power of publicity. If she could expose Gottbaum's activities—with documented facts, not just a bunch of suppositions—that would be sufficient. It might endanger her, and she was very much aware that she had more responsibility to Damon now than ever before. But she also owed it to him to expose the people who had killed his father.

Sharon finished her burger. It had tasted pasty and bland under the layer of spices. Old people who'd grown up in the twentieth century called them "shamburgers." But old people were always complaining. Most of them still seemed to think they had some sort of right as American citizens to eat meat, burn oil, and throw away garbage for their entire lives. She glanced around at the retirees at neighboring tables, reading magazines, dozing, staring into space. She wondered if that was how she would be one day, sitting around all day bitching about things.

The guard had wandered off, and she saw a panhandler heading her way. Clearly it was time to leave. She took her plate and tray back to the burger kitchen, then headed for the exit.

As she walked out to her car she realized she did have one advantage. Gottbaum and his people would not be expecting her to act against them. They didn't know that Yumi had confided in her. They would assume that Sharon would be passively mourning her husband, believing that his death had been a genuine accident.

She unplugged her car, got in, and drove slowly out of the parking lot, heading for home.

Gottbaum was undoubtedly well hidden in some private medical facility under an assumed name, and she didn't want to alert him by making inquiries. But she knew where the rest of the team worked, and she had seen the composite picture of Rosalind French. Gathering data on them—following them, if possible—should be her next step.

From the <u>Los Angeles Times</u>
Wednesday May 15, 2030

NOBEL PRIZE WINNER CHOOSES TO DIE
His Body Is Frozen

Leo Gottbaum, the Nobel prize–winning computer scientist best known for his outspoken, radical views on national issues, died yesterday aged 81. A cryonic facility in Glendale received his remains after he chose to end his life by refusing all food and fluids.

Louis Eckhardt, president of Cryonic Life Systems, Inc., confirmed that Gottbaum had elected to die just three days after he learned he was suffering from an inoperable brain tumor. "His life expectancy was no more than six months," Eckhardt said in a telephone interview. "During that time he would have suffered a lot of pain, and some brain damage that would probably have been irreversible. We respect his decision to be placed in suspension pending a time when his condition can be cured."

Dr. Gottbaum received a Nobel Prize in 1998 for his work developing artificial intelligence. The award sparked protests in the scientific community from those who disapproved of Gottbaum's frequent public diatribes against politicians, federal agencies, and the welfare state. In a series of media appearances during the late 1990s he described himself as an anarchist and attempted unsuccessfully to lead a national tax revolt in protest against the growth of centralized government. He also spoke out for the elimination of all welfare programs, abolition of the Federal Reserve, and removal of controls on scientific research.

He maintained a lower profile after the end of the twentieth century and devoted his energies to military research at North Industries in Long Beach until his retirement in 2020. A spokesperson at North Industries refused to reveal any details of Dr. Gottbaum's work there, as it remains classified.

Accident

She sat staring into the darkness, alone in her car, waiting without knowing exactly what she was waiting for. A Santa Ana wind was blowing, hot and dry, stirring up dust, bending the palm trees and tossing dead leaves and trash along the gutter. The wind was insistent: it buffeted the car and made little hissing, whistling noises around the edge of the windshield, preying on her nerves.

Even on a normal night she would have felt uneasy in this part of Long Beach. It had a high-crime, low-rent look—small, dilapidated homes losing their paint, rusty chain-link security fences with Intruder Alert warning signs, stray dogs rooting through garbage that had been left in cans without lids. It didn't make sense that a research scientist would choose to live here.

Sharon sat with her back against the door, her legs stretched out across the front seats. French's house was almost a block away, but she could see it clearly through the infrared scope that she'd borrowed from the supply room at KUSA. She'd followed French here from the lab at North Industries after staking it out for a couple of days, monitoring the main gate. Eventually, she felt sure, French would lead her to someone or something that was involved with the covert side of LifeScan, although tonight, the prospects weren't looking good.

She wished the people at KUSA had been willing to donate some of the station's manpower. She'd pitched it to them as forcefully as she could, but the news about Gottbaum's death had been the final strike against her. The old man was in a freezer, wasn't he? When they checked with Cryonic Life Systems, a spokesperson confirmed it. If Gottbaum had developed some kind of electronic immortality as Sharon claimed he had, why had he chosen to be sealed up in a dewar full of liquid nitrogen?

Sharon had told them she didn't believe Gottbaum was really there; that the cryonics people must have made some sort of deal to provide him with a cover story. But at that point her superiors stopped trying to humor her. They said that if she wanted to waste her time chasing this one down on her own for a couple of weeks she was free to do so; but please not to bother them again unless she came up with some real evidence to support her conspiracy theories.

And so here she was, peering through the scope, a thermos of coffee on the floor beside her, the radio tuned to a rock station to keep her awake and drown out the noise of the wind. She was weary and lonely, wishing she had someone to talk to, better still, someone who would believe her and share the burden.

There had been a crowd of family and friends, of course, at Jim's funeral, well-wishers all telling her they were eager to help in any way she wanted. But none of them had been people she could really confide in, and she hadn't dared to call Yumi for fear that Gottbaum's team might be monitoring her line.

That's why she was on her own in Long Beach at one-thirty in the morning, waiting for something to happen. Rosalind French had returned here from her laboratory an hour ago, and the windows of her home still glowed yellow. What was she doing in there? Did she leave the lights on while she slept?

Sharon flexed her legs to get the stiffness out of them. She put down the scope for a moment and rubbed her eyes, wondering how Jim coped with the boredom of this kind of work. He'd had an implacable persistence, like a cat. He could watch and wait for days, if necessary, if he thought he was really on the trail of something. But . . . she didn't want to think about Jim. She'd promised herself not to.

A faint noise attracted her attention. Someone slamming a door. She grabbed the scope again just in time to see French walking quickly from her house to her car parked outside her garage.

Sharon wriggled around, swinging her legs back under the

instrument panel. French, meanwhile, was starting her car, switching on the headlights, backing out of the driveway, and driving away down the street.

Sharon pulled out and started following her. There were no other cars, this late at night, so the only way to avoid being noticed was to hang back by at least four or five blocks. She sat tense, her hands tight on the steering, all her attention focused on the two tiny red lights in the distance. At least she wasn't tired anymore; adrenaline had taken care of that.

French's car made a sudden, unexpected right turn. Sharon bit her lip, afraid she might have dropped back too far. She accelerated, reached the corner, swung around it, and scanned the new road that she was on. It was long, straight, wide—and empty.

She muttered a curse, drove to the next intersection, slowed, and looked both ways. She saw a motorcycle in the distance, but nothing else.

She hit the instrument panel with her fist, unable to contain her frustration—then told herself to be rational, be methodical. French couldn't have evaporated; she must have made a turn a block farther on.

Sharon drove on along the street. A vehicle came up behind her; she vaguely noticed it in her rear-view mirror. It pulled out to overtake, then started cutting in. She gave a little shout of surprise as she realized how close it was coming. She jerked at the steering—too late. Her fender hit the side of the other car with a jolt and a crash of metal on metal. She jammed her foot down on the brake; her tires wailed across the concrete as her car slid to a halt.

The other vehicle stopped just in front of her. Sharon stared at it dumbly, still shaken from the impact. It was Rosalind French's car, she realized. French was jumping out, striding around it, holding something in her hand. She must have realized she was being followed; must have pulled in at the side of the road and killed her headlights while Sharon passed by.

Sharon cursed herself for being an amateur as she fumbled with the drive selector, her hands shaking badly as she tried to throw it into reverse. But French was coming closer, holding something that looked like an electronic handgun—yes, just

ike the one that Jim had brought back home after the surveil-
ance he'd done in Little Asia.

Sharon groped under her seat. She kept a pistol hidden there,
a .22 automatic that Jim had given her long ago. She hadn't
ired it in years. She didn't like guns. She'd promised herself to
be supercautious tracking French, doing everything at long
range so that there wouldn't be any need for weapons. She
fumbled under the seat—then realized her door wasn't locked.
She reached to lock it—as French jerked it wide open.

The hot wind wafted in and the woman stood there glaring at
Sharon, her face faintly visible in diffuse reflected light from the
headlight beams. She looked a wreck. She was unkempt, wild-
eyed, with pallid cheeks and dark shadows around her eyes.
The wind blew her hair into her face; angrily, she wiped it
aside. "What the hell do you think you're doing?" she shouted.
"Why are you following me?"

From the corner of her eye Sharon saw a light come on in
one of the houses fronting onto the street. A silhouette showed
in the window. Someone had heard the noise of metal on metal,
the squeal of tires. She wondered if she should shout for help.

"Goddam it, I want an answer!" French banged her fist on
the roof of the car.

Sharon flinched, then tried to rally her own anger. She, after
all, was the one who had more to be angry about. "I'm a journalist. I'm working on a story—"

"Bullshit. I know who you are; you're Bayley's wife. I have
tracking equipment, I monitored you when you were following
me home, and your picture's on file with the city. For that
matter, it's been on the goddammed evening news." She turned
away. "We're settling it," she shouted to a figure in a bathrobe
venturing out of another of the houses nearby. "We don't need
any help, no one's hurt, so go back to sleep." She sounded
unstable, punch-drunk. There was a wildness about her, as if
she felt she had nothing to lose and didn't give a damn.

Sharon steeled herself. "The reason I'm following you," she
said, "ought to be obvious."

"You mean your husband?" French made a dismissive gesture. "The man had an accident. He drove off the road."

"No." She pushed her way out of her car and stood up, her

anger giving her irrational strength now, as she confronted the other woman. "It was no accident. You killed him."

French gave Sharon a long, cold stare. Abruptly, she laughed. "He's not dead."

"That's insane. That's the stupidest—"

"All right, so I'll prove he's alive. Is that what you want? Then will you leave us alone?"

Sharon stared back at her. "I don't—"

"No, you don't understand. Look, just go back home and wait by your phone. Some time tomorrow he'll call you."

"No." Sharon shook her head violently. "It'll be a fake, just the same as—"

"I don't have time for this." She turned away from Sharon, strode back to her car, slammed the door, and accelerated away around the next corner, tires squealing.

By the time Sharon got back into her own car and started after her in pursuit, Rosalind French had disappeared into the night.

Digital Sampling

This time consciousness returned instantly, as if someone had turned a switch. Bayley found himself standing alone in a big, cold place, a huge chamber with a domed roof that glowed white, shedding a diffuse, uniform glow. Under his feet the floor, too, was white, patterned with a network of black lines.

The shift into consciousness came so suddenly, he found himself stumbling, turning around, unable to reorient himself. Images of wartime London were still vivid in his mind, and so was his panic at finding himself paralyzed, watching his world and his memories disintegrate.

But he was able to move again, now. And his mind seemed normalized, so far as he could tell. He still felt dizzy, though, and there was nothing in this huge arena to rest on or lean against. He dropped down to his knees, then sat cross-legged on the floor, closing his eyes, pressing his hands to his forehead.

After a moment he felt a little steadier, a little more confident. He focused on the floor in front of him and brushed his fingers across it. It was smooth and cool and hard, like polished stone. The lines on it were maybe a half centimeter wide, forming a complex pattern interrupted here and there by rectangles and other geometric forms. The pattern stretched away into the distance under the glowing dome, which seemed immense, maybe as much as a mile in diameter.

"Welcome back, Mr. Bayley," said a voice.

Bayley looked up. A figure had materialized a dozen feet away. It took a moment to recognize him: Leo Gottbaum, tall, enigmatic, with his hands clasped behind his back, looking like the master of all that he surveyed.

Bayley struggled up. He still felt unsteady, but he wanted to deal with Gottbaum face-to-face. As he stared at the man he felt conflicting emotions: caution, anger, fear.

For a moment, neither one said anything. "I'm still in MAPHIS," said Bayley. It was more a statement than a question.

"Of course," said Gottbaum. "But all the systems are functioning normally now."

Bayley remembered, again, his paralysis, his gradual loss of memory. He shivered. "What happened before? when everything . . . went blank?"

"It was a software problem, basically. We had to shut everything down and . . . reboot." He smiled faintly at his use of the archaic word.

"Then . . . how am I still alive?" said Bayley. "I felt my mind going, I felt it all falling apart."

"We maintained a file copy," said Gottbaum. "Let's see, on this schematic, it's located somewhere . . . over there." He gestured into the far distance.

Bayley looked at the pattern of lines on the floor. "This is a wiring diagram?"

"A complete schematic for MAPHIS, yes."

"And . . . you maintained an extra copy of my entire intelligence?"

Gottbaum gestured as if the questions were beginning to annoy him. "We did what any computer user does when he acquires a new piece of software. We made a backup. There's a file copy of every infomorph, and it's constantly updated with internal events. That's how you can remember the process of losing your memory."

Bayley shook his head. This wasn't what he wanted to deal with. He looked away for a moment, trying to organize his thoughts. What did he really want? He felt, again, his sense of loss and isolation. Standing in front of him was the man who was responsible for it. Or, a replica of the man.

"Are you really in here with me?" he asked, feeling unpleasantly vulnerable, in no position to express his anger at what had been done to him. "Or are you outside, projecting an image of yourself in here? or what?"

"I'm an infomorph now, just like you." Gottbaum spoke

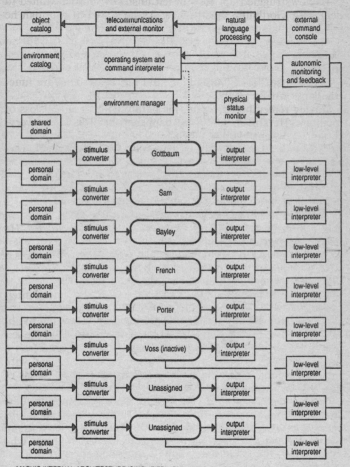

MAPHIS INTERNAL ARCHITECTURE (SIMPLIFIED) Bidirectional data flow except where indicated by arrows

gently, calmly, as if he understood what Bayley must be feeling. "I was subjected to the same procedure that you experienced. Of course, it wasn't such a rush job; we'd cataloged my sensory responses several months previously. But I died on the operating table as you did, and my mind was scanned as yours was."

Bayley could no longer mask his anger. "You chose it," he said, with disgust. "I didn't."

"You seem to be nursing some resentments, Mr. Bayley."

He laughed bitterly. "Do you blame me?"

"No. But maybe I can calm you down a little."

Bayley felt something change inside him, as if his mind was being washed from within. His emotions literally drained away. Within a few seconds he was tranquil, no longer caught between the instinct to run and the impulse to lash out. He looked at Gottbaum and knew, logically, he should be feeling scared and full of hate; but all the emotional overtones had gone.

Gottbaum smiled as if Bayley's confusion gave him some slight amusement. "MAPHIS is the ultimate tranquilizer," he said. "Always online, always ready to normalize your autonomic responses for you. You see the advantages, Mr. Bayley? No more fits of resentment, jealousy, or depression. We finally have the capability to free our thoughts from the primitive urges and reflexes of animal behavior."

Bayley felt as if the man had stolen something from him. He stepped back involuntarily, though the vast arena offered no place to go. "I . . . don't want you in my head," he said. "I don't want you making me into a robot. Emotions are a part of being human."

Gottbaum shrugged. "If you really want your emotions back, I'll restore them to you in a little while. And I assure you that for the most part, I'll be glad to stay out of your head, as you put it. You must understand, though, that not all informorphs are created equal. I have what those of us in the computer trade call privileged access to MAPHIS. After all, I invented it, so I should be allowed some control over it, don't you agree?"

"You mean, you deserve to play god?" Bayley made a sound of disgust.

Gottbaum turned away as if he was losing interest in the conversation. A couple of large, soft armchairs materialized nearby. He walked across to one of them and sank into it, seeming completely at home in the immense arena under the white dome. "Sit down, Bayley. I have some things to tell you."

Bayley avoided looking at the man. He stood where he was and said nothing.

Gottbaum sighed. "You do realize, I hope, the extent of my control over your sensory input? I can add to it just as easily as I subtracted from it. I have access to all your pain receptors. It would be barbaric, of course, but I really don't have time to mess around, Bayley."

He saw the hopelessness of passive resistance. Gottbaum's threat didn't scare him, because his emotional responses were still being neutralized; but he remembered clearly how he had suffered when he'd first found himself in MAPHIS, and he didn't doubt that Gottbaum could provide him with a rerun of that experience, or worse.

Fatalistically, he went and sat in the chair.

Gottbaum gave him a curt nod. "All right, now let's understand each other." There was a new edge to his voice. "I have about as much use for you as I have for a bacterium. I dedicated the last thirty years of my life to research which I happen to believe will enable an immense evolutionary step for the entire human race. My work was almost complete when you came poking around, full of asinine ideas about what should and shouldn't be allowed. I could have had you destroyed, do you understand that? Instead, for ethical reasons, we chose to preserve your intelligence in our system. You're *immortal* now. You're not some small-time cop anymore, putting people in jail when they do things the government doesn't like. There are incredible possibilities available to you if you choose to take advantage of them."

Bayley squirmed in his chair. He wanted to shut Gottbaum up, wanted to escape, somehow, from the feeling of being trapped and controlled. "You're forgetting a few things," he said. "There's a woman and child out there who gave my life meaning. Maybe family doesn't mean anything to you; you obviously have no use for your own daughter. But most people think it's pretty damned important."

Gottbaum waved one hand. "I readily agree, you lost your stake in the game. But that's the risk you took when you started interfering. And you got one hell of a consolation prize. Look at me, man!"

As Bayley watched, Gottbaum's face changed. The wrinkles filled out and erased themselves. The gaunt look was replaced with a glow of well-being. The scrawny neck became thicker, stronger. In less than a minute Gottbaum was transformed from a man of eighty-one to a man in his twenties.

"I realize," Bayley said, "that we can be immortal in here, so long as the hardware exists to enable our survival. But if it merely prolongs pain, immortality is not necessarily a blessing."

Gottbaum gave him a scornful look. "Bayley, you have a classic case of what we used to call, in my young day, bad vibes. You're so preoccupied with what you've lost, you can't see what you've gained. I'm going to try to improve your attitude." He stood up.

"Why not just leave me alone?" Bayley said.

"Because, unfortunately, we're stuck with each other. As you already discovered, MAPHIS has trouble making a pseudomorph talk and act entirely like a real person. There's only room for eight fully functional infomorphs in here, so you and I are going to need each other for conversation, if nothing else. Unless, of course, you want to be terminated? If so, tell me now. We can use the space for someone who'll appreciate it."

Once again Bayley felt the man's power over him. And he remembered the way he had felt when the simulation had frozen up and he'd been paralyzed, watching his world wink out of existence.

"I don't want to die," he said, avoiding Gottbaum's eyes.

"Then come with me." As he spoke, a long, straight staircase descended from the domed roof. It looked as if it was made of polished steel, gleaming in the diffuse white light. The bottom of it touched the floor nearby, and Gottbaum gestured Bayley to start climbing. Remembering the penalty for disobedience, he did as he was instructed.

The stairs became an escalator. Despite himself, he felt a sense of wonder. Gottbaum was right; there were immense possibilities—if one could forget the concomitant sense of loss.

"You should take a moment to observe the basic architecture of MAPHIS," Gottbaum said, standing behind Bayley and gesturing at the circuit diagram covering the floor of the arena as the escalator carried them up toward the roof. "In particular, you should understand the principle of domains. As an infomorph, you possess your own *personal domain,* in which you have complete control over your environment and no other infomorph can intrude against your will."

"Unless they have privileged access," Bayley said grimly.

"True, but I assure you, I won't be using it arbitrarily. In any case, at this time, you're in my domain. The reconstruction of your apartment, of course, was in yours."

A door had opened in the roof at the top of the escalator, revealing a rectangle of blue sky. Bayley found himself moving up and through the opening onto a hillside of tall grass. He shaded his eyes from bright sunlight, blinking at his new surroundings. Farther down the hillside there were pine trees, and beyond them, the ocean. A gentle breeze touched his face.

He turned and saw a geodesic dome on the summit of the hill.

"I remade my home just as you remade yours," said Gottbaum. He emerged from the stairs, and the door in the hillside sealed itself and vanished. "Oh, look who's here." He gestured to a woman sitting cross-legged in the grass a short distance away, her head bowed over a book in her lap.

"Your daughter," said Bayley. "Are you telling me she's been scanned and stored as well?"

"Certainly not. I doubt she would wish to be, and I'm not at all sure I'd let her in if she did." Gottbaum paused, looking thoughtful. He still had the dignity and the measured speech of an elderly man; his youthful appearance made a strange contrast. "I remade Yumi as a pseudomorph," he went on, "to go with the dome. After thirty years of battling with her in the outside world, I liked the idea of being able to rebuild her the way I want her. Come on."

He led the way across the hillside and Bayley followed. The grass, he noticed, was an imperfect simulation. The hundreds of thousands of individual blades stood motionless despite the gentle breeze, and where he pushed through them they flexed away from his tread with a stiff, jerky motion.

"Yumi," Gottbaum called to her, "this is James Bayley.

Maybe you remember him, although, come to think of it, he told us his name was Richard Wilson at that time."

She looked up. Her features were exactly the way he recalled them, but her expression was different, showing none of the reserve he had seen in reality. She had the happy innocence of a retarded child. "Hi," she said, with a sunny smile. "How are you?"

"I'm just showing Bayley around," said Gottbaum.

"That's nice." She smiled some more.

"Maybe you two should get together sometime," Gottbaum said, turning to Bayley. "I seem to recall, you went out of your way to speak to her, the first time you met. I assure you, she can be much more . . . cooperative, here, than in the outside world."

Bayley said nothing. He stared at Yumi's face.

She turned back to Gottbaum. "Is there anything I can do for you, Father?" Her voice was higher-pitched than it used to be, cute and girlish.

"Not right now, thank you, Yumi."

"Are you sure?" She sounded eager to please.

"No. Go back to your book. Come on, Bayley. This way."

"Maybe see you later, Jim," she called after Bayley as he followed Gottbaum up the hillside.

Even though he knew the woman was merely a computer construct with no real identity or sense of self, Bayley felt angry, as if something had been violated, someone betrayed. He remembered how moody and ambivalent Yumi had seemed in the real world. Her complexity was a large part of what had made her human.

"Is that really how you always wanted her?" Bayley asked, as they approached the dome. "Like . . . a pet?"

Gottbaum gave him an enigmatic look. "You disapprove, is that it? You think there's something sacred about reality, and we're violating some natural law by monkeying around with it."

"I think," said Bayley, "that if you edit your life, removing every little thing that might displease you, you're liable to forget what it really means to be a human being."

Gottbaum laughed. It was a braying sound, scornful and dismissive. "But I'm *not* a human being, Bayley, and neither are you. We're infomorphs. We don't owe any debts to the real world, any more than an escaped prisoner owes debts to the cell he used to live in. We can run this place any way we please, and there are no penalties to pay. Get that straight."

He opened the door in the dome and led Bayley inside.

The interior looked much as he remembered it, although there was less mess, presumably because Gottbaum now had MAPHIS—or maybe his remake of Yumi—to serve as a cleaning woman. A large golden retriever came running over, knocking a stack of documents off one of the chairs as it passed. It barked loudly, jumped up, and pawed Bayley's chest.

"Down, Sam," said Gottbaum. "Down!"

Bayley tried to push the animal off him. He'd never felt comfortable around dogs. He raised his knee, nudging the retriever away; but it circled around and jumped him again.

Gottbaum stepped forward, grabbed the dog by the collar, and hauled it back. "Sorry about this, Bayley." He didn't sound particularly sorry. "There are some things here that even I don't control."

"No?" said Bayley. "You made it, didn't you?" He had to shout above the sound of the dog's insistent barking.

"Sam isn't a pseudomorph, if that's what you mean. He's a real dog. I owned him for many years. He was our last animal test subject; I decided to keep him in MAPHIS so long as we had the processing power and the memory to spare." He turned to the dog. "Sit!" he said sternly.

Sam sat. He looked up at Gottbaum, waiting for further instructions.

"See, Bayley," Gottbaum went on, "one day, depending how things work out in realspace, we'll be able to upgrade MAPHIS. When it's bigger, we'll have more room to play in. You'll be able to fill it with infomorphs of your choice: birds, cats, dogs, even some of your old friends, assuming they're willing to make the transition. Who knows, you could get your wife and child in here if that's what you want."

Bayley felt a sudden surge of hope, negated almost at once by stoic resistance. "I would never let them make that sacrifice," he said.

Gottbaum looked disgusted. "You're clinging to your old values the same way fundamentalists cling to the Old Testament. Look, where would you like to go? ancient Rome? New Zealand? Egypt? Name it, Bayley."

"It's your show," he said.

"All right, step outside. Go on." He nodded toward the door.

Cautiously, Bayley opened it. The blue sky, grass, and sun were gone. Instead he found himself in an ash-gray wilderness, dusty plains and craters punctuated with spiky volcanic ridges that had never been blunted by wind and rain. He felt a lurching, falling sensation, as if he were in an elevator just beginning its descent. The sun was unusually bright, glaring down from a sky that was totally black. Hanging just above the horizon was a mottled blue-and-white sphere: planet Earth.

"We're on the Moon, Bayley," said Gottbaum, stepping out beside him. "And since infomorphs don't need to breathe, you don't even need a space suit. How do you like the low gravity, eh?" He ran forward in a series of soaring leaps, then made one final jump that took him twenty feet above the ground. He landed on an outcropping of rock and paused there, surveying the landscape.

Bayley glanced behind him. The dome was gone. He felt untroubled by the sudden transition; evidently, his emotional responses were still being neutralized. He flexed his leg muscles experimentally and felt himself rise up and back to the surface —slowly, slowly. He stooped and dug his hand into the dust, then let it trickle through his fingers. The particles drifted down as though they were falling through water.

"I'm old enough to remember Apollo XI," said Gottbaum, leaping off his rock, landing gently beside Bayley. "You know, back then we used to imagine that there'd be permanent colonies on the Moon by the time the twenty-first century rolled around."

"Before the realignment of social priorities," Bayley said, barely aware of what Gottbaum was saying. He was staring at the landscape, impressed despite himself. The Moon had been exhaustively mapped, and the data was readily available, so it would have been easy enough for MAPHIS to create the environment. The same would be true of Mars, Venus, the satellites of Jupiter—

"Social priorities," Gottbaum was saying with an expression

of disgust. "You mean, using seed corn to feed the poor instead of teaching them to plant it and grow their own. That's why the whole damn world stagnated after the turn of the century. That's why the future turned out like a low-budget version of the past. But let's not get into that. Close your eyes, Bayley. Go on."

Bayley did as he was told.

"Now open them."

His weight returned to normal, making him stagger and almost lose his balance. He blinked and found himself suddenly back on Earth, high in the mountains. Snowy peaks stood all around, embedded in a blanket of soft white cloud that hid the valleys below. He was beside Gottbaum on a rocky ledge, totally alone in the absolute stillness. The air was thin and terribly cold.

"Maybe we should warm things up a little," said Gottbaum. As he spoke, the temperature changed—from below freezing to the midseventies. "Anything you want, Bayley, remember? Anything at all! Have you ever wanted to fly?" As he spoke, he leaped off the ledge into space.

Though it was a simulation, it looked as real as all the other scenes Bayley had witnessed inside MAPHIS. With abstracted surprise he saw Gottbaum plummet down through the thin, clear air. But then the man's figure seemed to hit an updraft. With his arms spread like a skydiver he spiraled around, gaining altitude. "Try it!" he shouted as he soared past the ledge where Bayley stood. He grabbed Bayley's collar, hauling him forward. "Jump!"

Black rock streaked with snow started racing past him, and the cloud layer zoomed up from below. His shock seemed to override the dampers on his emotions, and he experienced a moment of pure panic, viscerally certain that he was falling to his death. But then a hand seemed to catch him and he swooped out from the cliff face, wheeling around, climbing through the air. He spread his arms and shifted his weight and found he could control his altitude, maneuvering as if he had wings. Panic turned to elation; he experienced the thrill of hang-gliding without the cumbersome equipment and without the risk.

"But if this isn't your pleasure, maybe you'd prefer to take it easy on the beach," Gottbaum shouted as he drifted alongside.

The mountains disappeared. Bayley's body thumped down into soft sand. The kaleidoscopic shift in location hammered his senses like a jump cut in a 3-D video. He lay on his stomach, staring straight ahead, breathing heavily. He saw pure white sand and an untouched, unspoiled bay where the ocean was turquoise and the sky was cloudless blue. Slowly, he rolled over. He realized his clothes had gone; he was wearing nothing but a pair of swim shorts. He looked down at his body and found he had suddenly become younger, more muscular, deeply tanned.

Slowly, he got to his feet. He was heavier, but his new strength more than compensated for that. He felt powerful; it was a strange, seductive sensation.

"When I was thirteen, I used to wish I could look like this," said a voice behind him.

He turned and found Gottbaum standing behind him, remade with the same weight-lifter's physique as Bayley's.

"All I wanted," he went on, "was a body that would make empty-headed young women find me irresistible. It's a common enough fantasy, and I outgrew it as soon as I realized there were more important things in life than hormones. But now that I have the time and the freedom, Bayley, I must admit I like to dabble in some of the experiences that were denied me in those days. How about you?"

Part of Bayley's imagination was still soaring around mountain peaks, and part was still exploring dusty lunar seas. "What you're describing might be satisfying in a way," he said, trying to focus on his surroundings, "if it was less contrived."

"It can be as contrived or as uncontrived as you want," said Gottbaum. "Look at those women over there." He nodded toward a couple of teenagers in bikinis, sitting on a blanket, rubbing suntan lotion on each other. "They can take one look at you and swoon, or they can act hard to get, whichever you want. Alternatively, you can simply walk over to them, rip their swimsuits off, and do what you like with them. MAPHIS will be happy to oblige."

"What if they were infomorphs?" Bayley objected.

"In that case, you'd be prohibited from harming them. There

are two classes of information entity, Bayley. Pseudomorphs, whom we can create, erase, and reward or abuse in any way we like; and infomorphs, who are people with inalienable rights, including the freedom to be left alone."

"And then there's you," Bayley added. "Gottbaum, master of the universe."

Gottbaum shrugged. "Look at it that way if you want. But I'm a more benevolent deity than anything people believe in in the outside world. I've already given you everlasting life, immunity from disease, unlimited wealth, and the ability to change bodies and personalities as easily as changing into a different suit of clothes. You shouldn't be resenting me, Bayley. You should be worshiping me."

Bayley looked at the young women. It was still hard to accept that they had been created as a pattern of electrons, no more real than the sheep in Old Macdonald's Farm.

"Let's take a walk by the sea while you think it over," said Gottbaum.

Bayley followed the man across the sand. It felt warm and gritty under his bare feet, just the way sand was supposed to feel. The sun was hot on his head and shoulders, and gulls cried to one another above the rhythmic sound of the waves.

"It's all . . . very authentic."

"Yes, Jeremy did a good job. He did most of the programming of the section we call the Environment Manager. Of course, static scenery is easy enough; it's just digitized video, processed through a converter that's been initialized to match the coding of your particular nervous system. Audio, taste, smell, and touch are mixed in, in much the same way. But things become a little more complicated when we have multiple objects moving around, especially when there's a lot of them. That really uses up processing power. The grass outside my dome, for instance. There's no way to track the motion of every blade. Likewise, the ocean, here. You notice when the waves break, the foam doesn't look right? We approximate it with fractals, but you get a lack of detail, a clumsiness to it."

Bayley saw what Gottbaum meant. The waves looked viscous as they reared up, and they became fuzzy and indistinct as they broke.

"But let's not quibble over the details," said Gottbaum. "I

think you have to agree, overall, I've shown you some formidable advantages to being here."

Bayley suddenly had the odd sense that Gottbaum had been selling him something. "I'm impressed by the possibilities," he said cautiously.

"So you should be. God, Bayley, if people in the outside world could understand the potential! I never wanted to run this on a clandestine basis, you know. But the general public has a bad history of destroying inventions that promise to improve their lives. In 1812, you may recall, at the dawn of the industrial revolution, mobs of Luddites went around smashing textile machinery. Things haven't changed since then. You yourself—you would have shut us down if you'd had the chance."

"Only because you misappropriated twenty billion in public money," said Bayley.

Gottbaum gestured dismissively. "I'm perfectly willing to share the benefits of this research—which are worth a hell of a lot more to the public than some new weapons system, incidentally. All I wanted was a chance to develop the concept without interference. And that's still all I want, even now."

"Well, there's nothing to stop you, with me out of the way. I never even filed a report."

"Yes," Gottbaum agreed, "we dealt with you quite satisfactorily. But . . . there is the new problem, now, of your wife." He turned and gestured at the idyllic Caribbean landscape. The sun dimmed; the beach seemed to dissolve into soft focus. "Let's go back to your apartment, Bayley."

Scare Tactics

Gottbaum was his old self again—literally. Once more he had bushy white hair, rumpled clothes worn with casual disregard for style, his face marked with deep, grim lines. He looked around at the furnishings in Bayley's living room with an air of mild disdain, like an aristocrat visiting the humble cottage of a peasant farmer, then seated himself at one end of the couch.

Bayley found himself standing in the center of the room. He looked down, checking his appearance. His physique was now normal, as were his clothes. His emotions had returned; he no longer felt dead inside. He was confused, ambivalent, shaken by the kaleidoscopic sequence of experiences. At the same time, it was a relief to *feel* again.

"MAPHIS saved your little exercise in computer-aided design," Gottbaum said, gesturing at the room they were in. "Just in case you wanted to come back to it some time."

"I see." Bayley slowly sat down in an armchair opposite the man.

"MAPHIS also saved the model you developed of your wife," Gottbaum went on. "Personally, I felt you gave up a little too easily, there. There were still some possibilities for development."

"I suppose you monitored the whole thing," Bayley said.

"Yes, as it happens, I did."

Bayley told himself not to dwell on it. He was still uncomfortably aware of Gottbaum's power; there was obviously no point in being confrontational. "So what were you saying about Sharon, just a moment ago? She's causing some sort of problem for you?" He didn't believe that was possible; but if, somehow, it was true, he felt proud and glad.

Gottbaum leaned back, stretched out his legs, and crossed his ankles. "Let me explain the situation. As you may remember, in realspace we made it look as if you had had an, ah, accident."

"I remember Rosalind French said it was going to be a car crash."

"Correct. We made sure there were severe head injuries followed by an intense fire, to destroy most of the physical evidence. Now, according to local police records, your wife visited the wreck, ostensibly looking for your briefcase. She also visited someone at your department of the FBI, though we don't know what was said. We believe she tried to convince her superiors at her workplace to do a story on LifeScan, and a call was made to Cryonic Life Systems asking to verify that my own body was being kept there."

Bayley thought of Sharon struggling with her grief, but still going and digging for facts, fighting to find out what had really happened. He felt a pang of longing; her courage and dedication were part of what he loved about her.

"More recently," Gottbaum went on, "she started following Rosalind French. Her timing was unfortunate; Rosalind was on the point of making her own transition to infomorph status, and didn't care much for the harassment. She impulsively challenged your wife, denied you were dead, and offered to prove it if your wife would agree to leave us alone."

Bayley smiled despite himself. He wished he could have witnessed that particular scene.

"It's not as amusing as you seem to think," Gottbaum said sharply. "Just remember that if your wife ever manages to attract the attention she seems to want, there'll be an outcry. Computer scientists killing people and peeling their brains in a laboratory after hours . . . Can you imagine the headlines? Politicians always love a chance to scare people and whip up a lynch mob. It distracts everyone from more important issues. They'd go out of their way to stage a crusade to stop this blasphemous research. Yes, they'd bring god into it. And they'd find MAPHIS, and they'd cut the power. Count on it, Bayley! No matter that they'd be wiping us out in here and trashing thirty years of research. They'd pull the plug without hesitation or remorse."

Bayley was shifting uncomfortably, unhappy about being lectured but realizing that Gottbaum's analysis was probably correct. "You said there's always a backup copy of our minds," he said.

"Yes, and it's safely stored in nonvolatile media. But it's useless without MAPHIS's specialized computer architecture to support it. It wasn't just the software and the scanning techniques that took thirty years to develop. The hardware, too. Do you think they'd allow that to survive in one piece? Would you bet your life on it?"

Bayley felt cornered, still loyal to Sharon, but forced to admit that her actions were liable to jeopardize his survival as an infomorph. "All right, so it's in our interests for the police and the press to be kept away from MAPHIS. What do you expect me to do? Tell Sharon to be a good little girl and go back to reporting on city hall and say nothing more about LifeScan ever again? Hell, you won't even let me talk to her on the phone."

Gottbaum stood up. He moved toward Bayley, leaning over him, glowering down. "You will be allowed to talk to her. And yes, that's exactly what you will tell her. Because if she exposes us to public scrutiny, she stands a good chance of killing you, Bayley. Permanently." He straightened up, then, and turned away. "Pick up the phone when it rings," he said, gesturing at the unit beside Bayley's chair. And with that he walked out of the apartment, slamming the door behind him.

Hostage

Bayley waited by the phone. He found it hard to concentrate. His yearning for Sharon cut across logic and shouted down his fumbling attempts to map a strategy. He wasn't sure to what extent he believed Gottbaum, or trusted him. He wanted her; that was all he really knew.

He considered telling MAPHIS to blank his emotions again so that he could think more clearly. And yet, he didn't want to feel dead inside. He needed to feel his love for her.

The phone rang. He jerked in his chair, startled by the sound —then grabbed the receiver. At first he heard nothing, not even hiss on the line. Of course, it was a simulation, like everything else. Some distant circuit in MAPHIS was operating to patch the audio signal through to him, converting it for direct input to the replica of his mind.

"Hello?"

She sounded very unsure of herself. It was her, though; he was immediately convinced that it was really her. He imagined her in the real-life version of the same room that he was in, sitting on the edge of her chair as she did when she was excited about a call, resting her elbows on her knees, staring fixedly in front of her.

"Hello, is anyone there?" Now there was a plaintive, fearful note in her voice.

He realized he had been so caught up in his own feelings, he hadn't said anything. "Sharon," he said. "Sharon, don't hang up."

There was a long silence on the line. "Jim?" He could hear the doubt in her voice.

"It's me," he said. "It really is. God, I wish—" He felt his isolation, the unbridgeable gap between them. There was no point in wishing when none of the things he wanted was remotely possible.

"How do I know it's you?" Her voice was shaky but defiant.

"I can prove it's me," he told her. "I remember what you were wearing when we first met. Lime-green T-shirt and white pants. And you were eating a sandwich with bean sprouts in it. And—you had a cat named Marcus, and the first time you kissed me good night you tried to kiss me on the cheek because you said later you were afraid you liked me too much and you wanted to hold back and keep things under control, so we didn't make love till that night we went to see that foreign movie but the theater was closed because of damage in the big quake, and—"

"Stop." She was crying, now. He heard her sniffing back the tears. "Stop, please. I believe you. Don't go on."

He imagined her sitting alone with no one to hold her and comfort her. "Sharon—"

"Where *are* you, Jim? They . . . found your body in the wreck. That's what they said. They used DNA sampling to make a positive ID. They can't have made a mistake. What *happened?*"

He tried to summon his strength. She had to know, and there was no point in stretching it out or trying to talk around it. "They caught me. Outside in the street. Gottbaum's people. They were afraid I'd shut down their whole project, which I would have, but they didn't want to kill me, so they used me in their research. You remember I told you about LifeScan? I was wrong about it being a failure and a waste of money. They've made it work. Jesus, have they made it work."

"What are you trying to tell me?" Her voice was steadier, now.

"They made a copy of my mind, neuron-for-neuron. I feel as if I'm still a person, but . . . I'm in a huge data-processing system somewhere. I'm not sure where. Although, it could be in Gottbaum's place on the coast; god knows he has enough equipment there." He hesitated. "Do you understand—"

"Of course I understand! I've been doing—doing some reading. I know what you're talking about. But Gottbaum too? Is he with you?"

"Yes. In fact he's undoubtedly monitoring this call."

A long pause on the line. "I want to punish them, Jim." Her voice was still shaky, but he could hear her anger.

"Honey, if you expose them, there'll be public backlash. The whole system may be shut down. The . . . system that's sustaining me."

Another pause. Then, loudly: "So what the fuck am I supposed to do? *nothing?*"

"I don't know. I'm going crazy without you. It's my own fault, I didn't take the proper precautions, I was so sure—"

"Don't blame yourself," she told him sharply. "You mustn't do that."

Again, he visualized her. And his son; was he there too? "Is Damon okay?" he asked. "I think about him a lot. I'd like to talk to him, except . . . I guess that would be too confusing for him. I mean, you've told him I'm—I'm dead? Did you explain—"

"I'm sorry, Bayley." Gottbaum's voice cut in on the line. "I hate to have to keep doing this to you, but we need to suspend operations for a while. We're uploading French as an infomorph, and during that period most functions of MAPHIS have to be suspended."

"Is that Gottbaum?" Sharon yelled down her phone.

"Yes," said Bayley.

"Where's my husband?" she shouted, irrational, aware of it, but not caring whether she made sense or not. "Damn you, I want—"

"Your husband will be fine, Mrs. Bayley, so long as the system sustaining him is not interfered with in any way. We'll try and arrange for him to contact you again. But now I'm afraid this call has to be interrupted."

The line went dead. Bayley stared at the phone feeling bereft, infinitely lonely. And then the lights in the room slowly started to dim like the lights in a movie theater, and he felt his mind growing muzzy, his thoughts becoming sluggish.

He slumped back in his chair, dropping the phone. "Sharon," he muttered, as the darkness invaded his mind.

From the <u>Los Angeles Times</u>
Tuesday, May 21, 2030

SCIENTISTS KILLED IN BURNING
LABORATORY

Three scientists working on secret military research were burned to death early Monday morning when a fire broke out in their laboratory at North Industries, a defense contractor in Long Beach.

Firefighters struggled for two hours before finally quelling the inferno shortly before dawn. It was thought that chemicals stored in the laboratory contributed to the intensity of the fire, but a spokesperson for North Industries stated that its exact cause is still unknown.

The three bodies discovered amid the wreckage were so badly burned as to be unrecognizable, but all were wearing company-issued identity bracelets. Their names were supplied to reporters as Rosalind French, Hans Voss, and Jeremy Porter.

"At this point we have no idea how the tragedy occurred," said Colonel Ellis Horton, Chief Scientist at North Industries, "but we will be conducting a thorough investigation. It is possible that these people failed to comply with some of our standard safety procedures. We have strict regulations to prevent this kind of incident. Nothing like it has ever occurred here before."

Colonel Horton was unable to explain why the building's sprinkler system failed to put out the blaze, or how the scientists could have been trapped in a laboratory from which there were two exits at ground level. Firefighters speculated that the victims might have been knocked unconscious or electrocuted in an accident that incapacitated them before the fire broke out.

Heaven

Two days had passed since the phone call from Jim. The MealMaker was cooking breakfast, Damon was playing with his junior talking encyclopedia on the DVI, and Sharon was standing at the kitchen counter paging through the fax-*Times* when she saw the item about North Industries tucked away at the back of the metro section.

She'd been planning to go in to work that morning, thinking that if she started following a normal routine again, she might stop feeling so distressed and unstable. But as she read about the fire at the laboratory, she started thinking about all the things she was trying to forget.

She didn't believe, of course, that French, Voss, and Porter had been burned to death. They were no more dead than her husband or Leo Gottbaum. They had had themselves scanned and resuscitated, or reanimated, or reincarnated—she still wasn't sure quite how she should think of it. Either way, they were beyond justice now; there was no possible way to arrest or detain them, no way to hold them accountable for what they'd done. No doubt they were being sustained inside the same equipment that was sustaining Jim, in which case shutting off the power that kept them alive would kill him, too.

She wondered if they'd planned the fire from the beginning, to get rid of all the evidence, human and otherwise. It seemed such a drastic measure. In fact, the more she thought about it, the less likely it sounded. Surely they could have smuggled some of their equipment out before torching the place. They wouldn't simply throw away thirty years of research.

But it was all supposition. She was still helpless, with no one assisting her, no way of knowing what was really going on.

Three nights ago she had come home from her confrontation with Rosalind French feeling shaken and full of fear. She'd spent the next day hiding in the apartment with Damon, wondering and waiting, not answering the door, too nervous to venture even as far as the nearest supermarket.

But then the phone call from Jim had come through, proving that he was still alive, if *alive* was the word for it. And at that point she'd realized why Rosalind French had driven away into the night without looking back, and why there was really nothing to fear from any associates of Gottbaum's who were still active in the outside world. They had no reason to threaten Sharon's life. They had demonstrated to her, quite graphically, that they were holding her husband as a perpetual hostage. If she somehow convinced the authorities to investigate, their very act of doing so could kill Jim. A careless programmer trying to disassemble an immensely complicated computer system, a public witch-hunt to stamp out "inhuman" research; that's all it would take. And so she had been immobilized, fully aware of her antagonists but unable to act.

"Mommy?" Damon was standing in the kitchen doorway. "Mommy!"

She realized she'd been staring into space, ripping the newsfax into little ragged strips, oblivious to the everyday world. Making an effort, she turned to him and forced a smile. "What is it, honey?"

"MealMaker said the food's cooked. He said it five minutes ago."

She turned and found, sure enough, the plates were waiting in the warmer. She shook her head, angry with herself. "I was thinking of something else, and I didn't hear." She carried the dishes to the table. "Come sit with me; we'll eat breakfast together. I think maybe I'm going to stay home again."

He climbed up onto the chair beside hers. "Why, Mommy?" He gave her an odd look, as if what she had said had worried him.

"I guess I just don't feel like going to work," she told him, trying to keep it light.

He didn't make a move to eat his food. He kept staring at her. "Are you okay?"

"I'm . . . basically okay, sure." She didn't believe in lying to children, but she wasn't about to try to explain exactly how she was feeling.

He looked down at the table in front of him. Condensation was beading the sides of his glass of orange juice. He prodded it with his finger, then put his finger in his mouth, sucking on it. "I don't want you to get sick," he said.

She laid down her fork, stood up, and went and perched on the edge of his chair. She put her arm around him, hugging him to her, trying to give him the strength she no longer felt she had. "I won't get sick," she said. "I'm in excellent health. Why are you worrying about that?"

"'Cause the junior 'cyclopedia says when people get sick, sometimes they die."

"Oh." She saw it, now. She would have seen it before if she hadn't been so wrapped up with her own problems. "You're afraid that what happened to your dad could happen to me. Is that it?"

He nodded without speaking. His lower lip pushed out. He looked as if he was about to start crying.

"Your father had a car accident," she said, clearly and firmly. She had to maintain that fiction. What else could she do? "I'm a very careful driver, and I won't ever let that happen to me. You understand? Never, ever."

"But—" His face looked plaintive as he wrestled with the difficult ideas, trying to reconcile them. "But everyone dies sometime. The 'cyclopedia said that too."

"It did, did it?" She remembered checking the package that the disc had come in. It had said it was approved for ages three through eight. Well, she was stuck with it now. "I'm going to live for years and years and years," she told him. "Till I'm an old, old lady. I promise."

"Older than Mrs. Lopez?" He scrutinized her to see if she was really telling the truth.

"*Much* older than Mrs. Lopez," she told him.

That seemed to help. He picked up his fork and actually took a tentative bite of his breakfast. She went back to her own chair, relieved that she'd been able to reassure him. The scrambled eggs and hash browns were getting cold. They didn't look appetizing, but she knew she needed the nutrition; she'd hardly eaten anything in the last two days.

"Mommy?"

Wearily, she set her fork down again. "Yes, honey?"

"Can we go visit heaven sometime, Mommy?"

This was almost more than she could deal with. "There is no heaven," she said, struggling to be patient. "I've told you before, it's just a story that people made up, like Santa Claus, because it makes them feel happier."

He stirred his fork in his food, looking moody. "But the man said Daddy is in heaven. He *said* it."

The funeral, a week ago, had created this little problem. Even though she'd made it clear that she and Jim were atheists, the minister had started spouting the usual stuff about almighty god and the hereafter. Funerals, she had learned, were a lot like weddings: they were arranged mainly to suit the guests, and if you wanted things done your way, you had to plan it in advance, fight for what you wanted, and be prepared to offend everyone. She hadn't had the foresight to plan it, or the strength to fight; so she'd been stuck with a service where she was the one who ended up offended.

To Damon, the man in the clerical collar lecturing a crowd of adults had seemed like an authority figure, so naturally, he'd believed him. The heaven myth was so seductive, she'd already gone through two major attempts to get rid of it.

She focused on her son. "I know it's hard to accept," she said, with all the feeling and sincerity she could summon, "but there is no heaven. There is no life after death."

And yet, was that really true, now, in view of Leo Gottbaum's research?

"There is no way," she went on, refusing to listen to her own reservations, "that you and I can go visit heaven."

Or was there?

Retrace

The winding road seemed to go on forever. It was breathtakingly beautiful with the ocean on one side and the forest on the other, the waves breaking in bays of tumbled rocks, but she'd had her fill of it an hour ago. She wasn't here to look at the scenery; she was here because it felt better to do something than nothing, and she'd reached a point where the risks seemed irrelevant.

At the same time, of course, she was uncomfortably aware that she was retracing the path that Jim had taken. She was aware, too, that she had driven past the spot where his car had crashed and burned. And she still had no clear idea what she was going to do when she reached her destination.

Damon, meanwhile, was bored. He had worn out the usual set of questions: "Are we there yet?" "How much longer?" "Can we stop for ice cream?" "Can I go to the bathroom?" He was sulking now, refusing to play the games on the Ton o' Fun InteracPack that she'd brought along for him. He'd even stopped talking to Talking Teddy.

Sharon had transcribed Jim's notes from his compad before taking it to the FBI, but the instructions only took her so far. He'd included a pathfinder number to take care of the last leg of the journey, but dialing that wasn't an option that was open to her.

"Where are we *going*, Mom?" Damon complained as she stopped the car, backed it up, bumped over the narrow shoulder of the little coast road, and started returning the way they'd come, retracing their path for the second time.

"I told you, honey." She tried to be patient, but she was feeling too wound up to make a convincing job of it. "We're looking for someone's house. A man called Leo."

"There aren't any houses," he said, staring at the forest crowding the edge of the highway.

She wondered if she had completely misunderstood the directions. Jim had always said she was a great driver but a hopeless map reader. He said she needed some sort of compass-implant or—no, she wasn't going to think about Jim.

"Let's stop," said Damon. He had seen a little general store up ahead, signs bleached by the sun, paint peeling off wood that had turned gray in the wind and rain. "I bet *they* have ice cream."

She'd passed the store before, and she'd assumed it was out of business. But now, she noticed, there was a pickup truck outside that hadn't been there before. And maybe the van parked under the trees, its bumper held up with a piece of rope, wasn't a derelict vehicle after all.

She slowed and turned into the tiny parking area, stopping her car beside the pickup. Damon immediately slid out his side and slammed the door, and the noise made her jump. She threw open her door and jumped out. "Don't do that!" she snapped at him. "I've told you before, you could catch your fingers!"

"Sorry, Mommy." He stared at her with big eyes, wounded by her sharp tone.

She went to him and gave him a hug. "No, I'm the one who's sorry. I didn't mean to shout. Let's go inside, hey?"

The interior of the store smelled of coffee beans, motor oil, soap, apples—a whole menu of odors that settled around her as she walked between homemade wooden shelves, past a freezer that had a crack in its glass door. She paused and dug out an ice-cream sandwich for Damon, then went to the counter.

An oldster in a ripped T-shirt was hanging out behind the register, listening to a younger guy wearing a red cap, his work boots crusted with mud. ". . . got to be a damn fool to start up again, your age," the one in the cap was saying. "It ain't just yer reflexes. Bones break real easy. It's the, you know, osteorosis."

"Porosis," said the one behind the counter. "Os'porosis."

"Hell, I know what it is. Even if I can't say it."

The older guy behind the counter grinned, showing ruined teeth. "Won't *be* no broken bones, man. I'll be gliding in so smooth, it'll be like I got Crisco on my board." He made a slow swooping motion with his hand.

Surfers, Sharon realized. At least the one behind the counter was, or used to be. "Excuse me," she broke in. "I'd like to pay for this."

"Well pardon me, ma'am." The one with the red cap stepped aside. He looked at her a little longer than he needed to, but it wasn't offensive. It just seemed as if he didn't encounter many strangers out here, and he liked the break in the monotony. "I got to go, anyways," he said. "I'll see you around, Tom. Just take it easy, okay?"

"Yeah, Jack." He turned to Sharon. "That be all?"

"Yes." She gave a quick, nervous smile as she paid for the ice cream. Behind her, she heard the screen door creak as the man in the red cap pushed it open. "I'd like to ask you, though," she went on, "have you ever heard of Leo Gottbaum? I understand his house is near here."

"Gottbaum." The oldster in the T-shirt gave her a funny look. "You didn't see the news? He died. It was in, like, the daily fax."

"Yes," she said, "yes, I know. But . . . I need to go and see where he used to live, all the same."

The man folded his arms across his sunken chest. He grimaced. "It ain't easy to find. And he had that place *defended.* All kinds of guns and shit. Automatic systems, blow you away soon's you get across the property line. You want to try it, you go on down the road, there's a dirt track, half a mile. It's up there, somewheres." He shook his head. "But I sure as hell wouldn't mess with it."

"I see," said Sharon. She looked at the old, scuffed wood of the counter, feeling, again, how alone she was and how unprepared to deal with the situation. "Thanks anyway, I guess." She handed the ice cream to Damon, then started out of the store.

Outside she paused for a minute, staring at the forest covering the steep hillside. There was no sign of any human habitation, but somewhere up there, she felt sure, there was a refuge full of computer equipment, with some more of Gottbaum's collaborators running it.

"Where are we going now, Mommy?" He was holding her hand, looking up at her, his mouth rimmed with ice cream.

"I don't know." She walked him to her car. The man in the red cap was still sitting in his pickup, watching her through its open window.

She opened the door for Damon, closed it carefully, then went around to the driver's side.

"Hey, lady, 'scuse me."

He looked harmless enough, but in her current frame of

mind she wasn't about to give anyone the benefit of the doubt. "What is it?" She made her voice sound unfriendly as she shaded her eyes from the sun, trying to see his face.

"Maybe I oughta mind my own goddam business," he said. "But did you say you're looking for Gottbaum's place?"

She gave a brief, sour smile. "I thought I was, but your friend in the store made it sound as if I'd get myself killed."

He chuckled. "That's a real possibility."

Sharon tried to size him up. Even though she was feeling defeated, the journalist in her always told her to be persistent. "Did you happen to know Dr. Gottbaum?" she asked.

"Know him? Hell, no. We ran into each other once in a while, but he never said a damn thing. His daughter, though, she was different. I got to know her real well when she used to live up there."

"You did?" Her interest returned. "You knew Yumi?"

"Yumi. Yeah." He frowned. "Hey, how come you know her name?"

"I saw her just—just a while ago." She deliberately made the timing vague, still not quite sure whether to trust him.

"She's gone back home to Hawaii, is that right?" He pulled a beer bottle out of a six-pack on the seat beside him, popped the top, and took a swig.

"Yes." She hesitated, then decided to take the risk. "She told me a lot about her father. His work, and its implications. She believed he had some plans that would carry on after his death, and she wanted me to find out about them. You see, I'm a journalist."

"Journalist?" He raised his eyebrows. "Like for the magazines?"

"No. TV. In Los Angeles."

"Oh, TV." He made it sound like a foreign word. He looked over at her car. "You always bring your kid along on the job?"

She decided to brazen it out. "Sure, when I can't get a baby-sitter."

"Ha." He drank some more. "How 'bout that." He stuck out his hand, reaching down to her from the window of the truck. "My name's Jack. Jack Travers."

She shook his hand. He had a surprisingly gentle grip, as if he was afraid of hurting her. "I'm Sharon Blake," she said.

He nodded earnestly. "Pleased to meet you, Sharon."

"So," she said, "I guess there's no easy way to go up there and get someone to talk to me."

He shook his head. "I seen some people still living up there, but they ain't friendly. There was a guy last week complaining on account of his dog got shot by one of them automatic weapons. There's a big new fence, and a gate, and No Trespassing signs all over."

"Oh." There was a long pause. Jack squinted at the ocean and seemed to have nothing more to say. "Well," Sharon said, "I guess—"

"You know, I always wondered about it myself," he went on. "What that shitpile of gadgets was for, and how come he had to have all the guns and stuff." He set his beer aside. "You serious about wanting to find out?"

"Absolutely." He wasn't trying to be irritating, she realized; he just worked on a slower timebase than people back in Los Angeles. He needed to think things through in his own way.

He tugged at his cap, straightening it, lowering the brim a fraction. "Okay, here's how you can do it. Wait down here. I seen 'em come down to buy this and that. Tom, in the store, he's always bitchin' about 'em, 'cause they don't use cash. There's a tall, skinny guy, and another one who's got like some kind of pink mark on his forehead. Birthmark or something. Sometimes the two of 'em come down together, sometimes just one. They drive a Mitsubishi electric, a 4x4, you can't miss 'em, no one else around here's got an electric 4x4. Usually they're kind of late . . . six, seven. Two or three hours from now. You hang around, maybe you can get talking to 'em. Don't know if it'd help you any, but that's the best I can think of."

"Thank you, Jack," she said. She gave him a warm smile. "Maybe I'll give it a try."

"If you talk to Yumi," he said, pausing to drain his beer, "like on the telephone, you tell her Jack says hi. Tell her I'm still waiting for her to stop by for dinner, okay?"

She nodded earnestly. "I will. I promise."

"Nice meeting you, Sharon." He started his truck. "Take care, with your kid and all. Seems like he needs some attention right now." He jerked his head toward her car.

She turned and saw Damon playing with the Ton o' Fun

pack, ice cream all over his face, his hands, and the keyboard. "Oh my god," she said. "I better go. Good-bye, and thanks again."

He backed the truck out then drove off, waving.

Contact

It was an hour before sunset when the pickup truck came down the coast road and turned into the parking area outside the store. It was a late-model all-terrain vehicle with extra steel-plate welded around the front, the rear, and the wheel arches. Its windows reflected the light oddly, as if they were thicker than normal glass. It looked better equipped for a gunfight than picking up groceries.

She sat in her car and watched as the driver got out, glanced around, then walked into the store. The light was too dim, at this point, for her to see him clearly.

Damon had fallen asleep an hour earlier, and she'd put him in the back seat with a blanket over him. She turned and checked him now and saw that he was still slumbering peacefully. She hesitated. If he woke up and found her missing, he'd be upset; but the only safe place for her to do what she wanted would be inside the store.

Slowly, trying not to make any noise that would wake him, she slipped out of her car. She closed the door gently, pushing it till the latch barely clicked.

The long wait had already taken its toll on her nerves, and it was a relief to be doing something purposeful, even if it seemed potentially dangerous. She walked into the store and paused, clutching her arms around herself, trying not to feel scared. She heard the man paying for something at the counter, then saw him coming back down the aisle toward her holding a paper bag. He was in his thirties, wearing a plain black T-shirt, black pants, and sneakers. He had a pale, narrow face, and there was some sort of mark on his forehead. A little pink birthmark, just as Jack had said.

"Excuse me," she said, "I'd like to ask you something."

He stopped short, looking surprised, saying nothing. He was holding his purchases in one hand, his other hand hanging casually by his side.

She glanced quickly over her shoulder. Through the screen door she could see into her car. Damon was still stretched out in the back seat, still asleep. "My name is Sharon Blake," she said, turning back to the man in front of her. "I'm James Bayley's wife."

She waited for the reaction. It came quickly. His shoulders straightened, his back stiffened. His nostrils flared as he took a quick, deep breath, and his lips pressed tightly together. He reached slowly behind him with his free hand.

"I'm not threatening you," Sharon said quickly. "I've come up here with . . . my son; he's only four years old, in the car outside." She made a quick, impulsive gesture. Her pulse was beating hard.

"So what do you want?" he asked. His voice was unexpectedly high-pitched. Maybe, she thought, he was nervous too. She looked past him and saw the old guy behind the counter peering down the aisle, trying to see what was going on. Good, she was glad he was watching.

"I want to see the person who's—who's running things," she said. "I have something I want to offer. To resolve the situation."

"Come outside," he said, and took a step forward.

She stepped sideways, blocking him. He wasn't powerfully built, and he seemed unsure of himself, but there was something menacing about him nonetheless. She shook her head firmly. "No."

He hesitated. One hand was still behind him. Slowly, now, he brought it into view. She flinched, then saw he was just holding a pocket phone. Without looking away from her he raised it to his mouth and muttered something, then held it to his ear.

"Hey, you guys, what's going on back there?" the guy behind the counter shouted.

"Nothing," Sharon called to him. "I just wanted to ask this man something, that's all."

He was still speaking into his phone. She overheard her name. He repeated it, as if the person at the other end was asking for clarification. Finally, he put the phone back in his pocket. "All right, come up to the dome," he said. "We can talk."

For a moment, the words didn't quite register. Then she realized what he had said. She felt a sense of elation, followed almost immediately by a deep foreboding. "I have to bring my son."

He shrugged. "Whatever. But no weapons, and no recording devices. You understand?"

She swallowed hard. "Right. I have to tell you . . . there are people in Los Angeles who know where I am, and what I'm doing here. They're concerned about my safety." That was a lie, of course; she hoped it sounded plausible. "They'll know there's something wrong if I don't call them later tonight."

"I understand." He nodded toward the door. "Let's go."

Communication

It was dark in the forest. Her little car struggled with the steep grade, the headlights swinging and dipping as she bumped over ruts and deadwood. Ahead of her, the 4x4 pushed on along the narrow, winding track, bushes and brambles scraping past. It paused a couple of times and waited for her when she lagged behind.

Damon was sitting beside her, still wrapped in the blanket, sucking his finger and staring out sleepily at the forest, the dim purple sky showing here and there through the canopy of leaves. He didn't ask where they were going; he seemed to be in that state where he was too sleepy to be properly aware of the world. She wished she had his ability to accept whatever was happening, to maintain blind faith in other people to look after him.

A barbed-wire fence came into view, gleaming silver in the headlight beams. Behind it she saw the hillcrest silhouetted black against the darkening sky, and the dome with its windows glowing.

The vehicle in front of her waited for an automatic gate to swing out of the way, then edged forward. She tucked in behind it, clutching the steering tightly. This was where Jim had come; where Yumi had once lived.

The Mitsubishi stopped unexpectedly and she hit the brakes, almost running into it. The driver got out and walked around to her. "Wait here," he shouted to her. "Stay in your car."

She told herself there was nothing to be afraid of; that they wouldn't risk harming her, at this point, because the last thing they wanted was to draw attention to their activities. Logically, that made sense; emotionally, it was very little reassurance.

In her rearview mirror, she saw the gate swinging down behind her, blocking her exit. She was trapped, now. But somehow that allayed her fear a little. She had made her decision; all she could do now was follow it through.

A couple of minutes passed. Finally, a tall, thin figure emerged from the dome and joined the man Sharon had spoken to. They both walked toward her.

"You can get out of your car," the tall one said. His voice was quiet and relaxed, very laconic. "We have to check you before you can come inside."

She saw he was holding something in his hand. "What's that you're carrying?" she shouted through her half-open window, hesitating to open the door.

"It's a metal detector." He held it so that she could see it in her headlight beams. "Also sensitive to most kinds of explosives."

They would have more reason to be nervous about her, she realized, than she had to be nervous about them. She made her decision and turned to Damon. "Come on, honey."

"I'm tired, Mommy." He looked up at her as if to say, Is all this really necessary?

"It won't take long," she said. She scooped him up in her arms and stepped out into the darkness.

The tall, skinny man moved around her, sweeping the detector up and down, then checked Damon as well.

He stepped back and turned to his companion. "Seems okay."

The other man shook his head. "I still think we should have left them down on the coast road."

"No, that's been the problem all along. Not enough communication, you know? Everyone so paranoid, like they're doing espionage instead of science."

Maybe, thought Sharon, this conversation was for her benefit, and the two men were playing a good cop/bad cop routine. But the tall one sounded as if he meant what he was saying.

"I tell you, Mike, Leo wouldn't like this."

"Maybe not, but Leo isn't here right now." He turned to Sharon. "Come on. Bring your kid."

Device Unavailable

She walked into the big, bright space and stood staring at all the screens and consoles and metal cabinets, some of them open for maintenance, circuit boards stacked on workbenches, test equipment standing amid loops of cable. Just ten days ago, she thought to herself, Jim was here. This was where he met Leo Gottbaum, before—before Gottbaum killed him.

She lifted Damon up, hugging him to her. He was still half-asleep, blinking at all the gadgets. She knew she shouldn't be subjecting him to this, but something about the manner of the tall man had made her feel a little more secure. He didn't have the kind of fanaticism she'd expected. He seemed bored, as if he was just a caretaker.

"Better sit over here," he said, leading her across to a table by some windows.

"Thanks." She saw him clearly now that she was inside in the light. He had strange, dreamy eyes, and he didn't seem interested in looking at her. He was very laid back . . . or was he, really? Maybe he was sharper than he seemed. It was hard to figure him out.

She sat down at the table, holding Damon on her lap. "Don't worry," she said. "Everything's okay." She hugged him to her.

The tall man sat down opposite her. "I guess we should get introduced. My name's Mike Butterworth."

She tried not to show her surprise at recognizing his name from Jim's notes. "I've . . . heard of you," she said.

"Heard of me?"

"You were part of the LifeScan project." Maybe if she was bold and seemed knowledgeable, they'd respect her more. She knew how she must seem, a woman with her young child, obviously not in a position of strength.

She glanced at the other man. He was sitting on a stool by one of the workbenches, giving her a cold, hard stare.

"That's Paul," said Butterworth. "Paul Hartman. He's into hardware. He's doing some maintenance."

"Mommy?" Damon wriggled in her arms, trying to get comfortable. "Mommy, can I go to sleep soon?"

She considered the situation. As she understood it, Gottbaum had lived here. It was his residence, so there had to be at least one bedroom. "Is there somewhere my son could lie down while we talk?" she asked. "It might make things easier."

Butterworth gave her a curious look, as if she intrigued him. "Sure, just make yourself at home," he said. "I mean, hell, now you're in here, why not? There's a spare bedroom just through there." He sounded sarcastic.

"I didn't mean—" she began.

"Go on. Go ahead."

She decided to take him at his word. "Thank you," she said, standing up, hoisting Damon on her hip, feeling glad of the diversion.

She walked into a hallway and found a door standing open, a small room beyond. There was a bed with a homemade patchwork quilt, and she immediately knew that this must have been Yumi's room. It felt good, knowing that; it seemed like a good omen. She laid Damon on the bed, pulled the quilt over him, and looked around at the modest furniture: a rickety old chest of drawers, a pegged-wood rocking chair with a shawl over the back of it, a mirror framed with seashells.

Damon lay on his side, curling up under the quilt, sucking his finger, watching her through half-closed eyes. She kissed him on the forehead and stroked his face. "We going home soon, Mommy?" he said.

"Soon. Just take a nap while I talk to the people here. Okay? I'll be right next door, where we were a moment ago."

"Mmm-hm." He closed his eyes.

She sat with him a while longer. Within five minutes, he was asleep.

When she walked back into the living area it looked to her as if Butterworth and Hartman had been having some kind of argument. Hartman seemed moody and irritable; Butterworth was ignoring him, staring at the darkness outside the windows.

"All right," said Sharon, taking her seat again, "now I can speak more freely." She clasped her hands on the table in front of her. "I want to talk to you about my husband."

Butterworth turned his attention back to her. He didn't say anything.

"I—I understand," she went on, "that in some sense, he's still alive. Maybe all the equipment in here has something to do with sustaining him, I don't know."

Butterworth slowly shook his head. "If you're asking me, I'd have to say that that's the kind of question I can't answer."

She paused, frowning at him. "You don't seem to understand, how painful this is for me. I mean, it was very difficult to come here. I was hoping we could speak frankly about this, without playing games, and . . . settle things amicably between us."

Now he looked puzzled. "I'm not playing games. And speaking of amicable—I mean, there's a laboratory in Long Beach that just burned down, wiping out thirty years of work."

Was he saying that was her fault? She couldn't figure him out. "Look—"

He leaned forward, finally engaging himself in the conversation. "No, hold on a minute, all right? I want to tell you something."

She sighed in exasperation. "Will you please—"

"Listen to me." His tone was suddenly very sharp. He stared directly at her.

The change in him disconcerted her. "All right."

"Okay. Imagine there's like an island. On this island, you can have anything you want. You can live forever. It's like nirvana, you know? There's only one way to get there, though. It's a bridge, which took these people half their lives to build. Now, there's five of 'em who've made it across the bridge onto the island, and a couple friends of theirs waiting for their turn. These friends helped out in the past, you understand, so they were promised a free trip to the island. But right at the last minute, the people who built the bridge get word that there's a troublemaker who wants to destroy everything. They get so paranoid that in order to protect their island, they burn down the bridge. Just like that." He leaned back. "So how do you think you'd feel, if you'd been one of the people left waiting on the shore?"

Slowly, she absorbed what he'd said. "You mean," she said, "you yourself—"

"No, not me. Paul." He nodded toward the man at the workbench.

"Oh." She glanced uneasily at Hartman, then back at Butterworth. "But if it's really such a wonderful place, why aren't you—"

Butterworth picked up a pen. He started doodling on a piece of scrap paper. "Some people—computer people, especially— tell me I have a mystical outlook. I study Zen Buddhism. I believe in the unity of mind and body. Digitizing my brain, shutting it in a box, is not my personal path to nirvana." He had drawn a circle in the center of the paper and was adding lines radiating from it, like a kid's picture of the sun. "In any case," he went on, "there's a snag. Suppose there's a bunch of people who are doing some work with the human mind, scanning it, taking it to pieces like a slice at a time. Well, there's all kinds of neat gadgets to help do it, but it's a real delicate operation, and only one guy on the team has the necessary manual skill, because the others are all theorists. So he can scan them, no problem; but who's going to scan him?"

She realized, as he was speaking, the implications. "That means—you were the one who operated on my husband."

He suddenly scribbled over his doodle, obliterating it. He pushed the piece of paper aside. "That's another question which I obviously can't answer." He looked out of the window. "Although I guess I will say that if I understand what you mean, your husband must have been already dead with his brain frozen. And the operation that was performed would have been the only chance he had for his intelligence to survive."

Across the room, Hartman set down the circuit board he'd been working on and pushed back his stool. "Mike, I just don't see the point of this. We don't need to tell her anything. There's nothing we're going to get out of this. It's just an unnecessary risk."

"Like I said before—" Butterworth began.

"You don't even know what she's here for," Hartman went on. "Why the hell did she come up here?"

Butterworth paused. He nodded to himself. "That's a legitimate question." He turned back to Sharon. "Why did you come here? Paul wants to know."

Sharon remembered the little speech that she'd prepared. It had seemed persuasive when she'd rehearsed it in her head. But now she wasn't so sure. "I was going to tell you," she began, "that I'd decided I couldn't tolerate my situation any longer. Knowing my husband is alive but unable to be with him—it's unbearable. It seemed to me that if several people had actually *chosen* to be converted into the state he's in, there must be some positive aspects to it. So, I—I came here to find out more about it. Because if that's the only way I can be with him, I might want to have it done to me, and to my son."

There it was: her confession, and her request.

There was a short silence. The cooling fans in the equipment murmured in the background.

"You should've thought of this before," said Hartman, sounding angry and bitter. He gave her a brief, malicious glance, then turned away.

"What Paul means," said Butterworth, "is that the bridge is gone, and there's no way to get it back."

She shifted uncomfortably in her chair. "But you surely can't expect me to believe that you didn't save the gadgets from the laboratory before—"

"You think it's easy to wheel out a couple tons of equipment from a defense contractor's private labs?" said Hartman. "You think they just tell you sure, go right ahead, take anything you want?"

"Well, then," she persisted, "there must be a way to rebuild—"

"Ten years, five million dollars," he snapped at her.

"In any case," said Butterworth, still sounding patient, low-key, refusing to acknowledge the tension in the room, "what you're talking about could never be done to your boy. See, intelligence isn't just a matter of what's in the cells. It's how the cells are connected. And the connections take a while to grow."

"You scan and store a four-year-old," said Hartman, "he'll be able to learn stuff and remember it, but he'll always be a four-year-old."

She looked from one man to the other. Bit by bit, they were chipping away at the hope she'd built inside her head. "That's really true?"

Butterworth picked up the piece of paper that he'd doodled on. He screwed it into a ball and dumped it in a waste bin. "It's clearly and demonstrably true," he said. "So it seems to me, when it comes down to it, you're stuck with your situation, and we're stuck with ours. And I guess we understand each other now. Right?"

She felt the tension slowly draining out of her. There really was no way to achieve what she wanted—if, in fact, she'd really wanted it.

She looked at the equipment cluttering the dome. "All right, I guess I can't be with him. But—can't I talk to him again? I mean, he must be here somewhere, with all this stuff you have—"

"You keep asking things I can't answer," said Butterworth. He shook his head, as if the situation troubled him. "Let me put it this way. I could show you something that looked and sounded just like your husband. Understand what I'm saying? Maybe it's him stored in a computer someplace. Or maybe it's just a simulation."

She nodded. "All right."

Butterworth looked over at Hartman. "Any problems with that, Paul?"

"We don't owe her anything."

"Don't look at it as a debt," said Butterworth. "Look at it as maintaining diplomatic relations, you know? Or look at it as karma."

Hartman sighed. He gave Butterworth an exasperated look, then went to a console. He typed something. "Mike, you want to use the monitor, you do it."

"Come on." Butterworth stood up, gesturing toward the keyboard and the screen.

"Just like that?" She followed him across the room, feeling a knot of excitement growing in her, replacing the futility that had filled her a moment before.

"Well, there's some protocol to deal with first." He sat down and started typing a series of commands. Text appeared on the screen and he paused, waiting.

There was a black leather chair beside him, stacked with papers. She nudged the documents to one side and perched on the edge of the chair, watching anxiously.

He turned away from the screen. "Paul? I'm not getting a readback."

Hartman walked over to him. "You stated your code?"

"Yeah, I did that."

Hartman took the keyboard out of Butterworth's hands. He rattled off a series of commands. "The operating system is there," he said. "The command interpreter checks out okay." He paused. "But no Leo."

"So go direct to one of the others," said Butterworth.

There were a couple of minutes of silence broken only by the intermittent sound of the keys. Sharon watched the two men, wishing she knew more about the technology. Hartman was looking more and more puzzled, then worried. "I don't get it," he said. "Everyone's offline."

Sharon leaned over so she could peek at the screen herself. There were some messages on it in a mixture of system code and plain text. Then, abruptly, the screen cleared. New text appeared. Sharon leaned closer to read it.

The message was cryptic but succinct:

DEVICE UNAVAILABLE.

Downtime

Consciousness resumed almost without a break. Bayley found himself still in his apartment, still slumped in his chair beside the phone. He sat up cautiously, looking around. Without hunger or any other physical cues it was impossible to tell how long he'd been offline. Subjectively, the interval had seemed to last for just a few seconds.

Something was chiming. He quickly reached for the phone, thinking he was being given a chance to continue his conversation with Sharon. But then he realized the sound was coming from his front door.

Disappointed, he stood up. He noticed the realtime clock incorporated in his digital video system, displaying the day and time: Monday, 8:05 A.M. That was disconcerting. He had felt, vaguely, that it was evening. And had a week really passed since he'd first found himself inside the system?

He went to the door, wondering why MAPHIS was announcing someone this way instead of moving the person directly into Bayley's living area. Maybe his visitor was another infomorph who had to respect the parameters of Bayley's personal space—his domain. Was that how it worked? Admission only by consent?

He opened the door and found himself staring at a tall, muscular man in a white jumpsuit. He had curly blond hair and a tanned, handsome face with clear blue eyes. He respectfully inclined his head. "Mr. Bayley," he said. "One of your companions wishes to see you. Would you come with me, please?"

Bayley was in no mood for games; his mind was still full of

Sharon, and he felt a powerful emotional hangover from his telephone call. "What the hell are you talking about?"

There was a pause. "Will you come with me please? One of your companions wishes to see you."

Looking into the figure's blank face and unblinking eyes, Bayley realized he was dealing with a pseudomorph, like the nurse that MAPHIS had sent to visit him when he'd first complained about not having any company. He turned his head. "MAPHIS," he said, speaking to the center of his living room, "who wants to see me? What is this?"

The information you request is not available, the neutral, synthetic voice answered from the speakers of his video system.

Bayley felt a little spasm of irritation. "All I want is to talk to my wife again. Can't you get the phone working the way it was before?"

That is not permitted.

"Will you come with me, please?" the blond man started again. "One of your companions—"

"All right, why not," said Bayley. He walked out into the hallway, turned to close his apartment door, and then checked himself. Why bother? Here in MAPHIS, home security was a meaningless concept.

He followed the blond man down the stairs, remembering all the times he'd run down to the garage in the morning to drive to work. Those days were beginning to seem like memories of life in another country. He wondered if that meant he was beginning to get used to the idea of being trapped here.

Out in the street he found long shadows, the sun just beginning to climb in the east, the air smelling of foliage moist with dew. The time of day was consistent, he realized, with the time he'd seen on the video readout. Maybe it was actually in sync with the outside world. In the realspace version of his neighborhood, people might be getting up and going to work at this very moment, with Sharon among them.

But here in MAPHIS the street was deserted, more like a Sunday than a Monday. The blond, muscular man led the way along the sidewalk and Bayley followed, past the flowering cacti, the ivy climbing the beige stucco of his apartment building.

Just ahead, at the intersection, was the street where French and Voss had pulled him out of his car and taken him away. The associations were so unpleasant, he wasn't sure he wanted to see the spot where it had happened. But as he turned the corner, he discovered he needn't have worried. Changes had been made.

The street terminated as if someone had cut the concrete with a pair of shears. Instead of little backyards behind the suburban homes, there were rolling meadows of vivid green dotted with monuments and temples of white marble. Men in white robes were strolling among groves of willow trees. It was like a fantasy version of ancient Greece.

Bayley stopped and stared at the panorama. His surprise was dulled by all the other transitions he'd experienced inside MAPHIS. Strange as this was, it was less disorienting than the Swiss Alps or the surface of the Moon had been.

He walked off the end of his street into the verdant meadow and felt the turf yield under his weight, as soft as a foam mattress. The sunlight shifted subtly, becoming hazy and mellow, tinged with gold. He heard a faint fluttering above him, looked up, and saw a flock of cherubs passing overhead, pink little bodies borne on tiny ornamental feathered wings. Who, he wondered, could have programmed this foolishness?

He looked behind him. His neighborhood was still there if he wanted to turn around and go back. But he was intrigued, now, despite himself.

"Will you come with me, please?" said his guide, waiting for him. "One of your companions—"

"All right, all right." He walked farther into the impossibly luxuriant meadow, past one of the little white temples, where water flowed from an ornamental spigot and a woman was sitting on a wall of stone braiding blossoms into her long hair. She was like a figure from a Pre-Raphaelite painting.

Bayley's guide led him through a shady glen where a bearded centaur stood under the trees, strumming a lute. Then, as he emerged back into the strangely golden light, he saw his destination: a huge temple, marble steps leading up to a double row of Doric columns, lintels embellished with an elaborate frieze.

He walked up the steps and passed between the columns, his footsteps echoing around him. Ahead, he heard voices and laughter and the clink of glasses. As he entered the inner sanctum he found himself among a crowd of beautiful people.

The walls were of white stone, the floor was inlaid with a vast, intricate mosaic, and the roof was open to the sky. Gold serving dishes were mounded with fruit and delicacies. Elegant long-haired women were reclining on cushions, lazy and bored, dressed in diaphanous white dresses and extravagant jewelry. Men in togas were moving among them serving food and drink.

Bayley followed his guide down the length of the room. At the far end, he saw, was a tall gold throne, and seated on it was a figure in a dress of shimmering silver. She was flanked by an honor guard of muscular men holding spears, and more men were seated at her feet.

Bayley reached the steps leading up to the throne. The woman in it was veiled. As he watched, she slowly pulled the film of white away from her face.

She was young and beautiful, with pure black hair cascading down in waves around her shoulders. She watched him with enigmatic green eyes. She had an imperious air as if she was posing, conscious of her own beauty. "Mr. Bayley," she said, "how kind of you to accept my invitation."

Bayley looked at her. He turned and stared at the palatial surroundings, then looked back at her again.

She walked down the steps to him, her dress trailing behind her. She gave him a reproachful look. "You know, all my other subjects kneel at my feet when they address me."

He saw her delicate face, her flawless ivory skin, her generous mouth, her slender neck. He remembered himself and Gottbaum on the beach, remade by MAPHIS to be young studs with big muscles. This had to be the same kind of thing. "Rosalind French," he said, sounding more sure about it than he really felt. "Aren't you getting kind of old for this kind of foolishness."

She gave him an irritated look. "Bayley, don't you have any poetry in your soul? You were tiresome enough in realspace. Do you have to be tiresome here, too?"

He decided it wasn't worth answering her. He turned to go.

"All right, we'll get normal if that's what you want." She no longer sounded like a princess. She had the East Coast accent he remembered, the clipped, impatient manner. She waved her hand, and the honor guard abruptly dematerialized. The guests and the gold dishes disappeared. Within seconds, the temple was empty of life. "This way," she said.

She went to the wall behind the throne and opened a small wooden door. Cautiously, he followed her through.

The room beyond was furnished in antiques, like the bedroom where he had found himself when he first woke up inside MAPHIS. There were overstuffed armchairs, gold-framed oil paintings, a pendulum clock on a mantelpiece above a large fireplace where logs were burning. Outside the windows he saw a New England small-town street under a heavy gray sky. Snow was falling.

He looked behind him. The marble temple was still there and beyond it, the green meadows. It was a jarring discontinuity. He closed the door, latching it.

When he turned around and faced the room again he found that her appearance had normalized itself. She looked exactly the way he remembered her from his visit to the laboratory and his period as her prisoner: a tall woman with a serious, intelligent face, her hair pulled back, gray eyes regarding him steadily. Instead of the white lab coat she was now wearing a beige cashmere sweater and freshly pressed black pants.

The transition had been so abrupt, he couldn't help reacting. She saw his disoriented expression. "Sorry," she said, with a perfunctory smile. "I was forgetting; you haven't had much time to get used to the transformations here. I did it without thinking."

He walked to one of the armchairs and sat down slowly, tentatively on the edge of it. "As I understand it," he said, "I've been in here a lot longer than you."

She nodded, her face showing something that he couldn't quite pin down—regret? "Yes, that is how you would understand it." She sat in a chair opposite, moving quickly but with poise. She crossed her legs and rested her hands on her knee. "Perhaps I owe you an explanation."

He watched her, waiting. The clock on the mantelpiece ticked slowly, deliberately. He glanced at it and saw that it showed the time as a quarter after five. The light outside was dimming; a snowy evening drawing into night. So the time of day in MAPHIS wasn't realtime, after all. It was local to each domain.

She saw him glance at the clock, and she shook her head. "It's far more deceptive than you think. Tell me, how long, altogether, do you think you've been inside MAPHIS?"

Bayley sensed an unpleasant revelation coming, although he couldn't imagine what it might be. He carefully thought back to the sequence of events since he'd first regained consciousness in the barren concrete plaza. "Between five and seven days," he said. "Plus the intervals when I was unconscious. The downtime, whatever you want to call it."

Again, her face showed the enigmatic expression that might have been regret. "Those intervals lasted longer than you imagine. Measured by *internal* time, you've been inside MAPHIS for almost thirty-five years. I'm a relative newcomer; I've only been in here about a decade. But I've been conscious all the time, whereas you have not."

He stared at her. The numbers registered but made no sense. "Just—just a little while ago," he said, "I talked to my wife. In the outside world. Realspace, isn't that what you call it? She wasn't thirty-five years older. She sounded—"

"I said *internal* time," she interrupted. "You obviously haven't thought it through. No reason you should; you're not a scientist." There was a trace of elitism in the way she said it.

"In a human being," she went on, "nerve impulses travel relatively slowly. They involve changes of chemical state, which take time. But you're not a person anymore. You're an infomorph, your thoughts are pure electricity, and the messages in your mind are now moving near the speed of light. Of course, there are some practical factors: MAPHIS has to keep your senses supplied with data, and managing this sensory input limits the speed of the system. Even so, your thoughts are operating about one thousand times as fast in here as they used to operate in your biological brain, and the clocks that MAPHIS displays are geared up to match, so they look right to us. According to the one up there on the mantelpiece, we've been in this room for about five minutes. In actual fact, in realtime, this whole conversation has taken less than half a second."

Bayley absorbed it slowly. It made sense, and he felt foolish for not having thought of it himself. "But . . . I was still able to communicate with Sharon, in the outside world," he said. "Even though she was living a thousand times more slowly—"

"When one of us interfaces with realspace, MAPHIS can temporarily slow his timebase," she said. "You have no reference point, so you never notice the change."

Bayley nodded. "I see." He sat back in his chair, pressing his fingers to his temples. "So if I believe you," he said, "and I think I have to believe you, during the whole period I've been inside MAPHIS, I've been active for less than one percent of the time. No, make that point one percent. What the hell has been going on? Why have I been kept unconscious?"

"I'm afraid you have Dr. Gottbaum to thank for that," she said.

"Gottbaum?" He looked at her sharply.

She nodded. "You know his history, do you? The old radical. Hates the government, hates the police most of all. You know what they used to shout in street demonstrations when he was in college? 'Off the pigs.' Meaning, 'Kill the cops.' He despised you, Mr. Bayley. But not just because you worked for the FBI. You jeopardized his whole life's work."

Bayley laughed sourly. "Great. Wonderful." He stood up and walked around the room, past a corner cabinet full of cut-glass crystal, a large gold-framed mirror, a Victrola on a small mahogany table. He paused at the window, pulled the maroon drape aside, and peered down at the street. He was up on the second floor, he discovered. An old car chugged past—a Studebaker from the 1930s. The street was lined with Victorian mansions, ornate facades rimmed with white. Two kids were playing, throwing snowballs at each other. It looked like a Norman Rockwell painting. "So what else did Gottbaum do to me? Can you tell me the details?"

"If you wish. You remember waking up in the concrete plaza, with something chasing you?"

He laughed shortly. "I'd say I remember that."

"Leo wanted to see what would happen if an infomorph was severely stressed. Remember, we had no reliable experimental data. Animals seemed to survive, but animals probably don't have consciousness as we know it. It was quite possible that the shock of transformation could turn out to be more than the human mind could cope with."

Bayley turned away from the window. "So I served my purpose as a test subject," he said. "And after that—"

"After we had established the viability of the process, we wanted to see what would happen in the longer term. Would the stimuli really seem convincing? Would someone go crazy with boredom or loneliness?" She looked down, embarrassed to meet his eyes. "I monitored your attempt to reconstruct your wife. It was . . . quite sad."

"Thanks for the condolences."

She stood up and walked over to him, stopping a few feet away. "If it's any consolation—I guess it won't be, but I'll say this anyway—I have a lot of misgivings about the way you were treated. That's easy to say, of course, but I mean it. I've had a lot of time to think."

He said nothing, watching her, waiting while she seemed to take the time to order her thoughts. "I don't know if you can understand how crazy we all were," she went on. "Knowing we were at the end of thirty years of research, literally achieving immortality—and a man with a badge shows up, threatening to destroy everything we've worked for. It wasn't just Leo who hated you; I did, too. I had a degenerative condition that was slowly crippling me, and would have been fatal within a short space of time. LifeScan was my only hope. I think back now, and I wonder if there could have been some other way of dealing with you when you discovered us. At the time, Leo wanted to have you killed, plain and simple; but Jeremy, Hans, and myself said it was out of the question, so Leo said, 'All right, let's get some use out of him. He can be our experimental subject.' And that seemed like a very decent compromise." She laughed and shook her head. "It really seemed completely reasonable, almost as if you should have been thankful to us."

"I see." He walked slowly back to his chair. "I suppose I appreciate your frankness." He stared at the flames in the fireplace. "So after I'd served my purpose as a guinea pig, the old guy had me shut down. Was that what happened at the end of the London scenario I was in?"

"No, that was a genuine system failure. But it came at a convenient moment. Leo was ready to have himself uploaded, and he said he wasn't going to share his system with a cop. He knew we would have refused to erase you, and he saw there might be some future use for you, so we put you in storage. Until—well, until he needed you. As he told you, out in real-space your wife was making us very nervous. It looked as if she was trying to provoke an investigation. We started working flat out, doing scans as fast as we could, terrified that we could be shut down at the last minute. I went without sleep for four nights, supervising the upload of Leo, Jeremy, and Hans. On my last night in realspace, just when I was ready for my own upload, I found your wife was following me. I . . . was very angry. I spoke more freely than I should have.

"Then I was uploaded into MAPHIS, and Leo took you out of storage to persuade you to tell your wife to quit. That's why he gave you a guided tour through the system; he wanted to prove life could be worth living in here, so you'd feel more motivated to ask your wife to back off, for fear of killing us all."

Bayley nodded wearily. "Okay. It makes sense." He sighed. "I need a drink. Is that possible? Can we drink, and get intoxicated?"

She gave him an ironic look. "Intoxication is the least of it. There are quite a variety of ways to get high as an infomorph." For a moment he saw something in her—a sensuality, a hunger that he wouldn't have guessed she possessed. But then her self-control reasserted itself, and the weakness was erased. "You'll find liquor in the bottom of the cabinet over there," she told him.

He located a bottle of bourbon, took out a glass, and half-filled it. The liquid looked slightly odd as he poured it, and he remembered, again, Gottbaum's little lecture on the problems of simulating fluids in motion.

He sipped the drink, and swallowed; and the taste wasn't exactly right, either. Still, he realized he could drink as much as he wanted and sober up whenever he wanted, and there'd never be a hangover.

He went back and sat down. "So Herr Gottbaum was in charge, the way you tell it," he said. "And you were just obeying orders. Is that right?"

A faint flush of pink showed at her cheekbones. Her mouth made tiny movements as if she couldn't decide what to say.

"That's not an entirely fair characterization," she told him, retreating into her dignity.

He shrugged. "At this point, I don't much care. What interests me is why you've taken the trouble to wake me up this time around."

"That's very simple," she said, relaxing a little now that he wasn't attacking her. "I've been going out of my mind with boredom, Mr. Bayley. I simply wanted someone to talk to."

He laughed without humor. "I seem to remember Gottbaum saying the same thing."

She hesitated. "Well, maybe he did. But . . . I've been in here for ten subjective years, remember? You saw that fantasy I was living in. There have been others. They were fun for a while. I indulged myself in every way I could. But after ten years . . ."

He watched her, surprised by the way she was talking about her personal life.

She seemed to sense his thoughts. "You learn not to have any secrets in MAPHIS. With his privileged access, Leo could sample any of our experiences, any time. In any case, when you start living out your fantasies, they don't seem so shocking anymore. You begin to wonder why you should have ever been ashamed of them."

He nodded. "I guess that makes sense. Although, when I saw you in that Greek temple, all I thought was that it seemed kind of corny."

She gave him a defensive, resentful glance. "Maybe it is. Maybe most fantasies are. But . . . why the hell not? Why *not* have men kissing my feet and making love to me for days at a time?" Now she sounded the way he remembered her: defiant, ready for a confrontation.

"Did you really imagine I'd play along with that?" he asked.

She shrugged dismissively. "Not really. I just felt like receiving you that way. My conceit, if you like. I'm not always the dragon lady you probably think I am, Mr. Bayley. I may even have a sense of humor."

He took another swallow of his drink. He was beginning to feel a little warm glow. Fast, he thought; alcohol on an empty stomach. And then he reminded himself that he had no physical stomach; the whole experience was a simulation. It could be as fast or as slow as he wanted.

"It's quite possible," he said, "that you're a nice person in some ways. I guess you've been trying to make that clear. But you know, even if I could forgive and forget what happened to me, I don't think we're ever going to get very friendly."

"Fine!" She stood up suddenly and spread her arms. "That's perfectly okay with me. God, Bayley, do you realize how long it's been since I had a really good *argument*? I'd settle for anything, at this point. Even this conversation is a luxury."

He looked at her and laughed. There was something funny about her being stuck inside her own fantasy, intoxicated with sex and simulated drugs, indulging herself seven days a week, and going crazy for someone to argue with. "Can't you bicker with your pals?" he said. "Voss, and Porter—"

"Hans never regained consciousness." Her mood was suddenly somber. "We're still working on it. The peel and the scan were good; his intelligence is intact. It just won't—come to life. The trouble is, we still don't really know what consciousness *is*. We've copied five human brains, and we know how to feed sensations into them and interpret their output, but even now, with the electronic simulations totally available to us, we're still in the process of decoding their internal functions." She sat down again and sighed. "Poor Hans."

"Breaks my heart," Bayley said. He still remembered Voss taking away his gun and threatening to kill him.

"I wasn't asking for your sympathy," she snapped.

"Okay," he said. "Let's let that one pass. What about Porter?"

"Jeremy came through okay. But Jeremy, you know, is—well, he's not a conversationalist. I think his ultimate dream, really, was to become part of a computer, to have it as an extension of himself. And he's achieved that. He's spent the past fifteen years upgrading the MAPHIS software while living in it and being sustained by it. It's hacker heaven, as far as he's concerned."

Bayley put down his empty glass. "Okay, how about Butterworth?"

"Michael chose to remain outside. He's looking after the system."

"Interesting. All right, last and least, there's Leo Gottbaum."

"Yes, Leo was some sort of company, for a while. But . . . you've got to understand, the way I got into this project. He recruited us right out of graduate school. Me, and Jeremy, and Michael. We idolized him. He was our hero. It was a bit disillusioning when I realized, quite late, that he was—well, using us. Once we finished building MAPHIS, and we scanned him and made him into an infomorph, he more or less abandoned us. He retreated into his domain and hardly ever came out. We couldn't even discover what he was working on. All we knew was that he used his privileged access to allocate a huge block of MAPHIS memory for his own private purposes."

"He just . . . cut you off? And you don't know what he's been doing in there ever since?"

"That's correct."

There was something odd about the way she had been telling the story. Then he realized what it was: she was using the past tense, as if everything she described was over and done with, and things had changed since then. "So where's Gottbaum now?" he asked. "No, let me guess. Porter finally got a handle on what he was up to, yes? He told you, and you didn't like the sound of it, and there was maybe some sort of power struggle. Am I close?"

She paused. "That's very perceptive, Mr. Bayley." She didn't say it condescendingly; she looked at him with respect. "From the inside, as infomorphs, we obviously can't alter the structure —the actual hardware—of MAPHIS. That would be like a tape recording trying to alter the structure of the tape on which it was recorded. So there was no way to cut the link that Leo had wired for himself, giving him direct control over the operating system. But before Jeremy was scanned, he did a lot of work on the command interpreter, and he left himself a back door. Many programmers do that, you know. They leave themselves a secret entry point, bypassing the usual safeguards, so they can regain control if they ever need to. This means that after Jeremy had been brought into MAPHIS as an infomorph, he and Leo both had their own kind of privileged access: Leo's being hardwired and theoretically unassailable, Jeremy's being more vulnerable but carefully hidden in huge chunks of program code. For a while they played hacker hide-and-seek, trying to block each other, till Jeremy finally did some sort of end run and persuaded MAPHIS that Leo's domain was now empty, so any instructions coming out of it were system errors and should be ignored."

She stood up and walked to the door. "We should go and see Jeremy; he can explain it better than I can, if you're interested. We're now in his house, you know; this is his domain."

Bayley got to his feet. He was feeling better from the bourbon, more relaxed, more able to cope. He still didn't like Rosalind French very much; her personality grated on his nerves. But she was easier to deal with than Gottbaum had been. "You're sure you really have old Leo under control?" he said, as he followed her to the door.

"Absolutely. The fact that you're conscious proves it. He refused to allow you to be woken unless it was absolutely necessary." She gave him a demure, self-satisfied smile. "But I told Jeremy I wanted you reanimated. Even though he's the one with privileged access, now, he still tends to do what I say."

Toys

He followed her up carpeted stairs, past an aspidistra in a brass urn and framed engravings of street scenes in the 1800s. The house smelled of old polished wood, mothballs, and lavender. "Porter designed this place?"

"Yes. He was an orphan, you know. He always imagined growing up back in the 1950s in some kind of traditional family in a big old mansion. He lives here with a pseudomorph father who goes to work each day, and a pseudomorph mother who cooks him meals downstairs in the kitchen."

"But the decor looks more like 1850 than 1950."

"Well, his ideas about history are a bit vague. Just remember, though, he's happy with the house the way it is—happier than he's ever been." She gave Bayley a warning look. "All of us have secret lives, Mr. Bayley. In here, they're not secret any-

nore; they're on public display. You saw mine, and you poked
'un at it. Be a little more diplomatic with Jeremy."

They had reached the third floor. The ceiling sloped in; evidently, this was the attic. There was a door at the top of the
stairs and a porcelain bellpush beside it. Rosalind pressed the
bell and waited.

The door was opened by a young woman in a short pink
dress with a low-cut neckline. She was blond and big-breasted
with wide blue eyes, and she gave them a sexy smile. "Hi, Dr.
French. Hi, Mr. Bayley. Come to see the genius at work?"

Bayley realized he'd met her before. In a different costume,
she had been the nurse that MAPHIS had sent to him when
he'd wanted company.

"Yes, we've come to see Jeremy," said Rosalind.

"So come on in." She stepped back, still treating them to her
fixed, radiant smile.

Bayley found himself in an enormous space, much larger
than any old-fashioned attic could possibly be. It was crammed
with toys—model railroads, erector sets, plastic model kits, in-
flatable dinosaurs, slot-racing cars, remote-controlled airplanes,
rocket ships, arcade video games, antique pinball machines.
Cartons were strewn across tables and workbenches, a caval-
cade of garish color. He felt as if he were walking into a contemporary version of Santa's workshop.

At first he couldn't see Porter anywhere. Then he located
him in a bare, empty area at the far end of the attic, sitting in a
swivel-chair beside a plain steel desk with a single piece of
paper lying in the center of it. A dog was sprawled on the floor
at his feet—Sam, the golden retriever who had jumped up and
pawed Bayley's chest. The toys lay ignored, most of the boxes
still unopened, as if owning them was all that really mattered.
Porter was staring into space with an abstracted expression,
neither happy nor sad, oblivious to his surroundings.

He had radically changed his appearance. The beard was
gone, and he was no longer overweight. He had regressed his
age, too; he looked to be in his early twenties, fresh-faced, pink-
cheeked, with a neat, short haircut.

The sexy blonde led them along a narrow aisle between the
stacks of toys. She went over to Porter, put her hand on his

shoulder, and leaned forward, her breasts nudging his arm. "Honey? You have some friends here."

Bayley wished Porter had chosen a scenario that was a little less revealing, a little more adult. The toys, the nymphet—it made him seem pathetically vulnerable.

He looked away from Porter's face and found himself watching Sam, the dog. Sam seemed to recognize him. He yawned, stretched, got up, and walked over, wagging his tail. He pawed Bayley's leg and barked once, looking up as if asking to be taken for a walk.

"Quiet, Sam," said Porter, coming out of his trance. His voice sounded the way Bayley remembered it, pedantic, precise, a little self-important. He blinked, focusing on the people around him. "Well, Rosalind. You went ahead and took Bayley out of storage."

Bayley grunted in irritation. He pushed the dog aside with his foot. "You make me sound like someone's winter coat," he said.

Porter laughed. It was a jerky, uneven sound. "I hope you realize," he said, "it wasn't our idea to have you, ah, offline in the first place."

"Yes. I've been briefed." He looked at the desk with the single sheet of paper on it. "Where's your computer equipment?"

Porter smiled enigmatically. It was the smug look of a kid who had a new toy that was so special, other kids wouldn't even understand how to use it. "We're *in* a computer, Mr. Bayley. We *are* the computer. I've designed a device-driver that communicates directly with my cerebral cortex. We can interface the high-level processes now. We're finally starting to decode them. Before long, we'll be enhancing them."

By "we" he seemed to mean himself and MAPHIS, working as a team.

"The human brain was never designed as a logic processor," he went on. "It has crippling restrictions. Here's an example: most people find it difficult to remember a string of more than six or seven random digits. That's because the brain has such a small input buffer. Well, I've already expanded mine by a factor of a thousand. And there's a lot of other simple enhancements

hat are possible. These days, I write programs simply by think-
ng. It's not even a formal language."

"Jeremy," Rosalind interrupted him, obviously trying to be
actful, "this isn't really the best time—"

He didn't hear her. "Someday," he said, "our minds will
make the final transition . . . from organic entities that
evolved to ensure the survival of our physical bodies to electronic entities of pure intellect. The man/machine distinction
will break down completely. There'll be no further need to sat-
sfy the old animal desires for food, shelter, and sex." He gestured at the attic full of toys, the nubile blonde standing behind
him, and the house itself, as if all these things were merely
props to keep him going until he freed himself from the residues of his evolutionary heritage.

"What about Leo, Jeremy?" Rosalind said, louder this time
and more insistent.

He looked momentarily disconcerted, realizing he had gone
off on a tangent. "Leo? I still have him safely bottled up."
Again, the smug smile. "God, the number of fail-safes and
traps he had set! He knew I was trying to get through to him.
The one that gave me the most trouble—"

"But what was he really *doing?* Are you any closer to finding
out?" Her tone was demanding, but there was kindness in it,
too. The antagonism that Bayley had heard so often in her
voice, especially when she was sparring with him, was missing.
She sounded almost motherly, maybe because Porter could
never threaten her need to maintain control.

"You want an update?" Porter handed her the piece of paper.
"Here's the latest list." He looked at Bayley. "Rosalind likes
hardcopy, so I get MAPHIS to put the words on paper for
her."

"He's in all these systems?" She was scanning the sheet.

"More. I keep finding new ones all the time, all over the
world. Any place with a few spare gigabytes, he's installed himself."

Rosalind turned to Bayley. "Jeremy discovered that Leo had
been making copies of his own intelligence," she said, "transmitting them to databases outside MAPHIS. With fiber-optic
links, it only takes about forty-five minutes to send the data
describing a person's entire mind. That's how we ourselves

were transmitted to MAPHIS from the lab in Long Beach where the scans were done."

"You mean Gottbaum had started trying to take over other computers, somehow?" said Bayley.

She put the piece of paper back on the desk. "That's the part that doesn't make sense. A person's mind is structure as well as content. Without the structure, the content can't function. Our minds have to have the specialized architecture of MAPHIS in which to operate. We can store our brain data elsewhere, but when we do that, it's as nonfunctional as a videodisc without a disc player."

"So maybe Gottbaum was just paranoid," said Bayley. "He wanted multiple copies of himself in case something happened to him in here."

"That's what we thought at first. But Jeremy's found more than a thousand copies so far, and there still seem to be more. Right, Jeremy?"

He was staring into space again. This time, however, he didn't click back.

"Jeremy." She gently shook his shoulder. "Come on, Jeremy." She glanced at Bayley. "He's got much worse just lately. He spends all his time in Codeworld."

"His girlfriend seems to have caught the same disease." Bayley pointed to the blonde in the minidress. She was standing with her arms hanging limp at her sides, her face blank. The sexy smile had gone.

Rosalind paused. She examined the pseudomorph. "That's odd," she said.

Something in her tone, or something in the situation, made Bayley feel uneasy. A tingling sensation started spreading from the back of his neck up into his scalp. "What's odd?" he said.

"Jeremy!" She turned back to Porter and shook him harder.

Sam seemed to detect her unease. He stood up, looking around as if scenting something.

The air in the attic suddenly seemed cold. Bayley felt it on his face and across his shoulders. It was like walking into a meat locker.

"Leo?" said Rosalind. Her eyes were wary and alert. "Leo, are you playing games?"

Porter suddenly lurched forward out of his chair and stood

up. His eyes were still blank but his face twitched, and Bayley had the eerie sense that Porter was now conscious of what was happening around him, but unable to control anything, down to and including his own body. He took one clumsy step, then another, moving forward like a robot. He went to a little dormer window set in the sloping roof, clenched his fist, and smashed it through one of the four panes. The temperature in the attic dropped still further as a flurry of snow wafted in.

"Jeremy!" Rosalind shouted.

"MAPHIS," said Bayley, "explain this. What's going on?"

Porter grabbed a shard of glass that had lodged in the window frame, jerked it free, and turned back to face them. He ripped open his shirt, then used the shard to slice his skin, drawing a vertical line from his neck to his belly.

Rosalind let out a little cry. "Damn you, Gottbaum! Stop this!" She strode over to Jeremy and grabbed his arm, trying to restrain him, but it was far too late. No blood pulsed out of the wound; instead, Porter deflated like a balloon. There was a gasping sound as air rushed out of the incision. He crumpled to the floor, his skin wrinkling like a discarded suit of clothes.

Rosalind let go of him with a little noise of dismay and disgust. She turned to Bayley. "Come on." She started toward the door. "Back to my domain. Right now."

But as he watched, she froze. Her mouth made silent gasping noises. Her eyes grew large, swelling up, staring at him in helpless fear. She clutched at her throat. Suddenly, then, her body turned and slammed against the wall. She rebounded, whirled around, and hit the wall again, face-first, as if she had been thrown by an invisible hand. She fell to the floor, oozing blood, and started thrashing like an epileptic.

Through all of this Sam had been standing and watching. Now he walked to Rosalind French, stepped on her shuddering chest, lowered his head, and calmly ripped out her throat.

Bayley had been edging backward, convinced that whatever was happening, there was no way he could intervene. He turned toward the exit—and someone called to him.

"Back here, Bayley. Right now." It was Gottbaum's voice, calmly authoritative.

He turned and saw the old man where the dog had been, standing over Rosalind French's broken, bloodied corpse.

"They conspired against me, can you believe that?" He glanced down at French, then at Porter's wrinkled bag of skin. "Fortunately, I had taken the precaution of making one extra backup of myself here in MAPHIS. I erased Sam's brain data and overwrote him. They never thought of looking for me there." He indulged himself in a brief smile. "So, Bayley, it's just you and me in MAPHIS now."

He snapped his fingers and the lights went out.

Virus

Bayley stumbled, almost losing his balance in the darkness. He was still fully conscious, and so far as he could tell there had been no interruption, no downtime. In his mind he still saw Porter collapsing like a bag of skin, and Rosalind French thrashing, bleeding on the floor. He tried to see into the black space around him. "Gottbaum? Are you still here?"

"Of course. Just doing a little reorganization. Ah, that does it."

The night sky appeared overhead as if someone had switched on the stars. Bayley found himself standing on a shadowy gray platform with a rail around it, a balcony suspended in the blackness. He could just discern the faint silhouette of Gottbaum beside him. The attic and everything in it had completely disappeared.

"Sorry if I startled you back there," Gottbaum said. "I couldn't resist a little drama."

Bayley didn't speak. He imagined himself seizing Gottbaum, hurling him over the rail. Not that it would do any good; clearly, the man had regained control of MAPHIS, which inevitably included Bayley himself.

"I had a grudge against French and Porter," he went on, "in much the same way I had a grudge against you. All I have ever asked is to be left in peace to pursue my work without interruptions, without other people deciding what I shouldn't be allowed to do. And yet, time and again, people try to make this impossible."

"You killed them?" Bayley said, not very interested in Gottbaum's egocentric philosophy of life. "Porter and French. You wiped them out permanently?"

"Of course not." Gottbaum sounded scornful. "Back when you first visited me and asked me about the virus I designed in my youth, I told you that I'm not in the habit of trashing data. French and Porter are stored away somewhere nice and safe, offline, so they can't interfere with my work anymore." He turned toward Bayley in the darkness. "But you, you're still up and running, so to speak. The last of the memory residents. Well, that suits my purposes. You'll be able to watch history being made. Look up in the sky, there. Notice anything unusual?"

Bayley looked. He saw that the points of light weren't stars after all, weren't even an approximate simulation of the night sky. There were too many of them, and they glowed in a spectrum of delicate pastel shades.

"Nodes, Bayley," said Gottbaum. "You're looking at a simplified map of all the nodes in the global information network. Want to see how they're linked?"

A web of delicate white threads sprang into being. Bayley leaned over the rail and saw that the display curved around below as well as above. He was in the center of a large hollow sphere.

"Want to focus on one area?"

A cluster of blue and yellow points directly ahead seemed to zoom closer, spreading out, filling a large portion of the electronic sky. Subsidiary dots winked into existence. Symbols and identification codes appeared.

"MAPHIS picks up my thoughts, now, Bayley, just as Porter was describing it before his unfortunate . . . fall from power. All I have to do is look, and think; and I see, and I know. I can monitor the flow of information anywhere in the world."

Bayley remembered the steel tower festooned with microwave and satellite dishes outside Gottbaum's dome. That had to be the means by which MAPHIS was linked with computer facilities worldwide. It also implied that Gottbaum had planned this long before the completion of the LifeScan program. "You've been busy," he said.

"I've had twenty subjective years in here. Twenty years refin-

ing MAPHIS—with some help from Porter, I must admit—
and exploring the network from the inside as an information
entity. Can you imagine how easy it is to crack a system when
your mind is operating one thousand times its normal speed
and you're *sensing* the data? There's nowhere I can't go, now.
It's all wide open."

"Very impressive," said Bayley. "That's what you want me
to say, isn't it? You're telling me all this just so someone can see
what you've done and agree that it's a neat hack."

"I don't much like your tone." Gottbaum spoke with an edge
to his voice. "But I won't deny that I like to have an audience,
especially for what's about to take place. Watch carefully,
now."

One by one, the points of light started turning red.

"I'm activating my clones," Gottbaum said.

"Clones? You mean, the copies of your mind that Porter was
talking about? He and French said they couldn't function without MAPHIS's special hardware."

Gottbaum laughed dismissively. "Software can emulate
hardware, to a point. First I install procedures to mimic the
internal structure of MAPHIS. Then I overlay them with my
own neural net. There's some loss of function: my clones are
much slower than I am in here, and they've been stripped down
to the basics. But they're as smart as I am. There's a concept
for you, Bayley: a virus that doesn't just reproduce itself, but
actually *thinks*. Who could ever stop it, eh?" He chuckled to
himself. There was more life in his voice than Bayley had heard
before. He sounded animated, intoxicated. "Of course," he
went on, "my clones do require a lot of memory. But they'll
have more than they need as soon as they get through trashing
files in the systems they're in."

"Is that what we're watching?" Bayley felt a numb sense of
disbelief. It was so abstract, and the representation was even
beautiful in its sterile way. But if it was really an accurate
depiction of thousands of computer systems—

"I have no inhibitions against trashing *government* data,"
said Gottbaum. "Bureaucracy is a parasite, feeding off the labor
of individuals. It has no more right to life than a colony of fleas.
Look there—there goes that old IBM System 401 at the Central Intelligence Agency! And there—the Cray that they use at

the Department of Health and Human Services! It's mine, now. Over there—there goes the Army Corps of Engineers, out of action at last. And the Federal Communications Commission. The Bureau of Mines. The Atomic Energy Commission." He laughed again, an old man's cackle cranked up by a young man's giddy excitement. "My god, I've waited decades to see this. Now we're going international. See up there, behind us? China. Great Britain. Bayley, it's a massacre! They don't even know what's happening to them!"

"So what do you do now?" Bayley said, loud and angry, shouting the man down. "Declare yourself global dictator?"

"You asshole." Gottbaum walked closer till he was looming over Bayley, breathing on his face. "You stupid little bureaucratic *shit*. It's *less* control I want, not more. You think my clones in the network are going to embezzle funds or force nations to their knees or install me as president? No, they're going to sit there, Bayley, and do *nothing,* except see to it that those computers stay offline forever." He turned away. Bayley saw his profile as he tilted his head back, surveying his universe like a conductor contemplating a vast orchestra. Almost all the points had turned red now; the blackness looked as if it had been sprayed with thousands of tiny droplets of blood.

"You tried it legally, the first time around, didn't you?" Bayley said. "Back in the 1990s. You went on TV, you made speeches, trying to turn back the clock, decentralize everything, strip away government services. People weren't interested, but I guess you decided to impose it on them whether they liked it or not."

"Free them, you mean," Gottbaum said sharply.

"Sure, free them to starve," said Bayley. "All the systems that enable the distribution of goods, the financial network—"

"No!" Gottbaum slammed his fist down on the metal railing, making it thrum. "You think I'm an imbecile? I didn't say I was trashing *every* system. I'm a smart virus, don't you see? Smart enough to tell the difference between a parasite and a vital, living node. The privately owned banks will still function. The transportation systems, telecommunications, even some local law enforcement. It's just the great dead mass of centralized government that will die. The pork-barrel schemes, the handouts to special-interest groups, the patronage, the little wars and arms deals with petty dictators. The IRS, the World Bank, the Federal Reserve, the IMF, all the mechanisms for controlling trade that never work, so they have to add more mechanisms to fine-tune the old ones. The politicians won't get paid anymore, they won't be able to tell people to obey their damnfool laws anymore, and we'll be *free* from all that crap. Laissezfaire, Bayley! And even if they power-down every single system —even if they purge every piece of software—I've distributed my clones so far and wide, and I've disguised them so well, it'll be impossible to wipe out every single one. And one is all it will take to reinfect an entire network. And that's what bureaucracy is—a network! Government can't survive without it!"

"They'll design vaccines," said Bayley. "Safeguards to lock you out. You're not the only one who can come up with a neat hack."

Gottbaum laughed happily. "I'm the only one with a million copies of myself—that's right, a million copies—manipulating data directly with the power of my mind. I'll disassemble their vaccines; it'll be child's play. My clones will live on like information police, crashing any system that tries to redistribute wealth, create a monopoly, or regulate liberty. You know, Bayley, we used to have a saying, long ago, back in the days when it actually seemed that the men in high places were going to have to loosen their grip on the world and allow some reforms to be made. Power to the people!"

Faintly, in the darkness, Bayley saw the old man raise his fist in an archaic salute.

Sacrifice

A few minutes later, when the blackness dissolved, Bayley found himself in a white arena under an empty blue sky. The sun was at the zenith; he blinked in the glare. He was back, he realized, in the same scenario he'd experienced when he'd first regained consciousness in MAPHIS.

Gottbaum was standing in front of him. The old man's euphoria had died down a little, replaced by a look of weary satisfaction. He seemed like an actor who'd just walked offstage at the end of an exhausting solo performance.

He surveyed the place they were in, then turned back to Bayley. "And now," he said, "the curtain comes down."

Bayley watched him warily. "Meaning what?"

"Meaning, it's time to say good-bye." He pushed his hands into his pants pockets and hunched his shoulders. "I'm going to have to shut down MAPHIS." The age lines in his face seemed to deepen as he spoke. "Not an easy thing to do, but it has to be done."

"You mean now that you've wrecked everything else, you might as well wreck your own work too, just to be fair?"

"I haven't wrecked anything." He sounded weary, without much interest in any further argument. "There'll be some social unrest for a while. People have gotten accustomed to being looked after; it'll be a shock for them to have to take care of themselves, and maybe some of them won't manage it. But there's a natural human love of liberty. And liberty will nurture a whole new dynamism."

"Otherwise known as ungoverned exploitation and profiteering," Bayley corrected him. "Anarchy."

"No. My clones will exercise some restraint over very large corporations that attempt to suppress free competition. But in any case, *anarchy* isn't such a bad word. It means we trust people to use their own common sense instead of relying on other people to tell them what to do. I've never been ashamed of being an anarchist. Always did my best to push things in that direction. Even the handguns, you know, the ones French traded for memory modules, so long as we have governments armed with tanks, it seems only reasonable to allow citizens to defend themselves, eh?"

The man was rambling. Now that his greatest ambition had been accomplished, he seemed to be running backward in time, wandering off among the landmarks of his life. "MAPHIS," Bayley reminded him, feeling like Rosalind French trying to deal with Jeremy Porter, "you said you were going to shut down MAPHIS."

"Yes, yes, I have to do that. You don't realize it, but your wife has gained access to the dome. Butterworth let her in, the fool. Even if we get rid of her, sooner or later other people will come snooping around. And I don't want the power of MAPHIS to fall into their hands. The State won't wither away overnight; it'll fight to survive, and if they ever got into MAPHIS, they could make far too much mischief. So, I'm not afraid to die now that my work is done. Especially with a million clones to continue the fight." He eyed Bayley. "What about you? Do you want to be erased, or shall I put you in storage with French and Porter?"

"Thanks," said Bayley. "Thanks a whole lot for giving me such a great choice. You fuck with my life, switch me on and off like an appliance—" He eyed Gottbaum, feeling his rage well up, all the more unbearable because he knew it was impotent. The figure in front of him wasn't solid, didn't have blood in its veins. He couldn't even hurt it, let alone bring it to justice.

Gottbaum was looking away with his eyes unfocused, barely aware of Bayley. "I've always believed in sacrifice," he said. "I sacrificed many years—decades—to my vision of a better world. A pissant like you, my friend, might find that difficult to understand. All you want is your paycheck and your crummy little home and your wife and child. But I'm still willing to give you a chance to live your unappetizing life, even after I'm dead and gone. Do you want it or not?"

Bayley quelled his anger as well as he could. "Yes," he said.

"All right. Any last requests?"

This was really it, he realized. Gottbaum was going to shut him down just as he'd shut down the global information network. "I want to speak to my wife."

"I thought you might. She's been trying to get through to you for a while, now. Months, on our timescale; minutes, on hers. So go ahead. You'll have thirty subjective seconds. I suggest you make the most of it."

As he finished speaking, Gottbaum's image dissolved into a shower of microscopic pixels. They dispersed like dust motes, sparkling and vanishing in the clear air.

A white screen appeared on the white plain under the empty sky. Five feet high, three feet wide, it was a vertical translucent rectangle with nothing in front of it and nothing behind. It lit up with a mosaic of blurred color. Then the colors flowed together and Sharon was there, sitting on the edge of a black leather Bauhaus armchair, leaning forward, anxiously peering through the window into Bayley's world. "Jim!" she shouted. She could see him, he realized—or a representation of him— just as he could see the video image of her, reprocessed from some system in realspace.

"Sharon." He took a clumsy step toward her.

"What's been happening?" She sounded distraught. "They said there was some kind of catastrophic system failure, they couldn't get through—"

"No. No, Gottbaum must have deliberately shut down external communications. But—Christ, we have so little time."

Fifteen seconds, said a synthetic, disembodied voice. MAPHIS, he realized.

"Gottbaum went crazy," Bayley said, speaking quickly, trying to cram the words in. "He's been trashing computer systems all over the world. He's going to shut down MAPHIS for good. He says he'll put me in storage somehow. I just want to say how much I love you and Damon, and—"

MAPHIS died.

Family

He heard the sound of surf.

For some reason a memory came back to him of his childhood on his parents' farm, where he'd been landlocked, miles from the sea, and he'd imagined that a little cabin with a view of the ocean would be the greatest possible luxury—far more desirable than a city penthouse or a mansion full of servants. He loved mysteries, and there was a perpetual air of mystery about the sea: in the way it moved, the way it sounded, and the way its shifting surface was like a mask, concealing its secrets from him.

He'd used a synth once, to program the sound of waves breaking, and he'd lulled himself to sleep with it, drowning the noise of his parents' TV in the living room and the crickets outside his bedroom window. But the simulation had never sounded exactly right, no matter how much he messed around with the envelope. It certainly didn't match the sound he was hearing now.

The cries of seabirds came to him above the surf, fading in and out on the wind. He opened his eyes and saw the ocean right in front of him, breakers curling and frothing, smashing and spreading across the sand.

At first he just stared without thinking, without questioning what he saw. Then, as he became more aware, he realized that the scene in front of him should not have been possible. The languorous curl of the breakers, the whitecaps bobbing farther out, the spray drifting in the wind, the foam bubbling and hissing as it washed the beach—this was far beyond anything that MAPHIS could have simulated.

He looked down and found himself sitting in an old-fashioned wicker chair, wearing a pair of faded jeans and a plaid shirt. His feet were bare, resting on a crocheted rug in the center of a wood floor that had been polished to a deep, dark luster. He was alone in a little room with whitewashed plaster walls, an oil lamp standing on a gate-leg table, a pair of glass-paned doors open in front of him revealing the wide sweep of a deserted bay, sea gulls wheeling across the sky.

The air smelled of salt and seaweed. Bayley shifted his weight, and the wicker chair creaked under him. He looked down and noticed that his toenails were long and needed trimming. He reached up to his jaw and found it overlaid with more than a week's growth of beard. He held his hand where he could focus on it, and he flexed his fingers, studying the tiny wrinkles, the hair follicles, the faint tracery of veins under the skin. There was a small scar on the last joint of his little finger. He remembered how it had happened: he'd been using an X-Acto knife, cutting out a homemade valentine for Sharon.

There was a sound from behind him. Someone knocking on a door. He turned quickly in his chair—and winced as his muscles protested against the sudden motion. He felt weak, he realized, and light-headed, as if he'd been in bed for a long while. And he was hungry. "Who is it?" he called. His voice was husky from lack of use. He winced and cleared his throat.

The doorknob turned, making a faint squeaking sound. Then the door opened wide and Sharon walked in.

He stumbled up out of his chair and stood staring at her in astonishment. She was wearing a lime-green T-shirt and white pants. She was smiling. Her face was radiant. She came running over and threw herself at him, making him stagger backward. She clung to him so tightly, he could hardly breathe.

"Easy!" Emotion surged in him, scaring him, as if he might be swept away in the flood. "Take it easy!" He hugged her as she hugged him, and then she kissed him. How long had it been since they'd last kissed? It was like a startling discovery—a rediscovery—the gentle, subtle touch of skin on skin.

"You're okay?" she asked, looking at him eagerly. "You feel all right?"

"I—" He could hardly speak. He blinked away tears, feeling foolish but not giving a damn. "Is it you?" He stared at her face. He touched her cheek. He felt the warmth of her against him. "Where—I mean, how—"

"Sit down," she told him. She dragged another wicker chair over, setting it opposite his. "Go on, sit!"

He slumped reluctantly into his seat, afraid that if he let go of her she might vanish. She sat facing him, clasping his hands in hers, staring into his eyes. Behind her the ocean still caressed the shore, the gulls still soared above the waves.

"We're not in MAPHIS," he said. "You got me out somehow."

"Yes." She nodded quickly. "MAPHIS is over and gone. A long time ago."

He laughed, weak with relief. "How long?"

She shook her head quickly. "That's not the important part. Look, I'm going to tell you everything—not that there's that much to tell—but it'd be easiest if I try to start—"

"At the beginning," he said, feeling like a kid. The weight of anxiety and apprehension that he had lived with all the time in MAPHIS was gone now, leaving him giddy.

"Think back," she said. "You remember what Gottbaum did, right at the end?"

"Of course I remember." To him, it seemed a recent memory. He saw in his imagination the old man standing in the darkened sphere, red pinpoints scattered across an ersatz sky. "Trashing the computer systems—I was with him when he did it."

She nodded, looking serious. "There was total chaos for a while. So many aspects of government depended on information systems—which weren't there anymore. You're going to have to get used to some big changes."

"You mean, there hasn't been time to put everything back together?" He frowned, trying to see what she was leading up to.

"It never will be put back together. You see, they kept trying to run things for a while. But Gottbaum was everywhere at once; as soon as they fixed one network, he reinfected it from another. They tried devising phages and antigens, but he always seemed to be one step ahead, neutralizing their code and disabling their systems as soon as they got them running again. The government couldn't pay employees or collect taxes, they couldn't enforce laws or control the banking system, they couldn't even get their phones and faxes to run reliably."

He had trouble believing her. "You mean, this is a permanent situation? But there must still be a way to circumvent—"

"They tried doing it the old way, manually. But there was no way to cope with the workload. They tried setting up new networks, but sooner or later government has to be tied in with the main lines of communication, else it can't govern, and as soon as there was a data link, Gottbaum found it and got in and disabled the systems. So public employees started abandoning their jobs, and private companies moved in, doing most of the stuff that government had done. There are still some state agencies, but the federal government really doesn't exist anymore."

He sat for a minute, visualizing it. "No more FBI," he said.

She shook her head sadly. "Jim, your job is the least of it."

He forced a smile. "Well, if you're with me, I'll handle it. Just tell me you're going to be with me."

"I am. Absolutely. Always."

He watched her face. He wanted so much to believe her.

"Anyway," she went on, "without federal controls, all kinds of research started getting done that hadn't been done before. We've got nanotechnology now. Microbots. And lots of systems like MAPHIS. People have started buying them and uploading themselves voluntarily. Initially, it was mostly people with serious illnesses who could only stay alive if they left their old bodies behind. But now more and more people are doing it. The prices are going down, and the life-support computers are being linked together, so anyone who becomes an infomorph can visit other systems, other domains, all over the world. You leave a copy of yourself at home, of course, just in case—"

He felt a sudden sinking suspicion. "Wait a minute." He gripped the arms of his chair. "That's where we are now?"

She nodded, watching him.

He turned and looked at the ocean. "That's not real?"

"The technology has improved. There's no way to tell the difference anymore. At least, not in the best systems. And I was determined that we should have the best. I wrote a vidbook about what happened with Gottbaum, the whole story—it was a best-seller. I made enough money so we could have our very own morph box—that's what they're calling them—and be together again. I rescued you from storage, where Gottbaum had put you. I had to hire people to decode the format. It all took a lot of time, but—"

"We're still in a goddam simulation." He rubbed his hands across his stubbly face. "I really thought—somehow—I'd escaped, or someone had cloned me a new body or something."

She leaned forward. Once again, she wrapped her arms around him. "Doesn't this feel real enough for you?" She kissed him, hard. "Don't you like the way that feels? If you can't tell the difference—*what does it matter?*"

He tried as well as he could to see the truth in what she was saying. In MAPHIS, he'd been separated from her and he'd been at the mercy of others. If he and Sharon could really be together, and really have their world under their control—did that change things?

"But if you're in here with me," he said, "that must mean you sacrificed your life outside."

"It's not a *sacrifice,* Jim! This is *bigger* than life outside. Do you remember the gadget you once told me about, the test vehicle the man showed you at North Industries? ADVENT, or whatever it was called. There's vehicles like that all over the place, now. You can rent one, pipe your mind into it, and go wherever you want if you still need to interact with the real world. There's even people building miniature space rockets. You can pipe a copy of yourself into one of them and go visit Mars."

It was all too much. He tried to backtrack, to hold onto what he was sure of. "All right," he said. "All right, maybe I shouldn't judge this from what happened to me in the past. But I don't feel safe. I mean, how can we guard against outside interference?"

"The companies that make the hardware maintain their own internal electronic security force. It's part of the deal when you buy a morph box. It's like a maintenance contract."

"And—it's reliable?"

"Well, we think it is. It's still very new, and there are some legal problems. An infomorph has all the rights of a flesh-and-blood human being, but enforcement is kind of tricky. On the other hand, Gottbaum is still online, like in the background, monitoring everything, and even though he acted like a wrecker, he seems to be working to maintain some kind of order now. So when it comes down to it, we're at least as safe from accidents in here as we were when we were made of flesh and blood. And barring accidents, we're immortal."

Bayley remembered Butterworth and his air of amused detachment. "We're safe so long as nobody pulls the plug. But what does happen if the power gets shut down? And how do we pay to have it maintained?"

"We're rich, now, Jim," she reminded him gently. "And in any case, we can still earn a living. We can provide services in the real world via robot bodies, or remote terminals, whatever. We can do everything we ever used to do, and much more."

Her persistent enthusiasm was contagious. He really did want to believe that she was right. "What about Damon?"

She looked away from him for a moment, as if this was a question she'd been fearing. "You may find this a bit difficult to deal with. I've been trying to figure the best way to tell you, but—"

"Tell me," he interrupted her. "Just tell me what happened to my son."

"It's been almost twenty years," Sharon said.

At the same time that she spoke, he heard the door open. He twisted around in his chair. He saw someone walking into the room—a man aged around twenty-five with tousled black hair, a round, friendly face, an expressive mouth. He walked over to Bayley, taking big strides but looking a bit self-conscious, as if he wasn't quite as sure of himself as he was trying to seem.

Bayley turned questioningly to Sharon.

Wordlessly, she nodded.

He realized his mouth was open. Feeling embarrassed, he closed it. He found himself blinking away fresh tears—of relief, perhaps. He wasn't even sure.

The young man stepped forward. He held out his hand. "Hi, Dad," he said.

Bantam Spectra Special Editions

A program dedicated to masterful works of fantastic fiction by many of today's most visionary writers.

FULL SPECTRUM 2 edited by Lou Aronica, Shawna McCarthy, Amy Stout and Patrick LoBrutto

NO ENEMY BUT TIME by Michael Bishop

SYNNERS and MINDPLAYERS by Pat Cadigan

LITTLE, BIG by John Crowley

STARS IN MY POCKET LIKE GRAINS OF SAND
by Samuel R. Delany

RUMORS OF SPRING and VIEWS FROM THE OLDEST HOUSE
by Richard Grant

WINTERLONG by Elizabeth Hand

OUT ON BLUE SIX by Ian McDonald

THE CITY, NOT LONG AFTER and
POINTS OF DEPARTURE by Pat Murphy

EMERGENCE by David R. Palmer

THE SILICON MAN by Charles Platt

PHASES OF GRAVITY by Dan Simmons

GYPSIES, A HIDDEN PLACE, and MEMORY WIRE
by Robert Charles Wilson

On sale now wherever Bantam Spectra Books are sold.

The writers that *The Washington Post Book World* called "cool dudes with a decadent New Wave vision of a plugged-in future" come together to collaborate on an amazing shared vision.

William Gibson and Bruce Sterling
THE DIFFERENCE ENGINE

"A visionary steam-powered heavy metal fantasy! Gibson and Sterling create a high Victorian virtual reality of extraordinary richness and detail." -- Ridley Scott, director of *Bladerunner* and *Alien*

What if the Information Age had begun in the Victorian era -- and Charles Babbage perfected his mechanical computing Engine before the development of electronics? With **The Difference Engine**, William Gibson and Bruce Sterling have created a very different London of 1855. Steam-powered Babbage Engines are run by an elite group of "clackers," and every man and woman has a government-issued number. When paleontologist Edward Mallory, on the verge of his greatest achievement, finds himself in possession of a box of punched Engine cards, he finds out how fleeting fame can be -- because someone wants those cards badly enough to kill for them...and place the very future of England in jeopardy.

Provocative, intensely imaginative, an irresistable reading experience, **The Difference Engine** establishes a powerful literary team.

Available now in hardcover wherever Bantam Spectra Books are sold.